Usurper's Curse

Ellen Foster (signature)

Usurper's Curse

By

Ellen Foster

2018

Book Seven

The Lady Apollonia West Country Mysteries

Lulu Press, Inc.

Copyright © 2018

First published in United States of America 2018

Maps and front cover photograph by Louis Foster
Drawing of Lady Apollonia by Michele Bishop Foster

ISBN 978-359-06328-4

Ellen Foster's Blog:
https://blogs.valpo.edu/ellenfoster/

Table of Contents

Acknowledgements...vi

Maps...ix

Preface xi

Chapter 1   Alwan's Unexpected Guest 1

Chapter 2   The Lady Apollonia's Queries...........................15

Chapter 3   Scholar and Knight 25

Chapter 4   King Henry's Dread...37

Chapter 5   The Tenacious Archbishop 49

Chapter 6   Murderers' Scheming 59

Chapter 7   Return to Aust..73

Chapter 8   The Pilgrim's Visit 83

Chapter 9   Abandoned with Salt.......................................95

Chapter 10   Blood Red Spring 107

Chapter 11   Classmates' Secrets 117

Chapter 12   MaryLizbet's Tale 129

Chapter 13   The Druid Returns to Aust.............................141

Chapter 14   Sir Julian Prepares 153

Chapter 15   Ferdinand's Vindication 163

Chapter 16   Clash of Allegiances......................................175

Chapter 17   Landow's Meddling, Lady's Grief 187

Chapter 18   Players' Gifts 199

Chapter 19   Seeking Forgiveness......................................211

Chapter 20   Affable Grace..223

Chapter 21   Growing Households 233

About the Author 243

Glossary 245

The Lady Apollonia West Country Mysteries
by Ellen Foster

Effigy of the Cloven Hoof
Plague of a Green Man
Memento Mori
Templar's Prophecy
Joseph of Arimathea's Treasure
King Richard's Sword
Usurper's Curse

Acknowledgements

It has always been a real pleasure for us to return to England to do research, visit family, and to explore our favorite home away from home. Each time I am able to finish a new volume of my West Country Mystery Series, however, I am especial grateful for the fresh eyes who examine the manuscript for me as early readers.

A good friend and regular early reader on the English side, David Snell has read and commented upon each new book in the series. On the American side, I am grateful to Sue Joys, the Reverend Jim Mitchel, and my favorite Episcopalian Bishop Ed Little, not only for their comments but also their encouragement. My thanks must also be shared with Mary Leonard, the Reverend Nancy Becker, and Philipp Brockington who have always offered new questions and helpful challenges in many chapters.

A new friend and contributor as early reader of the manuscript this year was Sandra Hass who brought professional criticism and comments that were to the point but also creatively encouraging.

Once again, I am especially grateful to be able to use the lovely drawing of my fourteenth century heroine, the Lady Apollonia by our daughter-in-law Shelly Foster. Our family has always been supportive of my writing, and a good friend as well cousin, Annette Aust has consistently been an early reader offering her teacher's insight into each new work. My husband Lou is here for me, closest to the successes and problems of the development of the story. He is my first editor, gracious listener, personal computer expert, and best-informed travel companion.

Lady Apollonia's West Country

Map Including Aust Manor

Preface

Usurper's Curse brings to a close the medieval mystery series featuring the life and career of the Lady Apollonia of Aust. Although the Lady Apollonia is a fictional heroine living in England during the late 14th and early 15th centuries, her stories, including *Usurper's Curse*, are based on historical fact.

This, the seventh book of the series, is set in England in the early 15th century, and several of its characters are historical persons, as is its medieval setting in the West Country of England. Her home village of Aust is an ancient village on the River Severn dating back to Roman times. "Aust" is the Latin word for south, and in Roman times, the village was the southernmost ferry crossing on the River Severn.

King Henry IV, christened Henry Bolingbroke, was of the royal family of Edward III but was a disputed and vulnerable king during these turbulent times because he seized the throne after the fall of Richard II and was not next in line to inherit it. As the Duke of Lancaster, he established the Lancastrian line of kings, but his reign was disputed by various members of the nobility who insisted that he was a usurper. In 1399, Henry had proclaimed himself King Henry IV and imprisoned Richard II who subsequently died in prison under mysterious circumstances. Richard was only thirty-three when he died, having come to the throne as a boy of ten.

Before taking the throne as Henry IV, Henry Bolingbroke was a famous knight, known for his triumphs in the lists. Rumours spread and persist that he had leprosy. Henry was afflicted by a series of serious illnesses. His skin diseases have not been identified, but scholars do not believe that he suffered from leprosy or Hansen's disease as we know it to be. During the opening chapters of my story, I did make use of the historical facts that King Henry had moved temporarily into Archbishop Arundel's palace at Lambeth and that Parliament did rule against having any foreigners involved in the care of the king.

Cardinal Henry Beaufort, half-brother of King Henry IV, was born as a bastard son to Henry's father, John of Gaunt and his mistress, Catherine Swynford, whom Gaunt eventually married. Although Archbishop Arundel did legitimise the Beauforts, he made a point that though legitimised, they were not eligible to inherit the royal crown.

An historical English nobleman of the period, Henry Percy, the Earl of Northumberland, makes a brief appearance in Lady Apollonia's fictional manor of Aust when he in historic time was fugitive from King Henry. Other historical figures of the period who are part of the story are the Archbishop Arundel, Prince Henry, eldest son of Henry IV, John Hawley, and John Purvey.

I do not deal with Lollardy in detail in the story, but references to it cannot be avoided during this period in England. Lollards were followers of the teachings of the English religious reformer and scholar, John Wycliffe. Wycliffe was never tried for heresy by the church courts during his lifetime, but during the period of my story, Thomas Arundel, as Archbishop of Canterbury and Chancellor of England, enacted laws against the Lollards as heretics. A well-known leader of the Lollard movement and its center in Bristol at the time of my story was John Purvey who is introduced as a good friend to the fictional knight, Sir Julian Thurgood. Lollard is a derogatory term which comes from the Dutch "lollen" and means to mumble.

By the time *Usurper's Curse* opens in the year 1406, John Wycliffe was long dead but had been introduced in the first book of the series, *Effigy of the Cloven Hoof,* as an acquaintance and friend to Apollonia and her beloved second husband, the merchant Edward Aust, as an Oxford scholar who held the prebendary of Aust parish church at the time when the Lady and her husband were living in the village raising their family. In my story, it was he who enabled the Lady Apollonia to obtain an English translation of the Bible.

Another historical person of the West Country to whom I refer in *Usurper's Curse* is John Hawley of Dartmouth, a merchant, mayor, member of Parliament, and privateer. By the time my story is set, however, Hawley is an old man and a famous example of a local hero of the southwest who rose to significant position and wealth during his lifetime. Hawley was elevated to armigerous rank by Richard II, and his memorial brass can be found at St. Saviour's Church in Dartmouth.

The sense that unusual natural events were signs of frightening problems in a community was common in medieval belief. A pool bubbling red, thought to be blood, was a concern, and the most famous example occurred in Finchampstead in Berkshire. A total eclipse of the sun was recorded in Northern Europe in 1406. The use of a packet of salt with an abandoned infant in medieval England was a sign that the child had been given up by its parents and required baptism and adoption. I have used each of these phenomena in *Usurper's Curse*.

"To usurp" is a medieval term which means to take a position of power by force. The word "usurper" was applied to King Henry IV as he was the leader of a group of nobles who dethroned Richard II, and then Henry made himself king of England. My title *Usurper's Curse* refers specifically to Henry IV who, though of royal blood, was not next in line to inherit the crown when Richard II was overthrown.

The medieval landscape of Aust on the Severn is the backdrop for Lady Apollonia's final stage of life. The Lady has become a vowess, a widowed woman during medieval times who takes a vow of chastity but remains in the world to serve the church. Her story describes deep loyalties mixed with wicked treacheries. Who is the stranger who appears in her manor, near death? Why are her villagers being poisoned? Who is trying to wound her...and why? With her abiding grace, deep faith, and extraordinary intelligence, she leads the way to solve these tangled mysteries and survive.

The Lady Apollonia of Aust

Chapter One

Alwan's Unexpected Guest

"Please God, no! Now it is snowing." He had never known such a brutally cold winter, and on this January day of the new year, 1406, as the skies darkened toward evening and the winds continued to howl from the north, he desperately wished that he had more clothes with him for warmth. He had been forced to flee from the palace with so little warning and since then had been sleeping rough. What was it, four, five days since? If only he had brought more money. If only he had had the good sense to pull on several layers of woollen undergarments beneath his doublet and hose. If only he had thought to bring his more rustic fur-hooded cloak. This fashionable cape that he wore would have been adequate for his daily rounds in the palace but never enough to maintain his body's warmth in this gale. He wore stylish boots, high to his knees with brass buckles at each side but made in the best of fashion, while walking about the king's chambers. He was not booted or prepared to be trudging on foot through the rough trails and deep, muddy earth of these country roads. At least the bitter cold had frozen the mud by now, yet he was forced to walk carefully to maintain his balance and not stumble into the wheel ruts sliced sharply into the country roadway. He had been told to follow this road to reach the village of Aust. Perhaps, someone in Aust could lend him more suitable clothing but cheaply, he thought, as his coins were few. He hoped he could find something more rustic to wear while completing his journey. He did not wish to stand out noticeably as a courtier. He wanted to appear as one of the locals in his dress, a rural traveller, on foot in the midst of this arctic winter.

He was determined to get to Wales, and to do that, he knew he must reach the ferry crossing at Aust. Surely, once across the River Severn, he would no longer be pursued. He knew several people with whom he could find safe refuge in Chepstow. Once there, he would begin to write to his friends at court and beg their intervention on his behalf. He would tell them the truth about the king, he said to himself, as he turned to look over his shoulder. Constantly looking backward, especially whenever riders appeared on the road behind him, he would rush into the woods and remain hidden until they passed.

"Surely, Aust can not be much farther," he cried out to himself. Then, suddenly, the sounds of hoofbeats pounding some distance behind him drove him again from the road into the trees and concealment in the forest.

He had become so nervously impulsive by this time, he ran more deeply into the woods in a desperate hope to find a secure place to hide from his pursuers and a bit of rest. He stumbled clumsily, his breathing heaved in gasps, and worse, he was thoroughly chilled by the raging snowstorm. He knew his hands were numb and he could no longer feel his feet. His aching hunger had begun to lessen in its hopelessness. Though he was driven to leave King Henry's England, he knew at this moment that he must rest, at least build a small fire, and find some bit of warmth to combat his body's mortal chill.

"Oh, praise be," he shouted when he saw it. A rustic peasant's hut stood in the woods ahead. It was simply but solidly built, well cared for, and surrounded by varieties of equipment for fishing and trapping. Best of all, there was light within and smoke pouring from its chimney. He ran to its low door and knocked fiercely upon it. That effort drained him of his last bit of strength. As if trying to pull his fashionable cloak more tightly around his body, he collapsed at the door, wrapped in his own arms.

* * *

Alwan was surprised to think that anyone would be at his door, unless of course, it was a messenger from his mistress, the Lady Apollonia of Aust. She and her household always made a point to express their appreciation to him as their forester for his regular supply of fresh game and fish to her manor kitchen. Frequently, a servant from the manor house brought him warm bread or pastry treats to complete his meals, but usually such deliveries would happen earlier in the day.

There was no treat to be found when he opened his door. In the bitter wind and blowing snow, Alwan was stunned to discover a man's body lying in a heap across the width of the entrance to his hut. The forester looked about his small, rustic yard quickly and could see no one else in the woods near his remote dwelling and, more strangely, no mount of any kind which could have brought this obviously stricken man to his door. Alwan stooped to touch the head of his unknown, unexpected visitor and found him to be feverishly unconscious but alive and breathing. Rather than waste more time in wondering, the Lady's forester moved quickly to pick him up by his shoulders and pull him inside the hut to the single cot bed. He gathered the few woollen blankets in his possession and piled them over the well-dressed young man because he could tell that his body was desperately chilled.

Alwan was quite at home living by himself in the woods, proud to serve as forester to the Lady Apollonia's manor. He was warmly welcomed whenever he would make his deliveries to her kitchen, but he was unprepared for this bizarre arrival of a stranger at his door, unconscious and desperately in need of care. How was the forester to help him? Alwan knew enough to try to warm his body, but he was no barber nor healer. Oh, if only Owen were still in Aust. The lad, now into his eighteenth year, had been Alwan's best friend since he joined the Aust household as the Lady's page a decade earlier. Alwan admired Owen's expanding education and preparation for knighthood, obviously a more sophisticated undertaking than anything the forester could consider. Yet, he remained one of Owen's best friends in Aust, and whenever Owen returned to the manor, he always went first to Alwan's cottage where they could share their news and adventures. In recent days, Owen had been home to Aust for a brief holiday but had returned only yesterday to his knight's service as squire to the Lord Ferdinand of Marshfield.

"Now, Alwan," he said out loud, as if Owen were speaking to him, "look closely at your guest. What do is silent body tell ya?"

"Well, ee be a young man and a gentleman, that be certain," Alwan answered himself. "Oi would guess ee ain't eaten for days and must be starvin." Then, as if a light flashed in his brain, he announced,

"Oi must get im to m'Lady's Mistress Nan. She'll know ow to nurse im."

At that, Alwan walked out from his hut and brought his cart around to the entrance. He filled the bed of the cart with a small quilt to make it more comfortable, then added the only small pillow that he owned. When the cart was prepared, Alwan went back into the hut to carry the emaciated young man wrapped in his remaining blankets outdoors and laid him gently onto its bed, placing the cushion beneath his head. The forester removed from his own shoulders the only fur-skin cloak that he owned, and normally wore on these cold winter days, to cover the sickly body. At last, Alwan harnessed his horse to the cart and began to drive out of the woods towards the manor house. "M'Lady's Nan'll know," he repeated to himself.

Apollonia's forester began to remember how helplessly pitiful he had been when the Lady of Aust first found him. He had walked into England as a twelve year old, having lost both his parents in Wales. He was a penniless orphan sitting in the village stocks, having been put there by the warden. Alwan had done nothing wrong, but the village warden did not wish to encourage beggars to come to Aust.

On that day when the Lady Apollonia approached with her maid, Nan, she could see him struggling to defend himself from garbage and stones being thrown at him as he was taunted by the village boys. The Lady's commanding presence made them cease their cruel attack as soon as she appeared while she sent Nan to bring the village warden to release the boy into her custody.

Each time he thought of it, Alwan smiled. He was now in his twenty-sixth year, he thought, and his badly scarred face seemed to have grown into a permanent smile. He knew it was only thanks to the Lady's grace and goodness to take him into her service that he had been able to find his way into an honourable life. He had not only become a respected member of the Lady's affinity, he was accepted as part of the village community. To this day, however, he knew he was still referred to by local folk, respectfully, as Alwan the Poacher.

During the brief drive to the manor house, Alwan could hear phrases murmured by his passenger that seemed to be some sort of fearful cries consistently ending with denials. "No, No, tis not true!" he seemed to be repeating.

The forester did not stop until he got to the barn of Aust manor where he leapt down from the cart and went inside to find the Lady's stablemaster. Gareth Trimble had been in the Lady's service since he was a teenager. Now, however, he was married and living in nearby Ingst with his young wife and family but faithfully reported for duty at the Lady's barn every day in Aust, where he was in charge of the Lady's stable and livestock. When Alwan entered the barn, Gareth greeted him warmly as a well-known fellow member of the Lady's affinity who regularly came to supply the manor kitchen. Today, however, Gareth could see that all was not as normally expected with the forester.

"Gareth, moi friend, Oi needs to bring moi cart into the barn. Can ye ask Mistress Nan ere to speak with me. Oi needs to know if she be free."

"Give a few moments, Alwan," Gareth said, already beginning to walk towards the manor house as he spoke. A man of few words, Gareth could see that Alwan's cart carried a recumbent young man. The stablemaster did not hesitate but went straight to the kitchen to speak with the Lady Apollonia's personal maid, whom he knew was chief among the household servants who were busying themselves to complete their chores.

Nan smiled as soon as Gareth entered the manor house. She was always pleased to see Gareth, for she had loved him since the earliest days of their friendship, devotedly, but silently. After his marriage several years ago, she had grown close to his young wife and loved to help with their toddler twin boys whenever she had free time. She never spoke of it with anyone, but she knew in her heart that once given the chance to marry Gareth, she had refused him and chosen the life of a spinster in service to the Lady Apollonia. Gareth and Lucy's boys were as near to her as having family of her own.

As Gareth approached her, Nan could tell that something was amiss. He whispered his message to her, so she took her woollen shawl from its hook and they left the kitchen together. When they entered the barn, Nan saw the gentleman's blanketed body lying in Alwan's cart with the forester standing nearby.

"Alwan, what in the world has happened? Who is this you have brought? Is he alive?"

"Mistress Nan, Oi can tell ya little as Oi found him collapsed at moi door. Ee came to me, alone with no mount in sight. Oi believe ee be starvin and needs ealin, but Oi be not able to know what to do for im."

"Gareth," the Lady's maid turned back to the stablemaster, "I shall return to the house and prepare a bed for this man. Once I am ready, will you help Alwan carry him into the house where we will put him into a warmed chamber. Then, you must go into the village to collect my Lady's doctor of physic. There is no doubt that she will wish us to do what we can for him."

"Som'ow ya must feed im soon, Mistress Nan," Alwan said.

"I shall see to that, Alwan, and you will please remain here until my Lady can speak with you, whilst you, Gareth, will hurry to collect Physician James."

* * *

The men of the household carried the young man to a small chamber at the back of the manor house where a fire was roaring in the small grate and Nan had warmed its bed with hot stones. In the midst of her maid's preparations, the Lady Apollonia came to see what was happening. Alwan was now holding the woollen blankets and his fur-lined cloak folded in his arms, and Gareth was gone on his errand. Nan had covered every inch of the young man with wool and fur from head to toe, but they could all see that was he was not resting. He appeared semi-conscious at times, looking about him terrified and continuing to tremble. Nan brought warm milk to his bedside, and lifting his head upon a cushion, she encouraged him to ingest its heat as well as its nutrition.

When their patient had finished his warm milk, Nan turned to Apollonia. "This fellow must be running from something, my Lady," she said quietly. "Whoever he is, he is completely unable to relax. He was terrified by my touch at first and continued to mutter, 'No, no, tis not true!'"

Though a petite, late middle-aged woman, Nan was commanding in her role as the Lady's personal maid who expected to have her will obeyed within the household and throughout the Lady's affinity.

Begging the Lady's pardon, she ran back to the kitchen to ask the cook to provide some warm chicken broth.

Apollonia was standing near the bed when Nan returned from the kitchen. The maid could see the Lady making careful note of the young man's condition and his confused, terrified appearance while Alwan stood patiently beside her.

"Nan, do we have any idea where he has come from?"

"No, my Lady. Alwan told me he simply appeared at his door, collapsed in the condition that you see him."

"Aye, m'Lady, Oi brought im ere cause Oi were certain Mistress Nan would know what to do for im."

"Gareth has gone to bring Physician James to us, my Lady," Nan told her.

"You have both done exactly as I would have wished, but you must come with me now, Alwan. I want you to describe everything that happened this afternoon. Nan, you will send the physician to me before he leaves. Just looking at this young man's soft hands, his fashionably trimmed beard, and his smart clothing, I can see he is a well-bred person, of good birth, and probably well off. He can afford to buy the very best the city has on offer, but what is he running from and why is he alone in the countryside without a mount? It is likely that he has come to Aust to take the ferry into Wales, but why in this condition?" She smiled, "You both know that I am never content until I have answers to all my curiosities."

* * *

When Apollonia began to leave the chamber, she nodded towards Alwan to accompany her upstairs to her solar, but at this, the Lady's forester was taken aback. He had never done such a thing by himself in all his years of service. His young friend Owen, when serving as the Lady's page, had always been with him on the few earlier occasions when he was called into the Lady's presence and provided a degree of confidence for Alwan that was missing now. The forester blushed a sudden rush of anxiety when he realised that he would be going alone upstairs into the Lady's private chamber. Fortunately, Apollonia did not miss his hesitation and made a point to add, "I must speak with you privately, Alwan, because I need to benefit from your counsel. Nan will be joining us soon."

Alwan nodded obediently and quietly followed when she walked past him. The Lady thought she could feel his sense of relief when he knew Nan would soon be with them. Alwan had been part of the Lady's affinity since his early teens. She knew he felt comfortable in her presence as her respectful servant who was more than willing to do any service she asked of him. In her own mind, Apollonia knew him to be devoted to her, but she was also aware that she must not ask personal questions of him. She would always grant him the complete respect of mistress to a loyal, faithful member of her household. She was seeking his advice, as she had said, because of *her* need.

When they walked into the Lady's solar, Alwan stood politely until Nan came. "My Lady," Nan said to their mistress, "the doctor of physic has returned with Gareth and is examining the young man. He knows that you wish to speak with him before he leaves."

"Let us sit near the fire, Nan. These wintry days are chilling my old bones. I pray you and Alwan will join me."

Nan walked to her chair near the Lady and indicated to Alwan to bring a stool. When they were seated together, Apollonia asked Alwan to tell her everything about the arrival of the young man at his cottage that afternoon and learned that his was not a long tale. The forester concluded his brief story by saying that he could not think what to do except to bring this obviously ill young man to her. "Oi knew Mistress Nan would know ow to care for im, m'Lady," he repeated.

"Be assured, Alwan, you did exactly as I would have wished, but I have other requirements of you just now as I need more information. It is possible that someone whom he fears is following this fellow. Will you use your excellent tracking skills to see if you can find any evidence of his being pursued, and from whence do you think he came? When the young man begins to tell us his tale, he may not wish to reveal the whole truth of his situation, so I should be grateful to have whatever you can provide me. I suspect there may be more puzzles revealed in this story as the days go by."

* * *

When the doctor of physic, James Morewell, finally came to her solar, he found the Lady accompanied by her chief steward, Giles Digby, going over plans for the new year's woollen sales. Apollonia could see that the physician was concerned for his patient, so she signalled to Giles to move slightly on his bench so that the doctor could be seated next to him.

"Pray sit with us, Physician James," Giles told him. "What can you tell us of this young man's condition?"

"I shall do my best for him, my Lady," the physician began, "but it is obvious to me that he has not eaten for days. More than that, he has the ague, with trembling chills, a high fever and severe pain in his head. When I listen to his lungs, I fear that he has caught his death of cold. Your staff and Mistress Nan are doing all that they can. They are keeping him warm and forcing him to eat and drink small portions regularly. It is clear to me that he is beyond the possibility of being bled. His recovery is now dependent upon God's grace and his young body's strength of resistance. He has returned to a more sensible consciousness, but I have given him a sleeping draught so you will not be able to speak with him until the morrow."

"My Lady wishes to inquire what the young man told you of himself or the purpose of his journey?" Giles asked.

"I only spoke of details of his body's symptoms, my Lady, but found that when he responded, he was driven by endless questions of me. He asked me immediately where he was? Was he in Wales? Who owned this property? 'Was the lord of the manor at home?' was the question he asked most anxiously. I told him that you, the widowed Lady of the Manor of Aust, is resident and in charge here and that you would call upon him on the morrow. He did not recognise your name and seemed to relax when he realised that he did not know of you. I shall return again on the morrow, but now it is best that he sleeps."

With that, the doctor of physic rose from his chair. Giles stood as well but continued speaking, "My Lady is grateful for your service, Physician James, and will look forward to your return in the morning."

James Morewell had served the Lady's affinity as doctor of physic for more than four years since he moved to his parents' home in the village of Aust. His father had been a successful merchant from Bristol who had been able to marry well and provide a good education for his son. Morewell knew the Lady to be a widowed vowess who rarely spoke, frequently preferring to use her personal servants to speak for her. With nothing further to share with her, he bowed as he prepared to leave and walked with Giles to the stairs. When Giles returned to the solar, he could not help but ask the Lady what she planned to do about their unexpected guest.

Apollonia did not respond to her steward immediately, but when she did, she took a deep breath and said, "I believe that we, too, must wait to see how our guest may fare in the days ahead, Giles. Physician James believes that we are doing everything possible for him at the moment. Past that, he says, the fellow's recovery is in God's hands, and I dare say, we must keep him there. I pray you will send Friar Francis to me. We will, as a household, remember him in our daily chapel."

* * *

Later that day, Apollonia was surprised by another unexpected caller who announced to Nan pompously that he was from the court of his grace, King Henry, and demanded to speak with whomever oversaw this manor. He seemed pleased, at first, to learn that one aged noblewoman was not only in charge, she was a widowed vowess who would receive him but could not speak in his presence. No doubt, he thought to himself, he would be able to exert his will into any discussion with her and would simply tell her what he required.

He entered the Lady's hall arrogantly, bowed before her as she sat in her chair while his young servant announced respectfully that his name was Waldef and wished to introduce his lord, Sir Hardulph of Leicester. Apollonia extended her hand in welcome to him but said nothing, all the while fixing her eyes on him and making careful note of his appearance and manner in detail.

Hardulph's face bore an aggressive expression with dark brown, bushy eyebrows that met above drooping eyelids. His mouth seemed unable to offer a friendly smile from his thin sneering lips, and when he spoke, Apollonia could see behind his straggly beard that he had one front tooth missing and the others blackly rotting.

"I am unable to spend much time in your ladyship's presence," he announced, "for I am on the trail of a traitor to King Henry who must be captured and returned to London."

Nan and Giles were standing on either side of the Lady, and Giles responded to their guest on the Lady's behalf. "My Lady of Aust bids you welcome, Sir Hardulph, and seeks to learn who it is that you pursue and what is his crime?"

"His crime is precisely how it must be described, my Lady of Aust. The man is no gentleman, much less a faithful servant of the king. He is an evil liar who claims to be a highly skilled physician trained in the south of Italy. In truth, he is guilty of putting about misinformation concerning his grace, the lord our King."

Apollonia passed a note to Giles who then spoke to the knight once again. "My Lady of Aust has heard that King Henry is suffering from serious illness, Sir Hardulph. Does he not require the care of a well-trained physician?"

"Not this physician, madam!" Hardulph shot back at her, rudely.

The knight could see that his aggravated response was not taken kindly by the Lady's servants and attempted to gentle his tone when next he spoke.

"I beg your pardon, my Lady, I respond aggressively because I am determined to take into custody this reprobate and see that he is imprisoned for his humiliating statements against King Henry. You must promise me that if he appears here in your manor, you will not receive him but apprehend him and send notification to me of his capture. I shall leave instructions with your servants. Adieu, my Lady of Aust."

As if resentful that he had been forced to give time to this interview with an unresponsive old woman, Hardulph turned abruptly and began to leave.

Giles, however, had one more question of him. "My Lady wishes to know if you can tell us the felon's name?"

"Oh that, well, if she really wishes to know, he calls himself the court physician, Mark Marimon, but be warned that you must trust nothing he tells you. He is known within King Henry's court for his wicked vice."

"And what is his vice precisely," Giles pressed him.

"Lying, dishonesty, deceit! I can think of no other words to describe his actions against our lord king. I shall not repeat the evil words he has spoken publicly about King Henry. Just see that he is captured if he should come to the Lady's manor," Hardulph called back, over his shoulder, "by order of the king."

With that, he strode from the hall as his servant Waldef, obviously embarrassed by the knight's rude behaviour, scurried to follow him.

After Sir Hardulph and his servant had departed, Giles barely knew what to say to his mistress. Worse yet, he could think of nothing that he could have done to protect her from the extraordinary roughness of the self-proclaimed servant of the king. Nan, did not hesitate to speak of it, however.

"My Lady," she exclaimed, "I have never known such crude and barbarous behaviour in your presence. Can this truly have been a knight of King Henry's court? How can anyone excuse such a lack of courtesy, much less such presumptuous behaviour by anyone in your presence?"

Apollonia could see that Nan was upset. She reached out to her chair and placed her hand on the maid's shoulder to calm her. "Gentle Nan, I shall privately inquire of this Hardulph of Leicester with my brother in Marshfield. Surely, Ferdinand will know of him if he serves the court. Receiving him with you and Giles at my side, I felt no threat, and I could care less of his ignorant barbarity, but I pray you will put our household on alert should he ever return to Aust. He is not to be allowed in the manor unless I am at home. His behaviour determined me to say nothing of our present guest. When I visit the patient tomorrow, I shall address him by name. If he is called Mark Marimon and is a physician, then eventually I shall hope to learn his side of the story.

"If he is the criminal this Sir Hardulph described," Nan frowned, "should we not summon Lord Ferdinand to us at once, my Lady? We must not allow Marimon free access within your household. Perhaps you should have him guarded through the nights until we can send him back to King Henry's court."

"Nan, dearheart, you have been nursing this young man. You know how weak and desperately ill he is. You have been at his bedside, feeding him and speaking with him when he is awake. Have you felt threatened by his company? What 'crimes' did Sir Hardulph accuse him of? He used the term 'vice' and said he was a liar, dishonest, and deceitful. Such accusations appear to be opinions of one man against another, but not threatening to us. Have you felt frightened in his company?"

Nan settled back into her usual practical self and after a few moment's thought smiled somewhat sheepishly towards Apollonia when she answered, "No, my Lady. His gracious gratitude to me has been expressed with gentility and kindness."

Chapter Two

The Lady Apollonia's Queries

A pollonia did not visit the patient until he received another day of her physician's care and restorative food and rest. When Giles told the Lady that Physician James was cautiously encouraged by his patient's improving condition, she asked Giles to go with her to the chamber. When they entered his room, Apollonia could see that Nan had propped the patient up upon pillows and was feeding him a bowl of hearty porridge. Physician James had not encouraged his patient to leave his bed yet.

Giles greeted the patient and said that as the Lady's steward he was accustomed to speak for her. "My Lady Apollonia of Aust is dedicated to the life of a widowed vowess, young sir, and speaks only when necessary, but has come to offer her extended hospitality to you until you have fully recovered."

"Forgive me, my Lady, for not rising in your presence," he said after greeting her. "Pray accept my heartfelt thanks for your hospitality and the excellent care your household has provided me since my collapse."

Apollonia found this young man to be straightforward and sincere in his words to her. He was a handsome fellow with brown eyes, blond hair, and beard. He appeared to be taller than Giles if he stood and spoke with the accent of the upper class. The Lady knew her Physician James wanted him to continue to rest so did not remain long. She had Giles assure him that her household would keep him in their daily prayers and turned to leave, but as she was walking through the door, she said quietly, "God's peace, Physician Mark Marimon," and left him open-mouthed for Nan to place another spoonful of porridge inside.

On her way back to her solar with Giles, she found a return message in the dovecote waiting from her brother.

"It appears that Ferdinand has responded immediately, Giles," she said as she opened the tiny note.

Apollonia unfolded it carefully and found its message to be brief, as required, but direct: "Polly, do nothing until I can come, F."

"Well, Giles, my brother says he is coming to Aust but offers no word as to when. I shall allow our guest to think on my greeting to him by name a bit longer and will return to his bedside later today. I believe he is the man whom Hardulph was pursuing and was obviously taken aback by my expressed knowledge of him although he knows nothing of Apollonia of Aust. I shall let him ask the next questions of me."

"What shall we, as your servants, do if he asks questions of us, my Lady?"

"Please answer honestly and tell him whatever he wishes to know. Then, let me know what information he has sought from you or the staff. Also, encourage him to feel free to speak openly with me."

* * *

Later, when the Lady returned to his bedside, Apollonia could tell that her guest did wish to question her. "Obviously you know my name and my profession, my Lady. How came you to be familiar with me when I am so uninformed of you."

Apollonia spoke tentatively but had now decided to respond directly to him and not mention anything of Hardulph's visit. She had decided to let Mark think that she knew of him because of her brother's attendance at the court of King Henry. "I daresay you are familiar with my brother, the Earl Ferdinand of Marshfield."

"Ah, yes. I have seen the Lord Ferdinand at court but was unaware of his relationship with the manor of Aust. How did he happen to mention me, my Lady, a lowly servant to his grace?" Mark asked cautiously.

"Ferdinand merely referred to you as the king's doctor of physic who had been trained by the world-famous physicians of southern

Italy." Apollonia stretched the truth a little, for she did not wish to bring up any mention of Hardulph of Leicester's search for him yet. "My brother suggested that it was because you had studied in the world's best medical schools that you had come to the attention of King Henry."

"Ah," Marimon acknowledged her comments but offered nothing more about his position nor anyone of the court who might resent him or would have been pursuing him."

"I have heard that our King Henry is seriously ill, Physician Marimon, so I cannot help but ask, why are you here in the West Country, far from court and without mount or servants in attendance?"

Now, it was Marimon's turn to stretch the truth. "T'was a dreadful accident of fate, my Lady," he began. "I was travelling through the West Country to visit family in Worcester and was robbed on the road. Everything was taken from me, my bag as well as my horse. I was abandoned blindfolded far out in the woods with my hands and feet bound. Eventually, I was able to untie my hands, remove the blindfold and other bounds, but I wandered disoriented, for days, I think. My first sign of return to humanity was sighting the cottage of your forester, Master Alwan. Thanks be to God, it was he who brought me to the excellent care of your household for which I am eternally grateful."

"Physician James tells me that you are making a good recovery, but your lungs are not clear. You must not leave your bed until he releases you," Apollonia said in her most grandmotherly tone. "Is there anyone to whom we can send word of your presence here in Aust?"

"No, no, please do not trouble yourself, my Lady," he said urgently. "When I have returned to good health, I shall…." Then he paused and seemed to reconsider. "If it is possible, could you send a message to Bristol to a dear friend, Sir Julian Thurston? He is currently residing in the home of the scholar John Purvey."

That name struck a vibrant chord in Apollonia's memory. She was not only aware of his name, she knew John Purvey was a colleague of John Wycliffe, the philosopher and theologian who held unorthodox religious views. Wycliffe was known to her in the early days of her second marriage. He had held the prebendary of the parish of Aust during the years of the births of her sons, and it was he who had helped her acquire her English translation of the Bible. Wycliffe was dead, but she had heard gossip that Purvey was known to lead a centre of Lollard teaching in Bristol. She could not risk exposing her household to any charges of heretical connexions, but perhaps she could ask her almoner, Brother William, if he would be willing to approach this residence of Purvey and carry a message to Mark's friend.

"Is Sir Julian an acquaintance of yours from King Henry's court, Mark?" Apollonia continued to press for specifics about his life.

"We have become friends fairly recently, my Lady, but have found ourselves to share a great many interests. Sir Julian has served the court since the latter days of King Richard but has now devoted his service to our present King Henry."

"How is it that a knight finds shared interests with the court physician?"

"I can not say how our friendship began, my Lady, but Sir Julian and I have grown to feel like brothers, not only in our mutual devotion to the king but also through our companionship with each other. Neither of us is married, and each has little family still living, so we are grateful to share any time together that we may."

"I shall ask my almoner, Brother William, if he will be willing to travel to Bristol with your message, Mark. My hesitation comes only because I have heard of this John Purvey as a known Lollard. If Brother William finds Sir Julian there and he is free to come, I will instruct William to tell Sir Julian of your whereabouts and bring him back to Aust," the Lady said, watching the eyes of their patient intently. In her own mind, she had not the slightest doubt that Mark's dilemma was more complicated than he was willing to reveal to her. It occurred to her that if he was not being entirely forthright, it was because he did feel a commitment to Lollardy.

"You must forgive me, Mark," she pressed him, "but even we in the far West Country have heard that our King Henry is seriously ill. As physician to the king, how were you able to leave the court?"

Mark's eyes looked away from hers, "It was a family emergency, my Lady. I had no desire to be gone very long but was struck down by the unexpected."

"Are you familiar with the heretical views of John Purvey, Mark?"

The patient continued to keep his eyes downcast as he said, "I only know him to be a scholar, my Lady."

* * *

After Apollonia left Mark's bedside, she walked to the chapel to speak with her chaplain, Friar Francis. When he had responded to her earlier call, it was to ask for regular prayers for their patient. Now, she wished to speak with him on a very different matter. She knew that Brother William would still be in the village, calling upon his regular list of those in need of pastoral visitation. When she found the friar, he was in the front of the chapel trimming the candles on the altar.

"Greetings, Francis," she said as she asked him to sit with her for a few minutes' conversation. She told the friar that she needed to share with him more of the complex story of their unexpected guest.

"Several unusual things have come to my attention since the arrival of Physician James's patient, Francis. You, of all my counsellors, have the gift of insight into my rampant curiosity and always help to direct my thoughts to order."

Francis assured her with a smile, "My Lady, I hope you will speak to my personal curiosity about our present guest, as well. Nan tells me that he is a doctor of physic from the court of King Henry. Why is he so far from London? What does he seek in the West Country?"

"These are important questions, Francis, but you must expand your inquiry to include, why should someone from the court be pursuing this Mark in anger, and if I am correct, why should Mark be trying to cross borders and escape to the safety of Wales from his pursuer?"

"Have you asked our guest any of these questions, my Lady?"

"He has been near to death, Francis, and I thought it best to focus on his recovery in these early days. At the moment, I have only introduced myself to him as the sister of the Earl Ferdinand of Marshfield with whom he has become aware in the court of King Henry. I will confess to you that I stretched the truth slightly to suggest why I knew his name and his position at court before he told me."

"Why did you resort to thus contrive your conversation with him, my Lady?"

"Because I received another very aggressive visitor to our door who seemed determined to take Mark captive," Apollonia said, raising her tone of voice.

"What caused you to question that visitor's motives, my Lady?"

"He was introduced to me graciously by his servant Waldef as Sir Hardulph of Leicester, Francis, but between us, I could only be impressed by this knight's lack of chivalry, courtesy, or gentility. Therefore, I choose not to reveal our patient's presence with us until I could know the truth of Hardulph's motives."

"You would not have done so without good reason, my Lady. I have always known you to grant grace to any in obvious need or honest inquiry."

"You are kind in overlooking my faults, Francis," Apollonia smiled, "but this is my real question of you. Do you think that Brother William will be willing to take a message for me into the heart of the Lollard community in Bristol?"

Francis was slightly taken aback, in part because he was not certain how he himself would respond to such an assignment from the Lady. After a bit of thought, the friar shrugged his shoulders and said, "William devotes his life to ministry, my Lady. I have never known anyone so faithful to the church, guided by God's grace, but also willing to question obvious church abuses and seek reform. I suspect that William's awareness of Wycliffe's views since his student days will go with him, but once there and given the opportunity, he will address his personal questions to his hosts in an effort to better understand the Gospel that the Lollards preach."

"Thank you, Francis," the Lady Apollonia said gratefully. "I knew you would advise me well. When William returns, will you kindly ask him to call upon me in my solar?"

* * *

Late in the afternoon, Nan brought Alwan back to the Lady's solar and sat with them while Apollonia's forester described what he had found in response to her tracking assignment for him.

"There be no doubt our visitor were tryin to get to Aust Ferry and were bein followed, m'Lady. That were probably why ee left the road to ide deep in the woods and stumbled upon moi cottage. Oi found fresh tracks of at least five orsemen ridin together on the road towards Aust, two of them came ere to the manor whilst the others waited at the Boar's Ead in the village."

"Well done, Alwan," Apollonia said, obviously pleased with his findings. "From whence did they come? Could you tell?"

"Oi can only say they was comin from the east, m'Lady, and they was ridin ard to catch somethin or somebody.

* * *

Brother William did not return to the manor until the hour of their evening meal. After the household had eaten, he approached the Lady because Friar Francis had told him she wished to speak with him.

"I want to send you on a mission for me to Bristol, William."

"Your servant, my Lady. What can I do for you in Bristol?"

"I want you to visit a centre for Lollard study and deliver a message to a knight who is resident there. The study centre is run by John Purvey, a renowned Oxford scholar who is known to be a follower of John Wycliffe. Are you willing to do it? I have no desire to offend your faith by requiring you to visit folk who are regarded by some leaders of the church as being heretics."

"I have read several of the pamphlets distributed by this John Purvey, my Lady, and though he is judged as heretical by some in the church, I find I must agree with several of his suggestions for reform. When I was a student at Oxford, I was strongly drawn to the teachings of Wycliffe, especially to reform the errors of church teaching and reduce its extraordinary wealth. Yes, my Lady, I shall go. Who am I to seek at John Purvey's centre?"

"I want you to find the knight, Sir Julian Thurston, who is a friend of Mark Marimon, the young man who is staying with us while he heals. Mark wishes to send a message to Sir Julian and, if possible, have you bring him with you back to Aust."

Without another thought, William said, "I shall be glad to do this for you, my Lady."

"Then, I beg you to come with me to Mark's bedside in the morning and collect his message to carry to Bristol. I have asked no questions of Mark about his friend, Sir Julian, or the possibility of their Lollard sympathies. I leave it to you how you regard those succeeding reformers inspired by John Wycliffe, but I believe that our patient, Mark, is in trouble with important people in the court and was being pursued by someone of evil intent when he collapsed on Alwan's doorstep. I am hoping that you will be able to bring Sir Julian to his friend's bedside here, for I should like to meet this knight with whom Mark feels a close friendship."

* * *

It was not long after Brother William had gone on his errand to Bristol when Apollonia was surprised to see her brother bursting with energy into the hall of Aust Manor that same morning. Ferdinand was accompanied by two of his friends, men who had known him and served with him since his earliest days in Marshfield.

"Polly, you know Sir Reynold and Sir Gervase. Have some food brought to us, I pray you. We have been hunting and have not yet broken our fast this morning. Then, you and I shall remove to your solar, for I have things I wish to discuss with you in private."

Ferdinand was eight years older than his sister and presumed control of everything as his right when he was with her. An extraordinarily vigourous man for his late sixties, Apollonia knew that when they were alone and out of sight of the household, her brother would wish to be seated comfortably near the fire with his aching back supported by cushions. Riding had become uncomfortable for him as he aged, but he admitted that to no one and would never be seen riding in a carriage.

The Lady rose to take her brother's hand as he kissed her and then pulled her with him to go directly up the stairs to her solar. Nan was aware of Lord Ferdinand's habits with her mistress, so after curtsying to him, she took his comrades to the table dormant in the hall where, once they were settled, she left for the kitchen to see that a hearty breakfast was prepared for all of them.

Apollonia had barely entered the door to her solar when her brother began to move several large cushions into a great chair near the fireplace. "So, Polly, what did Hardulph say to you? Why did you allow him to speak with you? What do you know of Mark Marimon? Is he still in England, or has he moved on to Wales?"

"Well, dear brother, that is at least five different questions, and I shall answer each of them to your satisfaction if you will tell me what you know of this Hardulph of Leicester?"

"First and foremost, Polly, you must have nothing to do with Hardulph. He is recently knighted, and I suspect that he bought his knighthood. He is known as a mercenary, to do anything for profit from his services to those in power and, as nearly as I can tell, is devoid of any gentle blood."

"That was obvious to me, Ferdinand, but I did allow him to speak with me because I wanted to know why he was pursuing Mark Marimon, the king's physician. Hardulph insisted that he wished to arrest Marimon, when he found him, for insults against King Henry. I decided that I would not cooperate with him because of all his aggressive presumption, brother. He is at best an arrogant nonentity who made it clear to me that he regarded his interview with an insignificant, old woman as an utter waste of his time."

"How did he justify his pursuit of Physician Marimon, Polly?"

"In truth, brother, he tended to speak in vague generalities, basically accusing Mark of spreading lies against the king."

"You speak of Marimon as if you have become acquainted, Polly."

"I can claim to know him, Ferdinand. He is here in Aust as my guest, recovering from serious illness brought on by starvation and severe cold. However, we shall keep that information shared between us for now."

"I am not happy to know of this acquaintance, Polly, and I do wish you would have spoken with me before you became involved in this way," Ferdinand complained.

"My forester will tell you, brother, that I did not move to intercede with Mark. It was he who came to us in a dreadful state, seeking help. I am a vowess, dedicated to serving others. I have sent a messenger off to Bristol to inform a close friend of Marimon's that he is here. I confess, I am looking forward to learning more from him if he will come to Aust. He is called Sir Julian Thurston."

"Oh, dear God, a Lollard knight. What next? I have no doubt of your devotion to the church, Polly, but I am also well acquainted with your burning curiosity. If there is mystery in the air, you will place yourself in the midst of it," Ferdinand growled.

"While you are here, do you wish to speak with Mark, brother?

"No, Polly, not yet. I do not wish to know where Marimon is, and I prefer to maintain my distance from him at the moment. I certainly have no desire to join you in the midst of your 'mystery', but if this Lollard knight comes to Aust, send me a message. I would like to know what you think of him. Most of all, is he truly Christian?"

Chapter Three

Scholar and Knight

The day was dark and bitterly cold. Brother William was grateful that he had dressed in layers of wool beneath his fur-lined cape because the sun was down by the time he rode into Bristol, and darkness had begun to spread throughout the city. It was not difficult to find the residence of John Purvey, however, for Bristol was well known for its sympathies with Wycliffe and his followers. A well-dressed merchant on the street was obviously glad to be able to direct him. The simple dwelling was alight and welcoming as Brother William knocked on the door.

He introduced himself to the man who answered as almoner to the Lady Apollonia of Aust who had been sent to bring a message to the knight, Sir Julian Thurston, from his friend, Mark Marimon. The man answering said that his name was John Purvey and urged William to come inside. A middle-aged man of medium height, Purvey was also warmly dressed but anxious to close the door against the winter's cold. Once inside, he led William to the fireplace where a tall, well-built, martial-looking companion sat reading.

"Julian, this is Brother William, almoner of the Lady Apollonia. He has come from Aust with a message for you from Mark."

"Come to the fire, Brother William," Julian said in a deep commanding voice as he rose in welcome. "Where is Mark?"

"Greetings, Sir Julian, I am glad to meet you. Your friend Physician Marimon is in Aust Manor returning to good health but has been seriously ill in recent weeks," William told him as he walked nearer the fire to warm his hands and give Mark's message to the knight.

Julian tore through the seal and read to himself. "Damn that Hardulph!" he swore angrily.

"I take it you know the knight," William asked him.

"I do not speak ill of any man, Brother William, but Hardulph's reputation contains no devotion to chivalry."

"I am to add to your friend's message that my mistress, the Lady Apollonia, invites you to return with me to Aust Manor to be with Mark during this latter stage of his recovery, if you can." Then turning to his host, he added, "I must ask you, Master Purvey, if you will put me up for this night? I shall return to Aust on the morrow."

"Brother William, I pray you will join Julian and me for our evening meal. I can offer you simple but hearty food as well as a warm bed for the night."

"Gramercy, a quick wash and I shall be ready to accept all, with my sincere thanks."

"And, I shall be pleased to accept your invitation to guide me back to Aust Manor, Brother William," Julian said candidly. "I had no idea that Mark has been ill. I must offer my protection to him, John. It appears that he is being wrongly accused and has been wickedly pursued."

The three men sat together round a table as they shared their meal, and Brother William began to ask Purvey of some of his earlier experiences. "On an entirely different matter, Master Purvey, would you be willing to speak of any of your memories of John Wycliffe? I never met him, but as I understood his teachings when I attended Oxford, he was convinced that the church was in need of serious reform. He denied the validity of transubstantiation, and he certainly taught that those serving the church should be poor, as Jesus and his disciples were poor."

"You understood correctly, William. Wycliffe was concerned that many leaders in the church today come from families seeking only to use its wealth and power. He felt that they sell the church's ministry for profit rather than minister to the poor, the weak, and those who need to understand God's gift of grace through faith. I am accused by the archbishop of preaching heresy, but I speak only from my translation of the Gospel. I have been imprisoned, and, God forgive me, when threatened to be burnt to death, I recanted. At this point in my life, I simply refuse to hold a vicarage so that I am free to preach being faithful to Jesus' Gospel in Holy Writ as I understand it."

"But, what is your most fond memory of John Wycliffe?" William pressed him. "What kind of man was he?"

Purvey smiled as he thought aloud. "I will always remember as a young man sitting across the table from Wycliffe when we worked on our translations. We shared an inkwell between us. Wycliffe could be an irascible soul but was always a dedicated friend to me. He insisted on speaking out against the corruption of Christ's church wherever he found it. And, I will always remember him first as one who worked tirelessly with no complaint, never asking for help despite his struggles with a palsied arm."

* * *

Early the following morning, William and Sir Julian mounted up to begin their journey to Aust. Brother William could see that the knight was uneasy about leaving John Purvey alone, but as John blessed both of his friends, he quietly said to the knight, "All is in God's hands, Julian. Do not fear for me. Go to Aust and see what can be done for our friend Mark."

Brother William looked down from his horse for a brief minute and expressed his thanks to Purvey.

"Gramercy for your hospitality, Master Purvey. I am glad to say that I know you as a man of faith even if I am unable to agree with you in all aspects of correcting the problems of our church. Surely, men of good faith and differing opinions will someday work together to share in its reform."

"That is the truth, William. Let us agree quietly that we are hopeful for reform together. Go with God, friends. I keep you in my prayers," Purvey said as he made the sign of the cross over them.

There was relatively little conversation between William and Sir Julian after they turned onto the road and began their journey, but eventually William could not resist asking the knight how he had come to know John Purvey.

Julian's answer was somewhat surprising to William. "I have heard that many call me a Lollard knight, whatever that means. I readily confess to be a Christian, but I have found understanding of my faith through the teachings of Wycliffe that John has shared with me. I do possess a copy of Purvey's revised English translation of the Bible, and as a fighting man of limited study, I am eternally grateful for John's scholarship to help me become literate in Holy Scripture. In recent months, I have seen that he is under threat by those who only wish to defend the temporal power of the pope. They accuse John of heresy to keep him quiet. John Purvey needs protection, William; therefore, I also feel called to do whatever I can to protect him."

"Why do you think that there are those in the church who seek his life? He is obviously a man of peace and dedicated to his ministry.

"Because he represents a menace to their power and profit," Julian said in disgust. "John has been imprisoned for what they call heresy and for writing to honestly expose the corruption of the church. He also told you that he was terrified when threatened with being burnt at the stake. At that time, he returned to orthodoxy by confessing and revoking his so-called heresies out of fear. Yet, I also know that he has grown ashamed for recanting," Julian said. "He now regards that as a betrayal of his faith, so he has left the church in order to continue to preach. Those who follow Arundel, our Archbishop of Canterbury, are actively seeking to silence all whom they call Lollards, especially him, and will use any means to do it."

* * *

One of the Lady's stable boys ran out from the barn to take their horses as Brother William dismounted with Sir Julian. Gareth also came out from the barn to welcome William home.

"Greetings, Gareth, come meet Sir Julian Thurston who is a good friend of Physician Marimon."

When Gareth doffed his hat to the knight, Julian said with real enthusiasm, "It is good to be here, Gareth. I have been to the Holy Land and back but have never enjoyed a more beautiful ride than this has been to encounter the mighty River Severn."

"Aye, m'lord, tis grand to enjoy Severn's views in all seasons of the year. Welcome to Aust Manor, and Oi ope you may enjoy many rides long Severn's banks." Gareth was a man of limited conversation but one proud of his home county and always glad to hear praise of his favourite river. "Pray, come with me to the entrance of Aust House. Oi knows that m'Lady be expectin you."

Gareth led the guests into the hall where Nan sat mending by the light of the fire. When the Lady's maid saw that Gareth and William had brought their hoped-for guest with them, she sent one of the servant girls to collect the Lady and her Steward Giles from the solar where they were working.

While Apollonia and Giles were descending the stairs, Giles greeted William and welcomed him home. "Come, let us gather by the fire, William, where we may meet our guest."

Gareth quietly turned to leave when he knew his service was finished and slipping out through the servants' entrance of the kitchen, he returned to the barn, his favourite dwelling as stablemaster.

Giles escorted the Lady and her guest towards the great fireplace in the hall, and once the Lady was seated in her chair, William stepped forward to present Sir Julian and introduce him.

"My Lady Apollonia, may I present Sir Julian Thurston, knight errant to his grace, King Henry."

Julian was pleased to be able to meet the Lady Apollonia and curious to know more of her as sister of the dour Earl of Marshfield. He bowed to kiss the hand she extended to him and was struck by her straightforward warmth and mature beauty. He found her to be a stately woman, elegant in her black gown decorated only by a gold cross lying upon her breast. Her face was that of an older woman but one who retained a classic beauty through fair skin, brilliantly grey/blue eyes, and perfect white teeth when she smiled. He could see that she made no effort to affect courtly manners and was examining him carefully in return.

Giles spoke next. "My Lady wishes to express her welcome to you, Sir Julian, and her pleasure to receive you on behalf of your friend, Physician Marimon. True to her vocation as a widowed vowess, she speaks only when required, but she thanks you for coming and wishes to know if you would like to visit with Mark."

Julian assured her that he would be grateful to speak with his friend, so Giles responded, "This is Mistress Nan, my Lady's maid. She will take you to his bedside, but you must know that the doctor of physic who oversees his care begs that all of our visits with his patient be relatively brief."

"Thank you, my Lady of Aust, for sending Brother William to find me in Bristol. I was unaware of Mark's illness and am especially grateful for your household's care of him. After we have spoken, may I return to the hall?"

"Indeed, Sir Julian," Giles said to him, "my Lady not only extends hospitality to you, she would be grateful to speak with you privately in her solar. I shall wait here until you return."

* * *

Apollonia was sitting in her great chair when Giles brought the knight into her solar. She gestured for him to sit with her, and then, to Julian's surprise, she dismissed Giles. With her spokesman gone, the knight was further surprised when she spoke directly with him.

"I am pleased to make your acquaintance, Sir Julian. Will you tell me more of yourself, whom you serve, and where is your home?"

"I come from a small village in Wiltshire, my Lady, and am the younger son of an ancient family dedicated to our feudal knighthood. I have chosen to serve my king as a knight errant wherever I am needed and serve my fellow man whenever my community is in need."

"Can you describe for me the difference between a knight errant and one who is called a mercenary knight?" Apollonia asked him.

"In my understanding, my Lady, there is a significant difference. Members of my family have been ever ready to lead our men to serve the king whenever we are called, while overseeing the lands and estates granted to us by the king. A mercenary knight is one who is paid for his service and may serve any lord in any land for a price."

"You are describing two very different kinds of knightly service, Sir Julian."

"Indeed, my Lady, and although I do not wish to value one kind above the other, my family and I prefer to serve our king."

Apollonia began to feel a sense of admiration for this knight as she continued to question him, "How do you find Mark, Sir Julian?"

"He believes that he has been near death, my Lady of Aust, and wishes me to add my heartfelt thanks to you and your household for saving his life."

"I am grateful to speak with you alone, Sir Julian, and happily acknowledge your thanks on behalf of Mark. My dear maid, Nan, has been at Mark's bedside day and night since a member of our household discovered him in such dreadful condition. He has lavished his thanks and rightly so, upon her. However, I mean to ask questions of you that I feel Mark has not wished to answer in my presence. My intent is not to ask you to betray your friend but merely to grant me, as his hostess, whatever understanding of his peril is possible."

Sir Julian continued to look into her eyes as his deep voice assured her, "I shall consider whatever you ask, my Lady."

"My questions began immediately when Mark was found on my lands. He was suffering from starvation and dreadfully ill, without possessions or mount, and in a state of terrour as if he had been pursued by an enemy," Apollonia said. "Then, the day after Mark was brought home by my servants and taken into our care, I received a very different caller, a knight, Sir Hardulph of Leicester, who told me of his search for Mark. He said he was seeking to arrest him for crimes against the king. That was a bit of a shock, but I confess that I did not respond well to Hardulph's aggressive attempt to bully me into obedience. I remained silent and told him nothing of Mark's temporary residence with us while he recovered.

"Suspecting some sort of personal conflict at court, I sent a message to my brother, the Earl Ferdinand of Marshfield, who regularly attends King Henry's court. I sought to gain information from him because Hardulph had told me not only Mark's name but also that he is King Henry's physician.

"Here in the West Country," she continued, "news from the palace comes slowly to us but we have heard that his grace, King Henry, has been seriously ill, so I had to ask myself why the court physician is not at the king's bedside?

"Finally, when my brother came to speak with me, his words were least helpful of all. He simply told me that he has heard of this Hardulph and his professed hatred of the court physician, Mark Marimon, and that I should have nothing to do with either of them. Ferdinand scolded me for involving myself in this situation all the while ignoring the truth that the 'situation' came to my door and is now resident in my household."

Julian sighed deeply as the Lady completed her story. She had spelled out in detail the reasons for her legitimate questions of Mark's predicament, but he felt there was little he was willing to say in response just yet. The knight looked into her eyes and smiled gently. When next he spoke, his base tones seemed honestly full of regret as well as understanding.

"My Lady of Aust, I beg your patience. I am truly sorry that Mark has involved you in this, but it was never his intent. Let me speak with him again, and I promise to provide you with at least some answers to your insightful questions."

* * *

When Julian next returned from Mark's bedchamber, he asked the Lady if she would be good enough to return with him so that they might speak with Mark together.

"I pray you will understand, my Lady, Mark says that he must ask you to accompany me alone with no other servants or members of your household present, not even dear Mistress Nan."

Apollonia rose from her chair and took Sir Julian's arm. Together they left her solar and walked downstairs. When they entered Mark's bedchamber, Apollonia dismissed Nan and asked her to keep the chamber undisturbed until her meeting with the young physician was over. When the chamber door was closed, Apollonia sat beside the bed and simply said, "Well, Mark, I have come to listen."

Sir Julian was the first to speak, "My friend wishes to offer his apologies for not being straightforward with you, my Lady, especially after the extraordinary amount of care your household has extended to him."

"Indeed, my Lady Apollonia," Mark told her, "I pray you will understand that I only kept my difficulties from you to protect you and your affinity. There are those at court who have sought to discredit me and go to any extreme to achieve it."

"Is Sir Hardulph of Leicester one of those?" the Lady asked.

"I am not certain," Mark said, "but I have no doubt that he has sought to belittle me in every way: as a well-trained physician, as a true subject of King Henry, and even as an honest and faithful Englishman."

"Do you know why he has declared himself to be your enemy?"

"I believe that he was involved in an underground effort to have King Henry declared a leper," Mark told her, "and, as long as I continue as the king's physician, I shall insist that is untrue. The King is afflicted with an aggressive skin disease that causes him to break out in bloody pustules on his face, but he is not a leper. I do not know why Hardulph has made himself my enemy, but perhaps someone whom he serves has tried to keep King Henry from receiving proper treatment for his real illnesses in his stomach, heart, and lungs. Worst of all, I suspect Sir Hardulph is covering for someone in power who seeks to have our present king deposed and sent to a leprosarium."

"But, why was Hardulph pursuing you, Mark?" Apollonia asked.

"He wants to keep me from the king's side by destroying my reputation as a physician and replace me with a doctor of physic whom he, or someone he works for, can control. Hardulph insists to the court that it is I who has spread the lies about King Henry as a leper king. More recently however, Hardulph declared that he can prove that I am a Lollard, and in the mind of our devout Catholic Archbishop Arundel, that discredits me as a heretic."

Apollonia listened carefully to everything Mark was telling her and could see at once why he had been so tentative in answering her questions of him. This young physician was facing decisions of life and death consequences for himself while struggling to provide the best possible care for their king.

"How came you to Gloustershire in such desperate circumstances, Mark?" she asked him.

"One of my good friends among the servants of the court was able to give me a last-minute warning of Hardulph's intention to take me prisoner and throw me into a dungeon as a Lollard heretic. The knight already had my horse impounded and a guard posted at my chambers, so I was forced to sneak out of King Henry's palace through a window and literally make a run for the West Country on foot. I travelled incognito, thinking to cross the border into Wales where I could gather my friends, well-respected people like Sir Julian, to help me."

"Why should my brother, the Earl of Marshfield, be so determined to maintain distance from you, Mark?"

"I can only think that Lord Ferdinand has been made aware of Hardulph's charges of heresy against me as a Lollard, and as a devout Roman Catholic, he fears that I may seek to affect our Catholic king with my heresy, my Lady."

Apollonia stood up from the bedside chair and thanked him for his willingness to tell her the whole truth of his situation. "I shall leave you to rest, Mark, but do understand that I continue to welcome you to remain my guest in Aust Manor. In an effort to display my trust in you, let me share a truth of my life that few people know. Years ago, John Wycliffe was prebend of our parish here in Aust, and he became a personal friend to my second husband, Edward, and me. Wycliffe spent evenings in our home and was a key influence upon our middle son's call to the priesthood. I will confess to you that I long to see many of our church's abuses reformed, but as a devoted vowess of the church, I will never leave it. I do not consider myself a Lollard, but my faith has been strengthened through the years by reading my personal copy of Wycliffe's English Bible.

"Your servant, my Lady," Mark said very quietly.

"May I offer you my deepest respect, my Lady," Sir Julian added. "Your willingness to share your personal faith so openly with us speaks of a sincere awareness of God's presence in your life."

* * *

When Nan returned to the Lady's solar, she was burning with curiosity. "What have you learned, my Lady? Who are these gentlemen really? Is Mark so untrustworthy and evil as Sir Hardulph accused him?"

"Nan, just being with Mark and his friend, Sir Julian, has been an inspiration to me. You know that I thank God daily to have been called to be a vowess, but most of all, I am now grateful to have been allowed to know two inspired Christian souls who serve God in widely different occupations. One is a gallant crusader knight and the other a brilliant young physician who is prepared to bring the best of healing into our world. What a gift to an old woman. So, dearheart, I shall continue to offer my protection to them."

Nan was a little confused by the Lady's response to her question, but she could not help sense that Apollonia's time spent to get to know both of her guests had been a kind of revelation to her.

"Well," the maid said happily, "I must say that all of the days I have spent caring for Mark have been good for me as well. He is a devout and righteous young man who assumes no superiority towards anyone and indeed shared collegial thoughts on healing with your

Physician Morewell. I did not like that Hardulph at all, my Lady, and could never regard him as chivalrous."

Chapter Four

King Henry's Dread

In a dark lower chamber of an aristocratic house in London, Hardulph walked back and forth in studied irritation. He had been told to meet here for further instructions, but the foreign count whom he served remained at his dinner in the great hall, carelessly unaware of the knight's annoyance. After all, he had been provided with wine, a crackling fire, and a lusty young maid to serve him.

"What takes him so long?" Hardulph glared at her.

"Oi know not, m'lord," she said quietly, filling his glass and rubbing the full length of her body against his. "There be a couch ere, large enough for two of us," she said suggestively as she pushed her ample breasts against him.

"Move away woman! Go up to the hall and tell your master I have things I must be doing. If he has instructions for me, then he is to come to speak with me."

"Ah, Sir Hardulph, you are as impatient as the rest of your English brethren," the count said as he walked into the chamber. Gesturing to the maid to leave them, he continued to speak, "In my native Kingdom of Sicily, no one questions my activities or my commands. Here in England, anyone of status presumes his opinions are commanding, and his time is of great value."

"Count Dravini, you continue to ask me to perform services for you but still have not told me what it is that you wish to do next. My men and I pursued the king's physician as you asked but were unable to bring him into your custody. In his absence, you have assumed control in the palace by offering King Henry the services of your so-called healer, though he seems more sorcerer than medical doctor of physic.

"Ah yes, and the king's disease continues to grow worse, tragically," the count said theatrically. "Have you noticed how the last of his hair has fallen out, how his face has become a mask of bloody pustules of late? He has been too ill even to attend sessions of Parliament. It has not been difficult to spread the word throughout the city that his grace is a leper," the count smirked, "while I assure him constantly that he is merely suffering from skin irritation due to his extreme fatigue."

"What is it that I am to do for you, my lord?"

"Oh dunce! You are to continue to search for the king's true physician, Mark Marimon, and when you find him, do what is necessary to guarantee he will never return to court. He has consistently told the king the truth of his condition and pursued proper healing for him. I will not allow anyone to acknowledge him as an excellent physician in my presence. When he refused to submit to my direction, I knew I must be rid of him. Surely, even you can see, Hardulph, that I desire to stay here as the king's guest for as long as possible. Good God, man, King Henry is the richest man in England. Just look at the exorbitant sums his grace pours into the coffers of every so-called healing relic, holy well, sacred spring, or saint's tomb. I am determined that such royal gifts will continue to fall into my hands."

"So, what precisely are you asking of me?"

"Must one spell it out? As a knight, you are a trained killer, and I have paid you well. I require no details. Just guarantee that Marimon and his truth shall not return to court."

"If he did escape into Wales, it is unlikely that I shall find him, my lord, but I will ride with my men back to the village where we lost him. Perhaps someone in Aust extended shelter to him. If I can find him, I shall complete my task."

"Get it done, Hardulph, but spare me the details."

* * *

When the Sicilian count returned to King Henry's court on the following morning, his personal healer told him that the king's condition was worsening. Dravini went straight to the king's chambers and begged to be received at the king's bedside, for he insisted that the royal suffering was breaking his heart. The count's healer had been in complete charge of King Henry's care since Marimon's absence, so none of the king's servants felt they could refuse him. Dravini rushed into the chamber and dramatically knelt at the royal bedside.

"My lord," Henry's servant insisted, "you must not expose yourself to illness in this way."

"Indeed, I shall remain here on my knees in prayer until his grace has returned to good health."

King Henry suddenly awakened, and though startled by his new friend's excessive display of devotion, he simply gestured to his servant to bring a chair for him. When the count was sitting by his bedside, the king reached for his hand as if he wished to make a confession to him.

"I had a terrible nightmare last night, Dravini. I thought I saw the angel of death hovering over me and woke in a trembling sweat. There can be no doubt, my friend, the Lord God has stricken me with leprosy as His judgement against me."

"You must not say such things, my lord king. I have never known a more devout servant of God."

"I am the worst of sinners, Dravini, I enabled the death of the deposed King Richard. More recently, I lost my temper completely and ordered the execution of the Archbishop Scrope of York for his share in the Percy Rebellion. One was king by divine coronation, the other a man ordained by the Holy Spirit. I not only killed, I usurped England's throne. This disease--this curse--continues to worsen and must be divine punishment for my sin. I shall never be well again."

"Do not say such things, your grace. My personal physician insists that you are suffering from the rampant fatigue of one required to rule in a rebellious state," Dravini lied. "He tells me that he will bleed you again to restore your balance of humours whilst I shall gather all the members of your court in the chapel to pray for your recovery. You are a believer, your grace. With ongoing excellent care, devoted friends, and all your servants offering their heartfelt prayers to each of our patron saints and the Virgin Mary, surely the days ahead will bring you a return to the sturdy good health of your years as champion of the tournaments."

* * *

Pietro Dravini was a man without principle, driven by compelling greed to take advantage of every opportunity he could find to be in the king's presence. Dravini was certain, and his opinion was encouraged by his healer's diagnosis of the king, that Henry was weakening. An egregiously egotistical man, the count was thrilled to be in a position to use the king's illness as potential for his profit. He was not interested in merely gaining privileges but driven by the possibility of receiving royal gifts of jewellery, relics, things made with crystal, gold, and jewels. Already, each of Henry's gifts to him had been quietly sold abroad for considerable amounts of cash carefully stored away in a safe place. Dravini paid none of his household's bills, and he lived at the king's expense. He kept every penny for himself, determined to disappear secretly when he was ready, a significantly wealthier man than he had ever been.

The count was a fraud as well as a manipulator, one especially skilled at using men's personal fears against themselves. He would find ways to suggest problems or frightening possibilities growing out of the king's illnesses to him and then simply brush them away as unlikely because, he would insist, King Henry was so well cared for and obviously loved by his subjects.

He had tried to bribe Mark Marimon, the king's physician, to do his will but had been coldly rebuffed when Mark was in charge. At that, Dravini's aggression sought immediate ways to destroy the young doctor, not only in loss of reputation and position but literally by sentencing him to death.

* * *

Waldef, the servant of Sir Hardulph, had been sitting in the shadows of the lower chamber where his master had been summoned to meet with Count Dravini. A mere servant, he knew his presence was ignored by both men, but he had been unable to believe what he heard them discussing. His lord, Sir Hardulph, had been told to murder the king's physician, and the knight had taken it in his stride as just another assignment. He even acknowledged that he had taken money to do criminal acts for this foreigner. In the days since that incident in Count Dravini's town house while Waldef worked to prepare for the journey back into the West Country, the page had not been able to think of anything else.

All his life, Waldef's great goal had been to serve a knight. From his childhood, he had been encouraged to believe that chivalry represented the highest form of social code in life, one of courage, honour, courtesy, justice, and a readiness to help the weak. Early on in his service with Hardulph's family, he became aware that Sir Hardulph, even though recently made a knight, had no interest in chivalry. Yet, what Waldef had heard discussed between his lord and the count was more than a disregard of knightly code. How could the knight be, as the count described him, merely a trained killer? Worse yet, Waldef had seen Sir Hardulph accept money from the count while agreeing to continue to seek out and murder the king's physician.

Waldef told himself that he must do something to give Marimon warning. He would be returning with his lord to the West Country to search for the physician. If they found any trace of him, Waldef told himself that he would look for a way to warn him of the real threat. But then, what would he do he asked himself desperately. How could he continue as servant to such a lord as Hardulph, one whom he now found himself required to betray?

"Now past my sixteenth year, I am a grown man," he told himself. "Further, I am a free man. I live as a servant but never a slave."

Hardulph noticed an irritating change in the behaviour of Waldef but gave it little mind. If anything, his page seemed more concerned to learn every detail of what they were planning to do in the West Country, constantly asking questions of his lord regarding their next venture.

"Ask no more of me, Waldef," the knight told him roughly. "You are to do as I tell you, when I tell you."

Waldef turned away from his lord at this rebuke but would not be turned from his true purpose. "No, my lord," he thought to himself. "I am required to serve you at this moment, but I shall not follow you into a life of crime."

* * *

Mark and his friend, Sir Julian, were sitting together in the hall of Aust Manor with the Lady Apollonia and her maid. Their friendship had become so comfortably relaxed that the royal physician seemed willing to allow his recovery to go on endlessly in this lovely peaceful village by the River Severn. Julian was also enjoying their visit in the Aust household but felt that he had to continue to remind his friend that they must seek to clear Mark's name and return to court.

The Lady Apollonia was well aware that neither man could be completely at peace and decided to ask if they would be willing to share any of their future plans with her. "Now that you have made such a good recovery, Mark, Physician James tells me that I can no longer keep you restrained. Will you allow me, as one with honest concern, to ask what you will do next?"

"My Lady, Julian and I never cease to discuss what should be my best plan. I feel I must return, gain access to the king, and serve him personally."

"Can you tell me what was the real purpose of the visit of Sir Hardulph to Aust, Mark? Why was that knight in pursuit of you?"

"That remains one of our troubling questions, my Lady," Julian said. "Neither of us can understand why Hardulph claims to have charges against Mark."

"I do not believe I have ever spent any time with Hardulph, my Lady," Mark said, "and I have no idea why he should have such hateful feelings against me."

"Is it possible that Sir Hardulph is bringing these charges in behalf of someone of power in the court, Mark? Who in King Henry's court may have complaint against you?"

"I am merely the king's physician, my Lady. I can think of no one whose enmity I have invited."

"What of that count who claims to be from the Kingdom of Sicily, Mark," Julian pressed him? "Did you not feel that he wished you to do questionable things, alter your diagnosis, and allow him to take advantage of the king's weakness during your care of him?"

"Count Dravini is a fraud and a selfish churl who has been abusing the king's largesse. I purposely kept my distance from him. Why would he seek to do me harm?"

Apollonia looked directly into Mark's eyes and asked quietly but purposefully, "Is it possible that this Count Dravini feels that you are a threat to him in any way?"

"He presents himself as a courtier, my Lady, and regards me as something less than a servant. In my eyes, he represents the most supercilious of companions to our king, but his grace enjoys his company. Dravini kept insisting to me that the king must be protected from any possibility of being called a 'leper king', and I insisted in return that the king does not suffer from leprosy. His warrior's body is sickened by severe stomach ailments and massive skin irritations, possibly brought home from his time spent in the Holy Land, but he is not a leper."

"Why then does Dravini continue to use the term 'leper king' when you have correctly diagnosed the king's ailments?" Julian asked. "You are the doctor; he is not."

"Forgive me, my Lady, Julian, I can not answer your questions. Dravini is a pompous man who claims to have some sort of royal Sicilian blood, and his company is welcomed to the court by King Henry. Regardless of his presence, it is there that I must go because King Henry needs my care. Even if I can not cure the king, I am able to ease his suffering to an extent that he may return to some degree of normal living. This time, however, I shall return with protection, my Lady. Julian has agreed to go with me."

Apollonia listened carefully to everything that Mark was telling her, but even with protection, she could not feel confident in the possibility of his safety. "Can you delay your return for a bit longer, Mark? I fear that we are missing some important aspects of an ongoing threat to you at court, and I would very much like for you both to speak with my brother, the Earl of Marshfield. He has reservations about a rumoured interest you both are said to have in Lollardy, but as a knight, I believe he is chivalrous enough to accept that you deserve his protection. I will share my awareness with him that you, Mark, have been pursued and persecuted unfairly.

"But for what reasons, my Lady? I have done nothing to deserve persecution," he added plaintively."

"Mark, I am making judgements from a distance," the Lady told him, "but it seems to me that the king's guest, Count Dravini, is regularly abusing his position as a royal favourite for his own gain. Dravini does not wish to have you in charge of the king's care."

"But why, my Lady?"

"Because you are not willing to be ruled by him."

"He boasts that he is nothing more than a courtier, one who only desires to provide companionship for the king. Why should he object to the king's physician?"

"I can not be certain, Mark, but is it not possible that his true motives have sought to promote the king's illnesses, and to do that, he must be rid of the healing care of the king's excellent physician."

* * *

When Hardulph of Leicester rode into the manor of Aust with his servant, the knight had calmed his manner significantly from his last visit. He wished on this occasion to appear as the height of respect for the old woman who seemed to him to be the only noblewoman in the area with significant wealth and insight into the events of the village and its surroundings. There could be no doubt that she was religious, a widowed vowess, he had been told. Surely, he would be able to get information from her if Mark Marimon had been seen in the manor.

Still, what could he tell her of his reasons for his continuing search for the court physician? Hardulph did not like to play the roles of what he described as feeble courtesy, so-called chivalry in knighthood, that he could only see as womanish behaviour, but that is what he must do, he thought. He would tell the Lady that he was searching for the physician to offer his apologies for having cruelly misjudged him, for having been misled by some in the court who were jealous of the physician's favour with the king. He must appear to express sincere regret and humbly confess to her that he had been mistaken.

"Women love to see themselves as instruments of restoration who enable wrongs to be righted. If the Lady of Aust knows the whereabouts of Marimon, I shall convince her of my need to correct a wrong that I have done against him and beg her help."

* * *

Waldef was considerably nervous about this visit to Aust, and when he walked into the Lady's hall to announce the return of his master on this occasion, he was trembling. He kept telling himself that he must look for any possibility to speak with someone of authority in the Lady's affinity without his master present, to ask if they had news of where Mark Marimon might be. After announcing Sir Hardulph, the young servant stepped back, and his master went to take the Lady's hand. Waldef looked anxiously around him. There were several people with the Lady of Aust. One woman obviously served as her lady's maid, and another man introduced himself as the Lady's steward, Giles Digby.

"Perhaps no one here has any word of the king's doctor of physic," Waldef thought. "Perhaps he has escaped into Wales, and we shall hear no more of him."

The Lady Apollonia signalled a welcome to Sir Hardulph, and her steward begged him to take a seat next to her near the fire. The knight walked quietly to take the chair as Giles continued to describe again her vocation.

"My Lady Apollonia says little, Sir Hardulph, for she has dedicated her life since her widowhood to that of a vowess of the church. I hope you will allow me to speak in her place. She wishes to offer you any help that you require. May she ask why you have returned to Aust?"

"Ah yes, my Lady, I have returned to Aust to take up my search for King Henry's royal physician. The king's condition continues to worsen, and Physician Marimon's skill is needed at court. May I ask you if you have learned anything of his whereabouts?"

"My Lady asks how it is that your opinions of the skills of Physician Marimon have changed dramatically since your last visit to Aust, Sir Hardulph?"

At this, the knight assumed a new character. His body seemed to lose its arrogant aggression, and his eyes looked to the floor as he said quietly, "I was wrong, my Lady. I had been evilly misled. I confess that I have now come to find Marimon to offer him my apologies, and escort him back to court."

Apollonia said nothing through this conversation, but she was listening intently, her eyes watching both of her visitors. When the knight completed his sentence, she could not help but notice how his young servant, Waldef, suddenly went rigid, his face grimaced, and his eyes looked towards Hardulph in disbelief.

"My Lady asks me to tell you that she is unable to help you in your mission, Sir Harduph, but she will be alert to any news of Physician Marimon. How is it that she may contact you?"

The knight of Leicester was already on his feet, irritated that he had once again wasted time in Aust.

"If you have any news of Marimon, I beg you to send word of him to Count Dravini at Sicily House in London. His healer is currently assuming charge of the care of King Henry."

"The Lady begs to know how it is that this visitor from a far country has been given such important healing responsibility for our English king?" Giles asked.

"Surely, everyone in England knows that the best schools of medicine in the world are found in Salerno, my Lady. Now, I beg to be excused for, once again, taking your time needlessly." Sir Hardulph's voice seemed to have returned to its earlier irritated strain as he gestured to Waldef and stalked out from the hall.

As he was being rushed from the hall, Waldef looked about madly searching for someone with whom he could leave his message. Giles, the Lady's steward, hurried to join them to escort the guests towards the door. Waldef stopped as Giles came closer and reached out as if to take his hand politely while his master charged ahead. Giles was surprised by the servant's gesture but having taken his hand immediately realised that the lad had slipped something into his palm.

After both were gone and the door closed behind them, Giles unfolded the tiny slip of paper which read: "Caution Dr. Marimon. His life is in danger."

* * *

Apollonia signalled to Nan to bring Mark and Sir Julian from their listening post on top of the hall screen after their visitors had gone.

"I hope you were both able to hear all of that brief conversation, Mark," Apollonia said. "Pray tell me why Sir Hardulph continues to pursue you?"

Mark seemed at a complete loss to answer. "My Lady, questions only multiply. He says he wishes to apologise to me, but again, I do not know this knight and care little for his regrets at having abused me to you. Further, I have no idea why my whereabouts should be of interest to Count Dravini. I do feel ever more strongly that Julian and I must return to the king, but I have no interest in reporting to Dravini."

Sir Julian was even more to the point. "My Lady, you have suggested that there may be evil afoot seeking to control Mark's healing access to his grace, King Henry. Should we try to learn more about the motives of this Dravini?"

"Indeed, Sir Julian, I believe that will be prudent. I beg you both to remain here until I can bring my brother, the Earl of Marshfield, to Aust. Ferdinand will have more to tell us of the condition of the king and the manner in which this Dravini is regarded by the rest of the court."

"My Lady," Giles said as he re-entered the hall, "we are not the only persons concerned for the safety of Physician Marimon. I pray you will look at this note from the young servant of Sir Hardulph."

Apollonia took the small slip of paper from Giles and read it aloud to the group: "Caution Dr. Marimon. His life is in danger."

"Who did this, Giles?" Mark asked.

"It was just now slipped into my palm when I took the hand of Hardulph's servant, Waldef," Giles said. "There can be no doubt that this young man seeks to warn you."

"May I keep this note until my brother can see it, Mark?"

"Of course, my Lady, but let us not make too much of it. We can not be certain who is behind this threat, and the young man does not name anyone."

"Yes, Mark, that is so, but keep in mind what we do know. First," she said as was her custom, pointing to her index finger, "you have been aware of attempts by one in the court who sought to manipulate your care of the king; secondly," pointing to her middle finger, "you have been pursued in an effort to capture you; and thirdly, now you have been told specifically of threat against your life. If you insist upon returning to the court as King Henry's physician, you must be aware of the danger that may await you there."

Chapter Five

The Tenacious Archbishop

"My Lord Archbishop," the servant said quietly, "your men are ready."

"Send Mawes to me for instructions," the voice from behind the desk growled without looking up and continuing to write furiously.

When Mawes entered the chamber, Arundel's instructions were to the point. "You will see that King Henry is brought here to Lambeth Palace for his recuperation. Soon, I will be Lord Chancellor, and I want his grace here where I can know precisely what is being done for him and see him daily. Most of all, I am determined to keep him from the influence of that insidious fop, Dravini."

"Yes, my lord. How shall I have authority to enter the palace, and with whom shall I speak?"

"The heraldry that you wear will certify your authority as my man, and you will be met by Prince Henry's man Darroby who will take you into the royal presence. King Henry expects you and will be prepared to have you transport him to my home. Just take great care and move him very gently. His body is painfully suffering, and he must not be jostled about."

"Yes, my lord, we shall move his grace as gently as possible."

"And Mawes," the archbishop added, "if that so-called healer in Dravini's service who has been with the king attempts to question your purpose, say that you are acting on my orders. Tell him that the House of Commons has demanded that all foreigners must be excluded from the royal household. Then, you will escort him out of the palace and send him back to his master with the message from the Commons to both of them. They are unwanted."

When he was alone once again with his personal servant, Arundel spoke abruptly, "What was the name of that doctor of physic who had been so successful in treating King Henry during his last serious attacks?"

"He was called Mark Marimon, your lordship, but we have not been able to find him anywhere in the city."

"Then you must send out a search for him once again. He has been the only physician able to ease the king's discomfort and help him deal with his reoccurring stomach ague and fever."

"But, my Lord Arundel, you were suspicious of his religious beliefs and made him know of your vehement judgement of the Lollards."

"Dammit. man, my Constitutions are in place. Preaching is regulated as well as the translation of scripture. We have made significant progress against Lollardy," Arundel said, purposely unwilling to remember his objections to Marimon at this moment. "I shall do as needs must. This physician has not expressed such heresies in my presence; therefore, I will presume nothing of his personal beliefs. I want him here to oversee the king's care in Lambeth where I control all who have access. His grace is suffering ever greater weakness and needs the best trained doctor in England. The word from those who are well informed says Marimon is the doctor of physic always recommended as the best. Surely, someone in the court knows where he has gone. Continue the search for him now."

"Yes, my lord," the servant said as he bowed and began to leave the chamber.

"Oh, and one more thing," Arundel bellowed, "I want someone to remain at the king's side daily, someone whom I can trust completely. Send a message to the Earl Ferdinand of Marshfield and beg him come to me. He is not the most brilliant fellow but by far the most loyal and devout of all the knights of the court, the epitome of chivalric service, if such things do still exist. I have never known him to seek favour or advancement for himself in reward for his service to the king. Unbelievable in these days of self-promotion," he muttered as he returned to his work.

* * *

Ferdinand was in Marshfield when he received the summons to Lambeth from the Archbishop Arundel. The Earl had no choice but to prepare to leave Marshfield immediately. In his haste, he went first to the dovecote to send a message to his sister. It was brief and to the point: "Polly, is Marimon still with you? Send him to join me at Lambeth Palace. The king is residing there."

Ferdinand was not precisely sure what it was that Arundel wished him to do, but it had something to do with the guardianship of the king whom all recent reports seemed to indicate was seriously ill. Worst of all, rumours continued that the king was suffering from leprosy. Ferdinand was a brave soldier, willing to sacrifice his life for his king, but he was terrified of the possibility of being exposed to a leper. He sent one more message to his sister in time to receive her response before he left: "Is the king a leper?"

The earl did not leave his home until he heard back, and Apollonia's response was brief and again, to his points: "Marimon on his way. He says, 'No.'"

* * *

Even at his best pace, it took two days for Ferdinand to reach the archbishop's palace at Lambeth on the south side of the Thames. When he arrived, he was ushered into the presence of Arundel immediately. On this occasion, the archbishop seemed more than usually welcoming and thanked him several times for his prompt response.

"I shall tell you as a secret shared by us alone that the king is truly not well; his suffering increases daily, and there seems little can be done to help him heal. Against my wishes, a fake healer, loyal to one who calls himself a Sicilian count, wheedled his way into the king's presence and blatantly used the king's confidence to enrich himself. I wish to keep his grace here at Lambeth beyond the reach of this Count Dravini. I am asking for your daily companionship with the king. Offer him your company, but especially guard him against any future attempt of contact by those who seek to use his weakness."

Ferdinand did not respond immediately and tried to think what it was he was being asked to do. Finally, he said to the archbishop, "I have no men with me to post a proper guard, my lord archbishop."

"It is your person whom I wish to post with the king, Earl Ferdinand. My men surround Lambeth and protect its entrances and grounds. I want you to be with his grace each day, speak with him, share your best tales of adventures in the field, stir his memories of triumphs, share his meals. First and foremost, help King Henry to think of everything except his illness and the torment that plagues him."

Ferdinand smiled slightly as he began to understand his assignment. "I have never thought of myself as one brought to offer nursing care, your lordship, but I can see why you are asking me to keep the king's mind occupied with triumphant thoughts and memories of his own knightly valour."

"Yes, indeed you are quite to the point, Marshfield. First and foremost, I do not wish anyone in the king's presence to suggest to him that he is unable to get well."

"Also, your lordship," Ferdinand continued, "I have contacted my sister, the Lady Apollonia of Aust, to ask about the condition of the king's physician, Marimon. He had been dangerously ill and only recently recovered, thanks to the care of her household. She has told me that Marimon wishes to return to court to continue his care of the king. I told her that the physician should come here to Lambeth Palace to continue the king's care. Obviously, you are hopeful that recovery will begin to happen here."

"You amaze me, my lord earl, and have anticipated my keenest wish. I have been searching for Marimon for weeks. This doctor of physic has demonstrated his ability to be the only physician in the kingdom able to bring relief to our king."

"I have told my sister that *you* wish for Physician Marimon to come here to care for his grace. She says that if the physician's journey goes well, he should be here within two days."

* * *

That evening, Count Dravini was in the hall of his townhouse, storming about as if a badly-spoiled child. All his fraudulent international culture and sophistication had been discarded, and he displayed the reality of his person. His healer had returned from court with a message from the Archbishop of Canterbury telling him that the

Commons of England had declared that there were to be no foreigners involved in the care of their king, and every aspect of contact had been forbidden to him. All the healer and the count's access to the royal bedside had been denied them, and Dravini was made aware that he had been totally outmanoeuvered.

"What can I do, Hardulph? I must find some way to restore my access with the king. Shall I declare that an international humiliation has been done against the Kingdom of Sicily by the Church of England and must be corrected?"

"Can not see how that will make a difference, my lord," Hardulph smirked. "Who is going to take your word against the Archbishop of Canterbury who will soon be Chancellor of England?"

"I must do something," Dravini shouted. "I will not be treated like this."

As Dravini turned from Hardulph, the knight's smirk broadened into an ugly broken-toothed grin that the count could not miss. "How dare you laugh at me. You scum, you worthless, foul filth. I made you what you are."

Hardulph's expression changed dramatically, and he began to walk towards Dravini with his hand on his sword. "You will guard your foreigner's mouth, my lord, or I will close it for you."

Suddenly, as if the entire episode had not happened, Dravini began to simper. "We are being ridiculous, Sir Hardulph. Pray, grant me your peace. I have misspoke--out of temper."

Dravini's eyes were still ablaze, but his voice seemed to have calmed dramatically. Though he offered Hardulph no apology, his now quiet comments seemed to make nothing of his outburst.

"Let us share a glass of wine, my friend," he said ingratiatingly to Hardulph whose hand was still on his sword, "a far better way to end the evening. I have a delivery of Bordeaux recently come that is among the best vintage in many years." All the while Dravini was backing away from Hardulph, he called to his servant and signalled that wine should be served. When each man held a glass in his hand, Dravini proposed a toast.

"To those who will be acknowledged," he said with gusto.

"To those who will be rewarded," Hardulph said in response.

* * *

The bedchamber at Lambeth Palace where King Henry lay was grandly royal, but Ferdinand, when shown into the king's presence, felt immediately that the monarch had already determined that he was incurably ill. Looking up from his bed, the king could only grimace at himself after greeting Ferdinand.

"My Lord of Marshfield, what a ruin you see before you. You must not feel that you should hide your feelings of repulsion at the sight of me. I was once a warrior, a knight, a leader in warfare. Now, you see before you the disfiguration of a man. Arundel is trying to hide the extent of my disability from the world, but you see the horrific truth."

The king began to tell Ferdinand how he suffered constantly from a discomfort that seemed to have no cure. "This disease attacks as if my skin is constantly burning." Ferdinand could see that Henry's face was swollen and its skin peppered with pus-filled pimples. His hair had fallen from his head, and his formerly martial body seemed bent and twisted in agony.

Apollonia's brother had never been a courtier known for complementary or chivalrous conversation, and the king knew him well as one from whom complete honesty could always be expected.

"Your grace, I have seen the grotesqueries of the battlefield. Horrific realities do not shock me, but I am sorry to see how you suffer."

It was as if the king experienced a breath of fresh air by the earl's coming. He urged Ferdinand to sit next to him, and they began to reminisce of battle experiences they had shared in Wales in earlier years. Ferdinand was older than his king but a loyal subject who had personally supported Henry's claim to monarchy, especially after Richard II's demonstrations of tyranny. The two soldiers did not hesitate to correct the other's recollections, and soon their chat grew into an animated exchange.

Ferdinand was not certain how long he remained in the royal presence, but a servant came to announce that, on orders of the archbishop's physician, the king must rest. As the earl stood to excuse himself, he thought the king's voice expressed a kind of urgency.

"You must promise me to return, Marshfield. I feel your company brings healing digression, and I so miss being at court."

"Indeed, your grace, I shall speak with whomever is in charge of your care as soon as I can and ask when next I may be with you."

"Come again on the morrow, I pray you."

Leaving the king's chamber, Ferdinand found himself very well received by the entire archbishop's household. He was shown to a nearby chamber for his personal use and given every comfort. It was obvious to the earl that Arundel was determined to control all access to the king. When he was alone with the household servant, Ferdinand asked if the king's physician had arrived at Lambeth to care for him?"

"Indeed, my lord, he is due to arrive tomorrow and reassume charge of the king's care."

"Would you ask him to come to me when he has a free moment? I should like to speak with him."

* * *

It was the following day before Mark Marimon was able to meet with Ferdinand, and when he did, he felt apprehensive about the earl's surprising request to speak with him. They found each other first in the busy hall of Lambeth, full of people seeking contact with the powerful archbishop. Ferdinand did not wish to remain there. He asked the physician to meet him after dinner in his personal chamber on the upper floor where he said they might speak privately. Mark's apprehension grew, but he reminded himself that this lord was the highly respected brother of a noblewoman dear to him, the Lady Apollonia of Aust.

It was late in the afternoon when Mark came to knock on the door of Ferdinand's chamber, but as it was opened so rapidly by the earl himself, Mark knew he was expected. Ferdinand was alone and led him to a chair by the fire. He began speaking as soon as they sat together.

"The key thing you must remember, young man, is never mention religion in this house in any questioning way. The archbishop is determined to stamp out all influences of Wycliffe in our kingdom. You and your friends must never be seen to question any aspect of church doctrine. Arundel has been told that you are the best trained physician available in England to treat our king, and that is the only reason why you are here."

"My Lord of Marshfield," Mark said after a few moments consideration, "I am truly grateful for your advice and shall seek to follow your every instruction. Members of the household of your blessed sister, the Lady Apollonia in Aust, not only saved my life, they enabled my recovery. I feel a huge debt of gratitude to your family and especially to her ladyship."

"Do not concern yourself with gratitude here—defend yourself with silence. That is all. You may go."

At that, Ferdinand rose and Mark did as well. The physician could see that their time together had come to an end, so he thanked the Lord Ferdinand for his willingness to speak with him, then bowed, and walked from the chamber. It would be several days before they would share conversation again.

Mark returned to the hall to find Julian Thurston. As he walked through the door, he could see the knight seated by the fire, reading as usual. They moved to a very quiet corner of the great chamber where they could speak privately. He was anxious to talk with his friend and especially to share with him the strange interview he had just had with the Earl of Marshfield.

"Hide away that copy of Wycliffe's English translation, Julian," he whispered as he seated himself. "We can not let anyone see us being sympathetic with any question of the church or holy scripture whilst we are here. I have been officially, but gently, warned by the Earl of Marshfield. Our devotion to Wycliffe's English translation of scripture and his desired reforms to our faith must never be known."

"I have never met Marshfield, but he is reputed to be a good man—honourable, dependable, and loyal, Mark. Even more to our interest, he is the brother of the Lady Apollonia."

"Indeed, I received his words as well meant. He is a gentleman in the best sense of the word."

* * *

Sir Hardulph and Waldef approached the public house on the river and could hear music and bawdy language pouring from its doors. The knight gestured to Waldef to remain below while he took the stairs to the upper level. He knew his evening's pleasure would take place there.

Unbeknownst to Hardulph and Waldef, Dravini's hired assassin followed them. He watched carefully to note where each went, and it became obvious to him that the servant was to remain below stairs while the knight sought his whore on the upper level. He signalled to his friend, the barkeep, to keep Waldef drinking.

He remained in the shadows until he thought the knight would be in bed and then crept quietly to the upper level chamber kept by Hardulph's harlot. As the inn was crowded, no one was suspicious of his movements, and he easily located the bedchamber where he also found the door unlocked. His entry was easily and quietly accomplished.

Hardulph had wasted no time tearing off his clothes, and his nude body was on top of his woman who seemed to be squealing in delight at every penetration. A real professional with a dagger in each hand, the assassin stole across the chamber silently and plunged one dagger to its hilt into Hardulph's back, forcing the knight's body to collapse onto the bed beside her while sinking the second dagger into the heart of the knight's prostitute. The noises from each exposed body degenerated into choking, gurgling moans, and soon their murderer knew he had done his job efficiently.

He left the chamber in silence, leaving both daggers in place, and returned to the lower floor of the inn. The barkeep had tried to keep Waldef drinking as he had been told, but the lad had consumed little. Waldef had no interest in powerful drink, and he was anxious to be gone from this place. When, suddenly, this burley creature brought his drink to sit next to his stool, Waldef grew nervous.

"Greetins young'n," he said in seeming good cheer. "Oi be Buldoc, do grant me your company a brief while."

Waldef smiled, not knowing precisely what to do. This stranger was frightening. Though short in height, he was intimidating and powerfully built yet seemed to be friendly. Waldef decided he would remain with him just until he finished his ale. What the lad did not see were the drops that were put into his cup. Before he had drained the ale, he had fallen into a deep sleep.

Loud enough so that everyone could hear, the assassin shouted to the barkeep, "Time to put this young'n to bed." He threw Waldef over his shoulder, carried him up the stairs into the murder chamber, and tossed his limp body across the foot of the bed.

When Buldoc descended to the lower level, he calmly walked to the barkeep and quietly told him to call the authorities. A murderous act had been committed upstairs.

* * *

Waldef could not pull his thoughts together. His mind was foggy and madly confused as to where he was. He was being roughly shaken into consciousness and forced to look upon a horrific scene of bloodshed on the bed beside him. He had no memory of this place, but he could see that the nude body of Sir Hardulph was lying to one side of a nude woman, both covered in blood and mortally stabbed. The officer of the sheriff was shouting at him. "You will hang for this."

Chapter Six

Murderers' Scheming

When the count's assassin returned to Sicily House that evening, he simply announced to Dravini that the young servant of Sir Hardulph had been arrested for the murder of the knight whom he served. "How can anyone be trusted in these days, m'lord?"

With those words Dravini knew precisely what had been accomplished. He was rid of the knight, and his silly servant lad with high ideals of chivalry was in gaol for the murder. Everything had been done in an orderly and competent manner. He tossed a purse into Buldoc's hands and said nothing, but the assassin knew he would continue in Dravini's service. He was extremely efficient at his job.

"Now, you must make yourself gone. I am expecting an important guest who may arrive at any moment."

As if to respond to his words, the bell of the front entrance rang, and Dravini's servant went to answer. As soon as Dravini was alone, the caller was led into the hall.

"My lord count, this is Sir Joshua Blackwood who has come with a message."

"Sir Joshua, you are welcome. Pray be seated. May I offer you a glass of wine?"

"Gramercy, my lord count. I am unable to remain but must ask you to read my lord's message straightaway. If you have no questions regarding its contents, I shall be off."

Dravini broke the seal and opened the single-page message, which said: "Dravini, I am aware that you are now refused entry to Henry's court. Come to me tomorrow evening at our usual meeting place for your next assignment. Paine"

* * *

The Baron Wenlock Paine arrived late at his meeting with Dravini. Making no apologies, he simply sat at the small table in the corner of the ale house where Dravini was waiting for him and began speaking in a low voice full of resentment.

"Everyone in England seems to think that we who serve the Lord of Northumberland have been shown considerable favour by the usurper King Henry. Now, he dares believe that he can rule us, and we will forget his earlier lies. Know this, I have nothing but hatred for him since our rebellion and the death of my Lord Hotspur. What do you know of the king's condition? Is he soon to die?"

"Ah, no, my lord, the king is suffering from a series of unknown illnesses. His appearance is disgusting, but now an excellent doctor of physic is returned to him at Lambeth. From what I hear, he is recovering sufficiently to appear before the next Parliament."

"Damn and blast! I thought you were going to sicken him to death."

"We were well on our way to success, but what could I do? It was the Archbishop of Canterbury who forbade me contact, my lord. He has assumed complete control of access to our king who now resides at Lambeth Palace."

Paine's frustration was obvious as he sat beside Dravini, considering his next move. Finally, the baron stood, ready to leave once again.

"For the time being, you will continue to stay in Sicily House at my expense, Dravini, but you must try to make contact with the King as a visiting foreign dignitary because of 'your respect for him'. Find a way to get someone inside Arundel's household to do the deed and be able to slip away. Do you have a man we can use?"

"Ah, yes, my lord, one who has recently relieved me of an uppity servant whom I could no longer trust."

"I wish to know no details, but once your man has joined the archbishop's household at Lambeth, complete my instructions regarding the King."

Paine turned slightly to add a warning over his shoulder as he left, "Keep your distance from me, Dravini. I will contact you only when I need. For now, there will be no further communication between us. I worked to see Richard deposed but now seek an end to Henry Bolingbroke's rule. I will use you as my agent in the weeks ahead, for I wish to see that those who support the usurper will find themselves persistently harassed."

* * *

Apollonia visited her dovecote daily, always grateful to find any news from her brother. Ferdinand described the king's symptoms as easing since the return of Mark Marimon to take charge of his care. The king's skin problems had improved, Ferdinand told her, because of the application of herbal creams that the physician made daily to soothe King Henry's face and upper body. "His grace tells me that his skin no longer seems to be burning, Polly, and though he rests regularly throughout the day, he has been able to return to some of his royal duties, even to attend Parliament. I hope to return home soon."

The Lady was grateful to receive this news but remained troubled at the inability of anyone to discover who was at the heart of what she was convinced had been an attack on the life of the king's physician and possibly the King. Who was this Count Dravini, and whom did he serve? Why would a foreign dignitary from Sicily have a personal interest in destroying the King of England's health? Apollonia could not help but suspect that someone in the English aristocracy was more likely behind this attempt to remove King Henry. Feelings among some of the nobility had grown into revolt several years earlier, though that rebellion had been quelled by the king's forces at the Battle of Shrewsbury. Apollonia knew there were still those who were determined to replace him with, they said, one who possessed a better claim to inherit the throne, a twelve-year-old Mortimer boy much more likely subject to their manipulation.

"Ferdinand believes that he will be able to return to Marshfield soon, Nan, and, I dare say, will be erupting into Aust Manor hall to tell me every important thing that he has done to serve King Henry. It is unlikely that we shall hear much from Mark Marimon, now that he is lead physician in charge of the king's care once again. He will have little time for correspondence, but if Sir Julian remains with him, perhaps the knight will send me word.

* * *

Apollonia, resident in Aust, was eventually made aware of a very brutal event that happened in London before Ferdinand could leave to return to Marshfield. Her brother told her of having visited an old friend who lived near Lambeth Palace and whose son was sheriff of the county. As they were remembering old times together, his fellow knight told Ferdinand that his son, the sheriff, had encountered an unusual request during his recent murder investigation.

"The accused murderer is a young lad who served the knight he killed. He insists that he is innocent and claims that he is a chivalrous person who would never commit a criminal act, much less murder his master. He says he has no memory of anything other than sitting in the ale house waiting for his master to return from an assignation with a prostitute on the upper floor. He claims the protection of the Lady Apollonia of Aust and continues to beg my son to contact someone in her household to speak for him. The Lady is your sister, is she not?"

"What is this churl's name?" Ferdinand demanded.

"He is called Waldef and was servant to Sir Hardulph of Leicester. Though hardly more than a lad, he was found sleeping, lying on the bed in the chamber where his master and the prostitute lay dead, stabbed to death and obviously murdered."

"Are you telling me that the murderer was found sleeping in the victims' bed? That seems most unlikely. If he did the deed, why would he be napping at the site?"

"Well, my son agrees that it is hard to believe that a real murderer would wish to be found resting on the same bed with his victims, but that is how he was discovered."

"Were there any witnesses to this lad's presence at the inn?"

"Yes," Ferdinand's friend told him, "the barkeep has told my son that this Waldef had been drinking heavily throughout the evening whilst he waited for the knight to finish his visit with one of their whores. He also said that the lad seemed mightily annoyed at being kept waiting so may have cruelly played out his frustration upon his master by stabbing him and his woman. As I said, both were found stabbed to death with daggers in their hearts on the same bed where Waldef was found asleep."

"This story seems preposterous," Ferdinand told him. "He may have been the murderer, but why would he choose to be found resting at the scene of the crime?"

"These questions are also being asked by my son who has put them to this Waldef extensively. All he can say is that he has no memory of anything except waiting for his master below stairs in the ale house, and that is no defence. He claims the protection of the Lady of Aust. Do you think that your sister has any willingness to speak for his character?"

"She seems willing to put herself into the heart of any mystery," Ferdinand muttered, "but I will send her a message. If she denies any knowledge of this Waldef, I shall get back to you straightaway."

* * *

When Apollonia received Ferdinand's message, she thought it to be worded in a very inferential way. It read: "Local sheriff has young criminal named Waldef being held in gaol for murder of his master, the knight, Sir Hardulph of Leicester. Found at the scene of the crime, he claims you will speak in his defence. Surely, this can not be so. F."

The Lady read Ferdinand's message aloud to Giles and Nan and remained silent at first as her thoughts raced back to her brief awareness of young Waldef whose only appearances in her home had been in service to the obnoxious knight Hardulph. She knew nothing about the lad and felt that she could make no judgement upon him, but he had been willing to share with her household a warning of threat to Mark Marimon's life. Finally, she asked Giles, "It was this young Waldef whom you told me passed on the note warning Mark that he was in danger, was it not, Giles?"

"Indeed, my Lady, I was a bit taken aback by his forwardness to reach out to take my hand before he left the manor but discovered he had purposely done so to pass on the warning note, which I shared with you. He obviously did not wish his master to know what he was doing."

"Yet, he made a courageous effort to warn us of danger to Mark," the Lady said quietly.

"I know of no other way to interpret his note, my Lady."

"Giles, would you be willing to travel to London and seek out the imprisoned young Waldef?"

"What is my purpose, my Lady?"

"I shall send a message to my brother to remain there until you can arrive. Ferdinand will be baffled by my instructions but not wish further details of the reasons for my suspicions. I want you to speak for Waldef on my behalf because of the risk that he was willing to take for one residing in my household at that time. Whoever is behind these brutal killings, it is likely to have been someone who had real motive for Sir Hardulph's death and who sought to use the life of young Waldef to cover his crime."

"I shall prepare to leave immediately, my Lady, but where am I to find his lordship?"

"Go to Lambeth Palace. Disregard Ferdinand's bluster, and simply tell him that I must know if Waldef is being unjustly charged for a murder he did not commit. He can only be in his teens and declares to me that he is innocent."

* * *

Brandon Landow had been moving up in society in his later years. Both of his parents were gone, having left him a tidy inheritance of money as well as land. As a pardoner, he had always pursued a life dedicated to abusing the power of the church, and he had recently moved to London to serve in the household of Thomas Arundel, the powerful Archbishop of Canterbury. Landow's purpose, when he had served as pardoner of the church, was to promote his sales of indulgences to seek control over others' lives while increasing his personal wealth. Now, he promoted his position in the capital as a member of the affinity of the one powerful man in England, second only to the King. He had come to the attention of Chancellor Arundel as one who could get things done, so Landow sought every opportunity to promote himself further in the eyes of the archbishop.

Landow knew, as did all the members of the Arundel affinity, that the chancellor as Archbishop of Canterbury was personally warring against Lollardy. Therefore, Landow also desired to be seen daily as an avid warrior against what he called the great heresy of the present age. Always on the lookout for any suggestion of a man's questionable beliefs, Landow was told of suspicious behaviour by a knight newly returned to court, Sir Julian Thurston, who was a close friend to the head physician to King Henry. Landow was aware that Arundel, as a close friend to the King, had rejoiced at the recent return of Doctor

Marimon. He seemed to be the only physician in all of England able to bring comfort to the suffering monarch.

When Landow pressed those whom he knew about "questionable behaviour" of the doctor's friend Sir Julian Thurston, he was told to watch his habit of constantly reading when not called to be of service.

"Surely, there is no crime in that," Landow replied skeptically.

"No, master, until one realises what he is constantly reading."

"And what sort of filth can that be?"

"Not filth, heresy. He reads a Wycliffe English translation of holy scripture."

At this, Landow's eyes widened, and he determined that, indeed, he would pursue this charge.

"What precisely are you telling me of Sir Julian Thurston?"

"It is thought that he is a Lollard knight and a very devoted one, always seeking to improve his knowledge of holy scripture, advised by the writings of Wycliffe."

With this revelation, Landow thought immediately that he could bring to Arundel's attention a serious charge against Thurston— specifically that he, as a Lollard, did not seek the mediatory role of the priesthood of the church. Landow thought he could report that Thurston was regularly seen interpreting scripture and seeking personal salvation on his own. He did not know Sir Julian but would continue to observe his behaviour and find an opportunity to make himself known to the knight.

Landow desperately wanted to achieve special recognition within the Arundel affinity, and the best way he thought he could do that was to bring charges of Lollardy against Sir Julian to the archbishop's attention. In truth, he did not care in the least what the knight's religious views were, but if it were possible to use this to promote himself, he would make his charges. First, Landow told himself, he must pretend to wish to know more about Thurston.

* * *

The following day, when Landow was walking into Lambeth Palace, he encountered Sir Julian sitting in the great hall alone, not mixing with other members of the court who were gathered there. The knight was reading quietly by the fire. Landow saw this as an opportunity not to be missed and approached him with no introduction.

"I say, sir knight, I have noticed your presence here regularly. I am Brandon Landow, member of the household of his lordship, the Archbishop Arundel."

Sir Julian put his book down and stood to greet Landow. "Good morning, Master Landow," his deep voice expressing honest welcome. "Pray forgive me, but I do not know any of the archbishop's affinity. I have come to the palace with my friend, the king's physician. My name is Julian Thurston."

Landow made note of this connexion and pursued his query, "You seem so engrossed in your scholarship. Each time I have seen you here, you are reading, Sir Julian. Unusual for a man of arms, is it not? May I inquire what it is that compels your interests?"

As soon as this stranger sought to question what he was reading, Julian's suspicions were aroused. In these days, literacy was not questioned, but precisely what one was reading could be dangerous. He and Mark had agreed to hide away their English copy of scripture for as long as they were called to remain in London.

"I have borrowed this copy of Geoffrey of Monmouth's *History of the Kings of England* and am engrossed in the life of my favourite warrior, King Arthur, sir."

"Ah," Landow said somewhat taken aback, "an admirable selection for a present-day warrior."

This was certainly not what he had expected, and for once in his life, Landow was left speechless. He mumbled his good morning and swiftly moved on to another chamber in search of the servant who had put him onto this embarrassing pursuit.

* * *

It was later that evening when the Baron Paine demanded that Dravini come to him in their usual meeting place.

"Well, have you done as I commanded? Have you got someone into the archbishop's household at Lambeth to do the deed?"

"No, my lord baron, the staff of Lambeth have become very withdrawn and surrounded by guards. My man was unable to get past the gate. He continued to insist that he was merely seeking a job, in the kitchen, cleaning the garderobes, anything, but he was turned away."

"Damn and blast. There must be some way to find access to Henry Bolingbroke and guarantee that his illness is fatal."

"I, too, have tried to be admitted into the king's presence as a friend, as well as diplomatic visitor from the Kingdom of Sicily, but have been consistently refused entrance."

"Then, I want you to get to know one member of the archbishop's affinity whom we might use to gain entry. This is an insipid church figure who has come up in the world and done well for himself, but I believe chiefly motivated by arrogance and greed. See if you can become acquainted with Brandon Landow, a former pardoner of the church, who may well find his ego enhanced by the attentions of a Sicilian count."

"I shall invite him to call upon me at Sicily House, my lord. Wine and endless compliments can frequently puff up humans to their most manipulative point, and I believe I am especially skilled at such buffoonery."

* * *

Landow arrived at Sicily House at the end of the week, having received a highly complimentary invitation from the Count Dravini. The former pardoner was told that his presence was requested for a meal with the count as he had been advised of his extraordinary services to Holy Church. The pardoner assumed it to be an endorsement of his earlier reputation, and although such a thing had never been described to him before, he accepted it was his due.

Dravini could see at once that this member of Arundel's household was a conceited and incompetent churchman, totally unmoved by any inspiration of spiritual goals, barely educated, and driven by nothing but self-aggrandisement. Landow was the count's favourite sort of human ploy, and though Dravini did not know just yet how he could use him, this Landow would, he had no doubt, be useful in gaining information.

After sharing a luxuriant meal consumed with endless refills of wine, Landow was feeling marvelously self-indulgent when Dravini invited him to sit by the fireplace to continue their conversation.

His host said to Landow, staggering slightly to a great chair near the fireplace, that he had heard of the king's residence at Lambeth Palace with the archbishop.

"You know, dear friend Landow, there have been endless rumours of the serious illness of King Henry. Some have been truly threatening as to the true nature of the king's illness. I do not wish to spread evil ruminations, so what can you, with your high-level, personal contacts, tell me of the truth of the king's condition?"

"Well," Landow hiccupped, "it has been obvious to me when I have spoken with the King, that he is much improved, thanks to the care of his excellent physician."

"Ah, you have spoken with the King?" Even Dravini truly questioned such an unbelievable possibility.

"Of course, dear friend," Landow lied, "I have been summoned to deal with several of his grace's personal religious concerns."

"Really, how impressive that a dear friend of mine has such royal contact. What sort of questions does King Henry bring to you?"

"Ah, dear count, I am unable to share with you matters of royal concern, spoken to me in the manner of the confessional," Landow continued to lie more pompously.

"Well, I have been amazed at the archbishop's control over his grace, dear friend. How much longer will the King be resident at Lambeth Palace?"

"Oh, my dear Dravini," Landow laughed, "King Henry is no longer at Lambeth. He has recovered to such a state that he is travelling north to visit a variety of his Lancastrian lands, taking his personal physician with him. You are behind the times."

"Well, I am a mere visitor from a foreign kingdom," Dravini said sullenly. "What would I know of such things?"

* * *

Upon his arrival in London, Giles went first to speak with the Lord Ferdinand. He could see that the Lady's brother was, indeed, baffled by his sister's interest in the recent murder of Sir Hardulph and his prostitute. Most of all, Giles sought to learn the details of the charges against Waldef and his claim to be under the protection of the Lady Apollonia. Ferdinand at first said that he could not understand Apollonia's desire to be connected in any way with this crime or the accused murderer, but he knew that even the sheriff believed that the young lad's discovery on the bed with the murder victims was unbelievable. Also, Ferdinand knew that Waldef continually declared his innocence to the sheriff, though he could not explain how he had been found at the murder scene.

The Lady sent a note to Ferdinand with Giles and begged him to intervene as her representative. She wrote:

> Dear Brother,
> I pray you will visit this Waldef with Giles and send me your opinion of him and his claims of innocence. He is very young, and I can not say that I know him, but he did a courageous deed on behalf of one who was resident in my household. Grant me your opinion of him soon as possible.
> Your loving sister, A.

Ferdinand agreed to visit the prison with Giles not because of his sister's bizarre reasons for her possible support, but mainly because he, as an upright person and a knight of the realm, could not allow false accusation against the truly innocent.

* * *

Waldef was so overwhelmed by the appearance of Ferdinand and Giles in behalf of the Lady Apollonia that he fell to his knees. Ferdinand appeared unmoved and spoke first, coldly stating his and Giles' purpose as representing his sister, the Lady Apollonia of Aust, whom he did not wish to have defamed in this way.

"She says she does not know you, churl; therefore, I must ask why you dare to claim her protection?"

"My lord, I confess I am unknown to the Lady, but I beg her intervention on my behalf because she is known to serve God as a vowess and protect the innocent. I declare my innocence of all charges against me. I did not murder my master nor the woman he was with. I have never held such weapons as the daggers used to kill them. I served my master faithfully for more than a year, determined to pursue the goals of chivalry in my life. In recent months however, I became aware that though my Lord Hardulph was a knight, he was a man without principle or moral guidance, described by the Count Dravini who employed his services as a 'paid killer'.

"My lord, with that revelation, I knew I must find some way to leave his service. I swear to you, and to all who will listen, that I have no memory of what happened in the inn that dreadful night until I was awakened by the sheriff, lying across the bed where Sir Hardulph and his woman lay dead."

"Do you think that my sister will accept such a story? Would not every criminal caught amid a crime claim such amnesia?"

"My lord, in the name of our Saviour Christ, I proclaim I can do no other."

Ferdinand had encountered many evil men in his days, but this lad expressed a kind of unbelieving wonder at what had happened to him. The earl was forced to pause and consider what Waldef was saying.

Giles spoke next and put his case very simply to Waldef, "My Lady Apollonia is an elderly woman living in a village far from this city. Why would she ever wish to expose herself or her household to the murderous evil potential of one charged with your crimes?"

"Master, I can offer the Lady nothing but my personal truth. Throughout my life, I have only wished to pursue the goals of chivalry: courage, honour, courtesy, justice and a readiness to help the weak. I follow the great commandment of our Lord Jesus to love God and our neighbours as ourselves. I can not claim perfection, but I struggle to do good."

* * *

When Ferdinand and Giles left Waldef's cell, they walked outside the gaol and paused to speak with each other, exchanging opinions of their interview with the accused prisoner.

"Well, Giles, what say you? Do you find this Waldef convincing?" Ferdinand asked him.

Giles seemed undetermined, but his first response was simply to say, "He is so young, my lord, and so earnest."

"Indeed, he is youthful, but in my experience, some youngsters seem to be born into crime."

"Yet, my lord, he insists he has sought only one goal in his life, to fulfill the code of chivalry."

"No doubt his lord, Sir Hardulph, as a knight swore to fulfill such a code as well. Still, my sister knew him to be a man of questionable morality with no desire other than to manipulate the weak."

"All that you say is correct, my lord, but Waldef declares himself to be a follower of Christ."

"I could not help but be moved by his declaration of the code of chivalry ruling his life as a Christian," Ferdinand said somewhat hesitantly. "I confess, I am moved to believe that he deserves a hearing."

Chapter Seven

Return to Aust

In recent years, Apollonia was pleased to be home in Aust. She enjoyed travel about the West Country of the kingdom, especially being able to share the opportunities she had to be with her sons and grandchildren. But the home village of her beloved second husband, Edward Aust, the father of their sons, was full of meaning to her because of the endless happy family memories it called forth daily. Aust and its parish church were beautifully situated close to the Severn River. While sustaining her ongoing sense of responsibilities as Lady of the manor, Apollonia felt a personal awareness of the village's historic significance as the ancient, southernmost ferry crossing of the Severn River going back to Roman times. The Lady knew the names of every family who lived in the village and was especially grateful to be close once again to her friends, Joshua and Jeanne Falcon, Nan's adopted family. They were living on Joshua's mother's nearby farm with their adopted daughter, MaryLizbet, now thirteen years old and devoted to the care of her younger twin brothers, Jerald and Jock.

MaryLizbet frequently brought the boys to the manor house to visit with their special Grandmama Nan. Apollonia's maid always had something for them, a special treat or a bit of time to play a favourite game of hide and seek. Apollonia was convinced that though Nan herself had had no childhood, she was thrilled with the opportunity of sharing in theirs.

Nan's recent return to the manor from a visit with her family was greeted by a new worry for the Lady in the name of a young man whom she barely knew but who had claimed her protection against charges of murder in faraway London. Nan told Apollonia that she could see no reason why the Lady would make her protection available to him, but Apollonia could not forget that the young man had risked his position in life by warning Physician Marimon, a visitor in her home, of a threat against his life.

Apollonia went daily to the dovecote, expecting to receive more news of the details of the case against young Waldef from her steward, Giles Digby, or her brother, the earl, who had been in London during the entire episode. What she had not expected, as she sat with Nan near the fireplace in her hall late in the afternoon, was to see Ferdinand and her steward returning to the manor house bringing with them the accused criminal, fifteen-year-old Waldef.

"Polly, have some food brought," Ferdinand shouted. "I must speak with you now for I plan to take a very early night and be on my way by dawn. This is the accused Waldef, and I suggest you will have him locked in the barn under Gareth's guard."

As always, Apollonia was prepared for her brother's abrupt demands of her as his younger sister. This time, however, the Lady knew that she had already used her brother's presence in London to help her understand the extraordinary position she was in, of being asked to offer her protection to Waldef.

The Lady sent Nan to bring food from the kitchen and then asked Giles to take charge of Waldef in the hall while she retreated with her brother to her solar. In an amazingly brief time, Ferdinand was seated in the great chair across from her eating hungrily and telling her what he had done.

"First and foremost, you must know that I have truly taken a risk for you, Polly, but I know the sheriff's father and could pull a bit of weight on your behalf."

"Would you kindly explain for me precisely what it is that you have done, Ferdinand?"

"I would think it is obvious—I have brought the accused murderer of Sir Hardulph and his mistress to you because he claims some sort of protection from your household."

"You call him an accused murderer; yet the sheriff releases him to my care as a favour to you, Ferdinand. How can that be? What precisely did you tell the son of your friend the sheriff?"

"He is as aware as anyone of this Waldef's constant declaration of innocence," her brother said defensively.

"There must have been more than that, brother. I have been told that he is the murder suspect actually found at the scene of the crime."

"Yes, yes, but I suggested to the sheriff that the extraordinary circumstance of his being found asleep, lying upon the murder bed, could be telling us that young Waldef had been drugged. He begs a chance to prove his innocence."

"You do bring things to an interesting point, brother, and now you have made my household solely responsible for Waldef until his innocence is proven."

"Well, Polly, it is always just what you want—to place yourself at the heart of any mystery. Now, the mystery is brought to you, and I am off to bed," he said as he stood to leave.

After Ferdinand had gone to his bed, the Lady descended to the hall to meet with Giles and be introduced to young Waldef. The lad remembered being here in the Aust household with Sir Hardulph, but his circumstances had changed so drastically that he was trembling in anticipation of being personally introduced to the Lady.

Apollonia spoke to Giles at first, thanking him for making the journey into London for her and then asked him to introduce her to his companion in the hall who was quietly being guarded by her stablemaster Gareth.

Giles simply said, "My Lady, this is Waldef, former servant to the knight Sir Hardulph, who tells me that he has called upon your household twice before. The Lord Ferdinand spoke on his behalf to the Sheriff in London, and therefore we were able to bring him to Aust as he claims your protection."

"I remember you, young Waldef in your capacity as servant to the knight, Hardulph," the Lady told him, at which point he threw himself to his knees and blessed her for her willingness to receive him.

"My Lady of Aust, I have heard of your extraordinary grace and goodness as a woman of the church and obviously beloved among your personal affinity. You are my only hope of salvation. I am innocent of all charges against me, but I have no memory of what happened to place my sleeping body at the scene of my master's murder...none."

"Pray, Waldef, bring a stool and come sit with us by the fire. Can you describe for me what you do remember on the night of Sir Hardulph's death?"

"I remember very well that I accompanied him to an inn where my Lord Hardulph had a favourite mistress. As was usual during his visits to that place, I was to remain in the lower level of the public house until he had finished and summoned me to return to serve him for the rest of the night. It was a long evening, I knew no one there, but a ruffian called Buldoc joined me where I was seated and asked me to drink with him. I confess that I found his presence frightening and decided that I would remain only until I had finished my ale. I do not remember anything more said between us. My next memory of the evening is being shaken awake by the sheriff's man as I lay upon the same bed where the bodies of Sir Hardulph and his mistress also lay, both stabbed to death."

"You are saying that you were found by the sheriff actually lying asleep *with* the victims on the same bed in the chamber where the murder took place?"

"I confess to you that I was found in an incriminating situation, my Lady, but I am not the murderer. It was my hope to leave Sir Hardulph's service, but I had no reason to kill him or his harlot. I have never owned nor even held the daggers that were used to stab the victims. Please believe me when I say that I have dedicated my life, whatever my profession may be, to serve the code of chivalry."

The Lady said little during Waldef's tale, but now she asked him to return to his feet. "The days ahead will be a difficult time for you, Waldef, but I will listen to all that you can tell me. We will find our way to the truth, but now you need food and rest. You must understand that you will be kept in a locked chamber in the barn through the nights as long as I am responsible for you." With a gesture to Gareth, she suggested that Waldef be returned to speak with her further in the morning and waved them off to the kitchen.

The Lady turned to Giles after the men were gone. "Now, faithful steward, will you please tell me everything that you found in London and why you and my brother decided to bring an accused criminal into my household?"

"My Lady, I believe his lordship, your brother, and I agreed that Waldef seemed to deserve a chance to prove the innocence that he claims. Lord Ferdinand is impressed by the young lad's dedication of his life to the chivalric code, but we both find a religiously inspired confession of innocence in him. Most of all, it is the manner of his being found asleep in the murder chamber on the same bed as the victims. That was preposterous, even to the sheriff, so my Lord Ferdinand suggested that perhaps he had been drugged. Then, since Waldef claimed your protection, the earl suggested that we would bring him under guard to Aust and allow him time to prove his innocence.

"Giles, as a leading member of my household, I shall need to have you with me in the morning when Waldef returns from the barn where he must be kept. You know that I prefer to remain silent as a vowess, but I can not remain silent through this. I want to use your inquisitive mind as well as your insightful questions of the lad to help me pursue the truth of this bizarre episode. Also, will you please tell Gareth that I will need to have his opinions of this lad as time goes by. He has a sharp eye for integrity and honest uprightness."

* * *

When Giles returned to the Lady's solar the following morning, he brought Waldef with him. The Lady could see that Waldef had evidently slept well the night before, and she had been told that he had broken his fast with a hearty meal in the kitchen this morning. It was as if he had fortified himself to appear before the Lady, prepared to answer all her questions of him. The lad knew that she was his one hope, and he desperately wished to convince her of his truth.

The Lady bid him a good morning as he bowed to her. She was not smiling, but her face declared a willing curiosity in his behalf. Giles bade him be seated and began their conversation by asking, "Will you begin by telling us the story of your life?"

"I am Waldef Gilbert, the only son of Merton Gilbert, a merchant of Bristol, my Lady. My dear mother encouraged me in all things to seek to fulfill my potential in life. She died when I was six, and my father encouraged me to remain in school after she was gone. I did continue my studies until I was twelve, but early on, I was driven to seek to understand the meaning of knighthood and its code, even though I knew I was of the merchant class and not from noble family.

"Sir Hardulph's brother in Bristol knew my father and offered me the extraordinary opportunity of serving as his brother's servant. I confess I leapt at the possibility and drove myself to read everything I could to prepare. From my early days with Sir Hardulph, I could see that he dismissed the chivalric code as womanish foolishness. He sought only one thing, to enrich himself, frequently, in ways beyond the law.

"My greatest concerns grew when he agreed to serve a foreign count who said he was from Europe but had become resident in England at the court of King Henry. I could see nothing noble about that man. He used my Lord Hardulph to pursue evil tasks for him and in my presence called my master a 'trained killer'. I heard the evil count tell him to murder the king's doctor of physic, Physician Marimon."

"How did you learn of this?" Giles asked him.

"I was in their presence when the assignment was given. The count told my master what he wanted done, and Sir Hardulph seemed to think nothing unusual about it. It was then that I knew, when given an opportunity, I must warn Physician Marimon and find some way to leave Sir Hardulph's service."

"So, it was here in Aust with your master, that you pressed your warning note into my hand, was it not?" Giles asked.

"Yes, Steward Giles. When I thought that the physician was known to the Lady, you were the one person of authority within the household whom I had opportunity to reach out to."

"I must tell you, Waldef, it was that gesture made in behalf of Mark Marimon that has brought you the Lady's protection."

"Praise God, my Lady," Waldef said. "I acknowledge myself to be unworthy, but I am eternally grateful to you."

Apollonia gestured to Giles that she wished to speak with Waldef. "Your thanks are somewhat precipitous, Waldef. Now you must help me find proof of your innocence of the murder of your master. You have told me that you meant to leave his service."

"Ah yes, my Lady, but simply that—I had to leave his service. I could not consider being part of his illegal and murderous assignments."

"Why should I believe you?"

"My Lady, I had no motive to kill my lord, I only wished to leave him. I longed to serve a knight but I had no desire to learn to kill. I carry no weapons, I am not trained in the use of the dagger or sword. I tried to dedicate my life to the religious and moral goals of service: courage, honour, courtesy, justice and a readiness to help the weak. Surely, such goals are possible in life without carrying a sword."

Giles looked at his mistress, and the Lady could see in his eyes the question, "Does he not seem sincere?"

Apollonia turned again to Waldef and changed the subject of their conversation. "What can you tell me about this count whom your knight was willing to serve?"

Waldef was frustrated by this question because he knew he could tell her very little. "My Lady of Aust, I can only say that he is from Europe, and his name sounds something like Dravenie. He says he is from the Kingdom of Sicily, but I do not know where that is. As I listened to him speak with my Lord Hardulph, he seemed to be a person devoid of moral concern or religious scruple."

"Do you know of any reason why the knight came to Aust Manor and attempted to bully my Lady as he did?" Giles asked.

"I have my suspicions that he sought to use you, my Lady, Master Digby, in his search, but they can be merely that. It was when Sir Hardulph was sent into Gloucestershire in search of Physician Marimon to kill the physician and then escape back to London where the count was waiting to re-establish his power over the king, I knew I could not continue my service to Hardulph."

"Have you been aware of any English nobleman who sought to use the count's influence?" Apollonia asked quietly.

"No, my Lady, but I did see one English knight who seemed to bring regular messages to the count from someone in the nobility. I do not know his name."

"Let us return to the night of the murder of your master, Waldef. You say that you can remember nothing until being shaken awake while lying on the bed, but you also told me that you had been left to drink in the lower level by your master. How much did you drink and were you drunk? Is that why you fell so soundly asleep?" Apollonia asked.

"In all honesty, I had only one flagon of ale, my Lady, and I remember quite vividly being spoken to by a ruffian called Buldoc. It was shortly after he came to join me that I remember nothing. I have no other memory after he sat next to me until I was roughly awakened in the murder chamber."

"Have you ever experienced being drugged in your young life?"

"No, Master Digby, but I know I decided to finish my drink hurriedly in order to leave the presence of Buldoc. I chucked it down, and thereafter my memory ceases until finding myself in the upper level chamber."

"It would appear that my brother was correct, Waldef," the Lady said. "He thought it possible that something was put into your ale, and once unconscious, you were carried into the murder chamber. Who would have used you so?"

"I know not, my Lady, my only sin was being in that place, but I have no memory of how I was moved."

"What did you know of this Buldoc fellow?" Giles pressed him.

"I had never seen him before, Master Digby, and I can only remember him as being a relatively short man but very sturdy and threatening in his demeanour."

"Who would you say might have wished harm to Sir Hardulph, Waldef?"

"Once again, I know not, my Lady. I remember one occasion after the count and his healer had been dismissed from the king's care when the count was roaring with anger at his treatment and my master smirked at his childish behaviour. The count turned on Sir Hardulph verbally, and my master actually put his hand upon the hilt of his sword, suggesting to the count that he must back down. The count instantly changed his entire demeanour and made light of what had just happened between them, suggesting that they should share a glass of his best wine."

"When did that altercation happen, Waldef?" Apollonia asked.

"Not long ago, my Lady, several evenings before my lord was found dead."

"Do you think that the count could be considered as one who wished revenge upon Hardulph?"

"I only know the count to be a nefarious person, whom I witnessed ordering the murder of men whom he resented."

"If that Buldoc person was working for the count, could it have been he who set you up, Waldef? It is possible that he is strong enough to have carried your unconscious body into the murder chamber?"

Apollonia continued thinking out loud, "And, if he could carry you, could he have been the muscular assassin who had already murdered Hardulph and his woman lying on the bed where you were found?"

Chapter Eight

The Pilgrim's Visit

During the past six years, Apollonia had been pleased to receive annual springtime visits from a very good Worcester friend, Robert Kenwood. The Lady and Merchant Kenwood had become acquainted during her days spent in Worcester at the home of her son Sir Hugh and his family. Apollonia respected Robert as a devout Christian who had, when they met, just returned from his long pilgrimage to Santiago de Compostela in Spain to visit the tomb of Saint James the apostle. Apollonia had never been on a long-distance pilgrimage and found Robert's descriptions of all that he had seen across Europe to be fascinating and wonderfully informative. The Lady knew her friend was a successful merchant. He was well read, always ready to discuss privately with her troubling questions of their faith, the church, as well as their personal concerns for the new Lancastrian King Henry and the reoccurring rebellions he continued to face from members of the English nobility.

Robert was a city man and younger than the Lady, yet he had come regularly to Aust in March of recent years, especially to enjoy her friendship and the springtime beauty of her home village. They always sought time for long rides together along the Severn Estuary. If truth be told, Robert was also very happy to return to the realm of Guise, the Lady Apollonia's excellent Norman cook. Above all was his admiration for the Lady Apollonia. She was like no other woman he had ever known. He knew her to be well educated, but even more. he acknowledged that she had an intelligence surpassing any man in his acquaintance. She had achieved wealth and independence as a single woman who remained in the world while serving others through the church.

On his visit this early March, Robert seemed more than usually full of enthusiasm. He could hardly wait to describe for the Lady his recent acquaintance in Bristol with a well-known West Country merchant and ship owner of Dartmouth by the name of Robert Hawley.

"Surely you have heard of him, my Lady. Hawley has not only been a successful man of business, he was a licenced privateer who captained his own ship, the Christopher, in battle and destroyed many of the king's enemies at sea. He has been so highly respected in his community that he was elected Mayor of Dartmouth fourteen times, as well as four times Member of Parliament. The tales he has to tell are beyond imagination."

Apollonia smiled warmly at her friend's boyish enthusiasm for this well-known hero of the West Country and responded quietly, "Indeed, Robert, I am familiar with Hawley's name and some of his reputation."

"Well, I had heard that Hawley, having supported King Richard early on, lent his active support to Henry of Bolingbroke who as the new King Henry. was quick to confirm all of Hawley's existing grants. During the first two years of King Henry's reign, Hawley acted as lieutenant to the admiral of England, Thomas Percy. By this point in his life, Hawley not only began to grow wealthy, he became a member of the landed gentry, eventually elevated to the squirearchy with a coat of arms."

"Well, to some along the southwestern coastal towns, he is regarded more controversially rather than heroic, Robert," the Lady said quietly. "My brother, the Earl Ferdinand, calls him a pirate rather than the king's privateer."

Her friend seemed a bit taken aback but merely changed his enthusiastic tone slightly.

"Well, I will admit that he is now an old man who enjoys telling tales and perhaps he enhances them a bit, my Lady. Yet, I must say, I was proud to meet him and am glad to say that I know him as an acquaintance. Some say that his having met Geoffrey Chaucer, Hawley is one who serves as a model for the author's Shipman in *The Canterbury Tales*."

"Really," she replied, "but as I remember the *"Tales,"* Chaucer does not hide the fact that the shipman deals in unscrupulous behaviour far worse than many sailors of his time, does he not? When capturing other vessels, the shipman was known to make the men he captured walk the plank. Are you telling me that the use of drowning deaths at sea was part of his heroism?"

"Well, Hawley was imprisoned in the Tower of London by King Henry but released when he pledged compensation to some merchants," Robert added with less enthusiasm, and then as if ready to change the subject, he noted that his hostess seemed distracted. "Is something troubling you, my Lady?"

Apollonia was more than ready to speak with Robert of her recent dilemma. This was their first evening together after his arrival, and they were sitting before the fire in her solar. Even her long-time maid and dearest friend, Nan, was not with them as she had gone off to spend some days with her adopted daughter and son-in-law, Jeanne and Joshua Falcon, who lived on their nearby farm.

"I pray you will forgive my distraction, Robert, but I have found myself involved in a serious predicament, one of my own making, but one which I would be very grateful to share with you and seek your advice."

"Dear Lady, you have offered the best of friendship and hospitality to me. I would be remiss," he said earnestly, "if I withheld any assistance to you. Pray, feel free to share the details of your predicament with me."

Apollonia began by going back in time to tell Robert of the recent unexpected arrival of a gentleman in Aust, seriously ill and suffering from exhaustion, who had collapsed at the door to the cottage of her forester. As he appeared to be without any means of assistance, or even a personal mount, her servant Alwan, the forester, had brought him to be cared for at the manor. The Lady went on to describe an arrogant knight who, the same day, arrived at her door searching for the man whom she had taken in and from whom, she learned, was King Henry's lead physician, Mark Marimon. Due to her suspicions of the aggressive motives of the knight, Sir Hardulph, she told Robert that she shared nothing with him but did notice in his company a very polite young lad named Waldef who served Hardulph.

"To make a long story more brief, Robert, the knight, Hardulph, was found murdered in London in the bed of his mistress. His young servant, Waldef, was found lying across the foot of the bed asleep. The sheriff's men were called to the scene, and Waldef was charged with his master's murder. He has consistently declared his innocence and sought to place himself under my protection. I have extended my protection to him and have received him here at Aust because of a life-and-death service he provided for a visitor in my home."

"Gracious Lady, you leave me speechless! Are you telling me that you are keeping an accused murderer here in your household?"

"Indeed, I am, Robert, but the situation is not simply extending my protection, and that is why I am also asking for your counsel. Will you be willing to meet Waldef? Allow me to share nothing more with you about him at this moment. I desperately wish to have your first impressions of him."

She was not surprised that Robert did not respond to her question immediately. He sat very thoughtfully in his great chair and asked her several questions instead.

"How old did you say this Waldef is, my Lady?"

"He is past fifteen, nearly sixteen."

"Where is he from?"

"He is the only son of a successful merchant's family in Bristol."

"He is old enough to hang, my Lady."

"Yes, Robert, but he insists he is innocent of all charges."

After remaining silent for several more minutes, Robert announced to her, "I daresay that all accused criminals declare their innocence, but one thing I have learned in my life is that, as Christians, we are all sinners in God's eyes. Still, He offers the possibility of His salvation to us. I am daily in need of God's grace; therefore, I must extend that grace to this young Waldef."

"In the morning, then, if you are still willing, Robert," the Lady said, "I will take you out to the barn where the lad remains guarded by my servant, Gareth. I shall only stay long enough to introduce you to him as my special friend and then leave you to speak with him alone. Ask him every question you may have, but I pray you will not only listen to all that he says but also observe closely his person. When you have finished speaking with him, return here to my solar where I might then take full advantage of all of your observations."

"I shall do as you say, my Lady, but I can promise nothing in advance of meeting this young accused criminal."

* * *

Robert did not sleep well that night. His mind was unable to rest, constantly bedeviled by endless worries of how he could help the Lady in her recent dilemma. Obviously, she had taken this young man under her protection because of an important service that she felt he had offered to her household. She definitely believed that he deserved an honest consideration of his pleas of innocence. Then, Robert reminded himself, the Lady is a loving mother and grandmother. He also knew her to be a devoted vowess of the church as a thrice-widowed woman. Was it not possible that this young brat was simply taking full advantage of her gentle weaknesses as a devout Christian woman?

He tossed and turned in his bed and continued to think of all that he knew of the Lady Apollonia, how educated she was for a woman, how intelligent, and what a devout church woman. He also knew her to be an unusual person who had always been willing to question the regrettable behaviours of some contemporary leaders of the church, whether bishops, abbots, monks, or priests. He had seen her deal with serious human and family problems, and he knew he had always admired her for making difficult decisions. Still, he reminded himself, she was not on trial here. This young Waldef is. He must do as he promised the Lady to keep an open mind when meeting with him and focus on his person.

* * *

Apollonia was waiting for Robert when he emerged from his bedchamber to break his fast the following morning. She greeted him warmly but added nothing more to their conversation of the evening before. When they had finished their meal, they walked together to the barn where Gareth was already at work with young Waldef helping him. Her stablemaster, Gareth, had always been a reserved man and one not known to be extensive in conversation. He recognised Master Robert and greeted the Lady and her guest.

"This lad be a good worker, m'Lady," Gareth said, pointing to Waldef. "Ee be a willin elper in everything Oi asks of im."

Waldef smiled slightly as he bowed to the Lady and her guest. Though Apollonia returned his smile, she greeted Gareth and simply asked Waldef if he would come to the manor where her guest, Master Robert, wished to talk with him."

Waldef put down his pitchfork and brushed himself off indicating his willingness to follow her instructions. The Lady, Master Robert, and Waldef walked together back to the house where she led them to a small chamber, slightly larger than a storage closet near the hall where she kept her collection of bound and unbound manuscripts.

"This is not an elegant chamber, Robert, but it is my private space where I can see to it that you are not disturbed."

Then she turned to Waldef. "This is Master Robert Kenwood, Waldef, a good friend of mine whose opinions I respect. He is willing to speak with you and listen to every word of your memories from the night when the murder of your master occurred. When he has finished his questions, I pray that you will return to the barn with Gareth."

"Yes, my Lady," he said as he bowed to her again. "I am pleased to meet you, Master Kenwood, and especially grateful to be able to tell my side of this dreadful story, though I fear it is pitifully incomplete."

* * *

Apollonia was waiting in her solar when Robert returned from having spent more than an hour with Waldef. She looked up from her reading to greet her friend with a questioning smile. "Pray, seat yourself here by the fire, Robert. I shan't ask you anything yet; instead, give me your very first impressions of Waldef."

"I have met many people in my life and travels, my Lady, but this lad is an unusual young fellow. I find his devotion to the code of chivalry extraordinary for one so young who has no hope of knighthood. He comes from a merchant's family but speaks of courage, honour, courtesy, justice and a readiness to help the weak as if it sums his devotion to Christ's holy word. He has no desire to enter a monastery, but he has designed a morality for his personal life that can only be one of a truly devout young man."

"Did he speak with you about his service with Sir Hardulph, Robert?"

"He said quite frankly that he had decided to leave the knight's service and described for me his disillusionment during the time he spent with Sir Hardulph, my Lady. He is unable to get out of his mind an evening when the knight was addressed in his presence as a trained killer."

"Did he speak with you of his memories of the night of the murder of Sir Hardulph?"

"That is the great frustration, my Lady. Waldef has none except to be shaken awake by the sheriff's men on the bed at the feet of his murdered lord and the prostitute."

"This is where I require your excellent common sense, Robert. Waldef does remember being spoken to by a ruffian named Buldoc earlier in the evening whilst he waited below stairs at the inn for the knight to return from his assignation."

"Yes, my Lady, but he has no idea who this Buldoc is or why he made a point to speak with him."

"Robert, is it not possible that Buldoc sought his company merely to put a drug into his ale when the lad was unaware?"

"I must admit that it seems quite possible that he was drugged, my Lady."

"Then, I put a final question to you, Robert. Could this Buldoc have been the assassin hired by one who had his own reasons for wishing the death of Hardulph?"

"My Lady, such speculation is possible, but how is one to prove it?"

"I have not been able to move past speculation, Robert, but I am thinking that young Waldef has been cruelly set up as killer of Sir Hardulph by the real murderer who may be working for someone else. I shall not allow my speculation to die whilst I can try to prove the lad's innocence."

"This is beyond the realm of predicament, my Lady. It appears to me that you have taken upon yourself a life-and-death mystery that could bring dangerous threats into your household."

* * *

As if to lighten their minds and bring a bit more balance to her present concerns, Apollonia asked Robert if he would be willing to walk with her along one of her favourite pathways next to the Severn. It was a bright day with a gentle breeze. The Lady found a sense of peaceful return to God's creation on her woodland walks and she knew that Robert, too, always looked forward to such walks on his returns to Aust.

Faithful to Nan's constant instructions, Apollonia took her stick with her and offered Robert a walking stick as well. He selected a tall, manly wooden stick similar to one he had used on his pilgrimage and seemed to enjoy having it in hand once more as they left the manor house and strolled towards the Aust ferry crossing. A cool breeze was blowing, so their woollen capes helped to warm them while the exercise soon built up their bodies' heat. They said little at first, obviously enjoying the blooming colours of spring and varieties of birds' songs they heard as they walked along.

They reached a point near the river bank where there was a fallen tree, large enough to provide a space for them to sit together. It was a peaceful and pleasant view. The two friends made little comment between them, but their quiet smiles expressed mutual enjoyment of being able to spend this time together. Finally, as he sat next to the Lady, Robert was driven to say, "I hate to take your mind back to your predicament, my Lady, but have you spoken with Waldef about who may have been an enemy of Sir Hardulph? Does the lad have any sense of one who might have had a reason to wish his lord's death?"

Apollonia turned to him straightaway. "In truth, Robert, since Waldef's arrival in Aust, I have been struggling to find the best reasons to believe in him, his version of what happened, as well as trying to make him remember any sort of details of Hardulph's last days that might help us. But, you are more to the point. We must ask him about the knight's enemies. Does Waldef believe that Dravini would have had reason to kill his henchman Hardulph?"

"When we return to the manor, my Lady, I think that we should invite the lad to come to speak with us again privately. Two minds are always better than one. Perhaps together, we can question him gently and help him to give us possible names."

"Indeed, Robert," the Lady jumped up and used her stick to pick up her pace as they began their return walk back to the manor. "Why have I not thought to ask more questions about Dravini with the lad before?"

"Still, we must not make the lad think that we are pressuring him to name a suspect, my Lady. Let us keep our questions general as if we are seeking to better understand his reasons to leave Hardulph's service."

* * *

Later that afternoon after the Lady and Robert had returned to the manor, Apollonia invited Robert to join her in her solar and sent a message to Gareth to bring Waldef to speak with them. As usual, Gareth was prompt in responding to any of the Lady's requests. He arrived with the lad in the hall and was shown to the Lady's solar where she and Robert waited. Gareth's responsibility complete, he excused himself and promptly returned to the barn.

Waldef could be seen to be somewhat nervous about this abrupt request for another interview, but the lad hoped that the Lady and Master Robert had his best interests at heart. He picked up his courage and faced them ready to respond to any inquiries honestly. The Lady surprised him somewhat by asking him to bring a stool and sit with them, for she said they needed to have more information from him.

When he was seated by the fire, she began by saying to Waldef, "Master Robert and I need you to help us learn more about your master, Sir Hardulph. We know nothing of this knight or those whom he served. Can you at least give us some names of people to whom he reported?"

"My Lady, there was only one person who required his service within recent months, and as I have said previously, I can tell you very little about him."

"Search your memory and share with us any detail you remember of that person."

"He claimed to be a count from the Kingdom of Sicily, wherever that is," Waldef told them. "I was frightened by him, not because of any actions against me—he barely made note of me as merely another man's servant."

"Why were you frightened of him," Robert asked, "if he did not threaten you? Why should you care?"

"He insisted that he be referred to as a count, a member of foreign nobility, but I could see nothing noble about him. He was a skulking person, untrustworthy, unprincipled, a power-seeking villain, Master Robert. Worst of all, he laughed at morality and anyone who expressed respect or grace to others."

"More specifically, can you tell us why you describe him as a man without morality, Waldef?"

"Because I heard him tell my master, Hardulph, of the ways in which he had abused the king's presence when he had been allowed to be near King Henry's sickbed, my Lady. I believe he tried to manipulate the king's physician, and when he was rebuffed, he caused the physician to be run from the palace so that the count could insert a so-called healer of his own choosing. He laughed when he described how he put about the word that our King Henry's illness was that of leprosy and did whatever he could to make our king be thought of as a leper."

"Dear God, Waldef, you are telling us that this foreigner was trying to destroy the reign of our king?" Robert asked incredulously. "Why should anyone from a far-off kingdom be sent to England to do such a thing?"

"I have no idea who this man really is, my Lady, Master Robert, but I do remember that he had contacts from some English knight as well."

"Who, Waldef?" Robert asked urgently. "Do you remember any part of this Englishman's name?"

"Master Robert, I am only telling you snippets of things that I heard and saw while in Sir Hardulph's service. My lord spoke quite openly of those in England who did not wish for King Henry to remain on the throne, especially some of those lords who have continued in rebellion against him."

Seeing that Waldef was frustrated by his inability to answer their questions, Apollonia rose to dismiss him. "You have been most helpful. Grammercy, Waldef," Apollonia told him, "but now, you must return to the barn. Please send Gareth to me."

The lad bowed to the Lady and to Master Robert and then quietly left their presence. Apollonia could see that Robert was dumbfounded by what Waldef had told them, and he remained silent when Gareth came in response to the Lady's call.

"Gareth," Apollonia said to her stablemaster when he came into her presence, "I know well that you have not been home to Ingst with your wife and family since young Waldef was brought to us. I pray you will no longer feel a need to guard him or bother to lock him up during the nights. Continue to use his help in the barn during the days, grow to know the lad, but return to your normal family schedule. I do not think that Waldef is a danger to my household."

With a great smile of relief, Gareth bowed to the Lady and left her. She and Robert could tell immediately that though her stablemaster was always ready to serve her, he was more than ready to return to his own home and family in the evenings. Also, the Lady was aware that Gareth had grown to like the lad and expressed no distrust of him in any way.

"Well, Robert, we have some possible suggestions of motive for the murder of Hardulph, and though we can not say who is the murderer, I am convinced that it is not Waldef. More likely it is that so-called Sicilian count had reasons to be rid of Hardulph."

"Indeed, my Lady, but key to our mystery is the further question of who among the English nobility is behind this bizarre threat to our king."

"Will you continue to work with me through this dilemma, Robert? Your common-sense questions and devoted loyalty are of great support to me. I will continue to offer my protection to Waldef, but now that we have also become aware of threats to the reign of our king, whoever is behind those must be recognised and overcome.

* * *

The Lady arose earlier than usual the following morning. She had found herself unable to turn off her thoughts during the night. Finally giving up on sleep, Apollonia dressed and prepared to meet the new day before sunrise. She was sitting in the hall by the fire waiting for Robert to come down to break his fast with her when she heard a knock on the front entrance. No one called at such an hour, but she called to her new recently hired butler, Garmon, to answer it.

Unexpectedly, Garmon ran directly back into the hall after answering the knock. "My Lady, you must come. I know not how to deal with this."

"Deal with what, Garmon? If you need help, I shall ring for someone else."

"I pray you will come, my Lady. You must tell me what to do."

Apollonia lifted her stick and stood to walk towards the entrance hall. Garmon had closed the door but opened it quickly when she approached. The Lady could see immediately why he was reacting so strangely. There, on her step, sat a good-sized basket, but the shocking thing was its contents. Inside lay an infant wrapped in swaddling clothes. That was all, a sleeping infant but no adult; no one else waited at the door. The Lady stepped outside to look about and sent Garmon to walk around the yard to see if he could find anyone abroad at this hour.

The baby was sleeping, but as the morning was cool, the Lady gestured to Garmon to bring the basket inside. He carried it into the hall and set it gently upon the table dormant. Looking more closely at the child, Apollonia noticed a small cloth pouch lying upon it. Apollonia reached to take out the little pouch, and when she opened it, she could see some white substance inside. Putting her moistened finger into the contents, it soon became apparent to her that the little pouch was filled with salt.

"Oh Nan," she said aloud, "please forgive me, but I need you to come home." Then, she turned to Garmon and sent him to bring Waldef from the barn to her. When the lad entered the hall, he was taken aback to see a sleeping infant lying in a basket on the hall table but said nothing.

"Waldef," the Lady addressed him quietly, "I pray you will take a message to Mistress Nan for me. She must return to the manor, for as you can see, there is a new arrival here and I need to have her with me to deal with this."

Waldef said he knew where to find Mistress Nan and would be glad to take the Lady's message.

"Wait until Nan can return to the manor with you Waldef. She will not believe our newest guest."

Chapter Nine

Abandoned with Salt

One of the Lady's kitchen maids had given birth in the past year, and Apollonia had her brought to the hall. Pointing to the newly arrived basket and its contents, she said, "I need your advice, Mattie. This infant was abandoned on our doorstep this morning, and I am determined to see it taken into care. Mistress Nan will return home later today, but I shall need your help. Mattie."

"Of course, m'Lady, ow may Oi serve you?"

"Will you take leave from your kitchen duties and carry the baby upstairs to the bedchamber that once was the nursery here at Aust Manor? Then, I pray that you will stay with the child and be prepared to feed it and care for it."

"Yes, m'Lady. Oi ave plenty of milk for this littl'un and me own."

"Nan is not far away, only staying with her family at the Falcon Farm, and I shall have her return, prepared to remain. She will see straightaway why I need her presence."

"M'Lady, this be a newborn and just wakenin." As the baby began to cry, Mattie lifted it from its basket and could tell the reasons for its discomfort. With a big smile she said, "Oi shall dry its linens, m'Lady; then, Oi shall see if the little one be ungry."

"Do we have a baby boy or a little girl, Mattie?"

Mattie lifted the infant into her arms and moved about the swaddling clothes. "This be a precious baby girl, m'Lady," Mattie said with a smile.

"After having a household full of boisterous boys when my family was growing all those years ago," Apollonia told her, "I believe I shall especially enjoy observing the care of a little girl."

* * *

Nan returned to Aust Manor late in the day and brought a lovely surprise with her.

"MaryLizbet was determined to come, my Lady, for she wishes to offer her help to you in caring for this foundling. Dear God, what is the world coming to? Infants are to be loved and cherished, not left on doorsteps."

"My Lady," MaryLizbet said as she curtsied to Apollonia, "I am very pleased that Mistress Nan would bring me. It is my pleasure to be in your household once again, but I especially wished to be with you now to help care for the infant. Is the foundling a boy or a girl?"

"I am pleased to tell you that our precious foundling is a girl, MaryLizbet, and I will encourage my entire household to help with her care. She is a beautiful gift of new life to us."

"May I see the infant, my Lady?" MaryLizbet asked.

"Indeed, I will be grateful if you will ascend to the nursery and release Mattie to return to her kitchen duties. She has been good to give her time whilst waiting for you and Nan, but she has agreed to serve as wet nurse for as long as the baby requires."

The Lady called Garmon to her and asked him to take MaryLizbet to the nursery while she and Nan continued their conversation. When they were gone, the Lady looked to Nan with a questioning smile. "Dearheart, I am grateful to have you home, but I am in a bit of a quandary as to what we are to do next."

"My Lady, you of all people know that we must live our lives one day at a time. We shall see what tomorrow may bring, but can you tell me any further details of how this happened?"

"All I can say, Nan, is that there was a knock upon our front entrance before dawn this morning, and when I sent Garmon to answer, he found the infant waiting for us, asleep in a large basket."

"Were you aware of any girl or woman within your affinity who may have been carrying a child, my Lady?"

"No, Nan, but I pray you will continue to make such inquiries throughout the household in case it will help us find the mother."

"Indeed, I shall, my Lady, and I will be pleased to take charge of the infant's care with Mattie and MaryLizbet to help me. They will do most of the work, for as you can see, Mary Lizbet's enthusiasm for a fourteen-year-old is sincerely beautiful."

"There was one strange thing that arrived with the infant, Nan," the Lady said as she produced the small pouch. "I found this in the basket with the child."

"What is it, my Lady?"

"It is filled with salt, Nan, but what would be the purpose of putting a pouch of salt into the infant's basket?"

Nan's frown grew as she seemed to be harkening back to an old memory. "I can tell you very little, my Lady, but I remember one occasion when an elderly woman of the village told me something of this. She said that the one who abandoned the child has left the salt as a message."

"What message, Nan? What is it meant to tell us?"

"If I am remembering correctly, this is part of a ritual which says that whoever abandoned this infant with a gift of salt to you wishes that the child should be cared for and baptised. As you know, for many poor people, salt is very expensive."

"Well, dearheart, I shall take its meaning seriously."

"Think of the desperate straits to which some young woman has been driven, my Lady. Quite likely she is unmarried or may be a prostitute, without support and probably uneducated. Whoever she is, she begs you to take her child, care for it, and see that it is baptised into the church."

"With your help, Nan, I will certainly see to the future for this child, and we shall begin today. Bring Friar Francis to me that we may arrange the little one's baptism. Also, speak with MaryLizbet, and let us think of the best name for our little girl. She will have some good ideas."

"Oh, yes, my Lady, MaryLizbet has already mentioned her choice of names if the infant is a girl," Nan said with a great smile. "She told me that she thought the infant's name should be Arild, the name of a Gloustershire saint whose relics reside in Gloucester Abbey."

"Then, perhaps we might consider calling the child Arild Marie in honour of her elder 'sister', MaryLizbet. What say you, Nan?"

"Arild Marie is a beautiful name, my Lady, and I believe MaryLizbet will be especially pleased with its choice."

* * *

The Aust household became a whirl of activity preparing for the baptism in Aust parish church on the following weekend. Everyone was invited to the celebration, all the Lady's affinity and Nan's adopted family. The Lady sent Giles to speak with Joshua Falcon and his wife, Jeanne, specifically to ask if they would be willing to be godparents to the baby, Arild Marie. When her steward returned, he brought a note to the Lady:

Gracious Lady,

We have found a wet-nurse for the infant and will be delighted to become godparents for Arild Marie. Yet, we beg your permission to adopt her as our own. Our daughter, MaryLizbet would truly love to have a baby sister.

Joshua and Jeanne

* * *

The early April Sunday of the baptism arrived, and Apollonia was especially pleased to find that her brother, Ferdinand, appeared at the chapel. She had sent a brief note to him just to describe the extraordinary discovery of an infant on her doorstep with no message but a small packet of salt. Ferdinand was a widower who had lost his wife a year earlier. Finding himself frequently alone in his Marshfield home, he simply announced to his sister as he entered, "I am an old man, Polly, but I still enjoy family celebrations, and my squire, Owen, has been looking forward to an opportunity to return to Aust for a visit with his friend, Alwan."

All the household of Aust Manor could be seen to be anticipating the celebration, and Apollonia was pleased. "I hope that whoever was forced to give up our infant will know that she is being cherished, Nan, celebrated and valued as family."

"My Lady, you are creating an episode in the village that can not be missed by anyone. I dare say they will all be in church this Sunday."

"Wonderful. Then, Francis will issue an open invitation to the baptismal feast after the service so that everyone in the village will feel invited to join us here in the hall for the meal. I pray you will keep your eyes watchful, Nan. Note any girl or woman of the village who might show symptoms of recent delivery. You know that I am glad to do our best for the child, but it would be such a blessing if we could help the mother who was forced to abandon her."

* * *

In the evening after the celebration of Arild Marie's baptism, Ferdinand was pleased to be sitting comfortably with his sister in her solar. There could be no doubt that it had been a celebratory day. The Falcon family were delighted to return home with two daughters, MaryLizbet and her infant sister. Apollonia was especially gladdened by Joshua and Jeanne's desire to adopt Arild as their own. The Lady knew that their growing family would provide the best opportunity for the infant to grow midst loving parents, brothers and an elder sister. Such family life was a gift she could no longer provide for the child though she knew she would find other avenues of support for her as the years progressed.

Apollonia noticed that her brother appeared more quiet than usual, as if his mind was occupied by some inner concerns. As he continued to seem distracted, Apollonia could not help but ask him why.

"I am facing a mysterious difficulty in Marshfield, Polly, that I do not know how to correct."

"Is it something that you can share with me, brother? You know that I am always desirous of being helpful."

"I believe this strange occurrence is beyond even your gift of solving mysteries, but yes, Polly, I would be grateful to speak with you about it."

On many occasions in their relationship as younger sister with her older brother, Apollonia could sense that Ferdinand was glad to have her opinions and her insight.

"Pray, brother, let us think on this difficulty together. Two are always better than one."

"I can not describe this problem as rational, Polly, so please forgive me if I simply ask you to listen and give me your opinion. It began recently, since I returned to Marshfield from London. Do you remember the spring-fed pond in the woods behind my home?"

"Yes, Ferdinand, it is one of my favourite spots for strolling about in the summer when I visit, always quietly lovely with multiple birdsongs to add music to its beauty."

"A favourite retreat of mine as well, sister. My dear wife and I especially enjoyed walking there once spring returned each year. Well, since I have been back in Marshfield from having been with the king, a bizarre phenomenon has occurred. Several workers on the farm described it to my steward who reported it to me after seeing it himself."

"What sort of phenomenon, brother?"

"I was told that blood is seen to bubble up from the depths of the pool."

"Blood, Ferdinand, how can that be?"

"I have heard of such a thing happening in Finchampsted in Berkshire but never here in the West Country. You know that I do not think of myself as being a credulous fellow, Polly, so I made light of the reports until just before I received your announcement of the celebration of Arild's baptism. Before leaving home, I made a point to walk into the woods to see for myself, and it happened, Polly. I could see blood-red water bubbling up from the spring in the centre of the pond."

"How would you describe the colour of the water normally, brother?"

"It is a spring-fed pond, and usually in April, its water is very clear."

"Yet, now you are telling me that you actually saw the water turned blood-red before you left Marshfield. Is that correct?"

"Yes, sister, and the local folk are declaring that this is happening because of my support for King Henry, one with blood on his hands."

"Ferdinand, did you actually see this happening in the light of day?"

"Yes, Polly, and I assure you I had eaten a good meal while breaking my fast that morning before I walked into the woods, and," he said meaningfully, "I had consumed no wine."

"I know you to be a sober and sensible man, Ferdinand, and I have no doubt what you are telling me is what you saw. Yet, I can also understand why you are troubled by the interpretation of the locals as to why this phenomenon is happening."

Apollonia and her brother sat quietly together, saying little more, both deep in thought. Finally, the Lady asked Ferdinand if he could remain in Aust another day before his return to Marshfield.

"Would you be willing to share your story with a very good friend of mine who is also visiting with me now, Ferdinand? He is a successful cloth merchant of Worcester by the name of Robert Kenwood, devout in our faith having made the pilgrimage to Santiago de Compostela. It is his obvious good sense that has impressed me, and I find his critical mind helps me keep to the point."

"Polly, I have no desire to share this tale with anyone except you. Surely, you can see that your friend will see me as a wretched old man, suffering delusions at best, losing my senses at worst."

"I pray you will meet Robert, Ferdinand, share your story of recent times spent with our King Henry, and then judge his rational powers to understand the bizarre situation you are now facing at Marshfield. Will you at least meet my friend?"

"Of course, I shall meet him, Polly, but if I choose not to speak of certain specifics just now, I trust to have your confidence as well."

When Garmon brought Robert from the hall to the Lady's solar, Apollonia could see that her friend and her brother welcomed each other's acquaintance. Robert was considerably younger than Ferdinand but an intelligent man who had travelled extensively and achieved considerable success in his life dealing with people of all classes. Ferdinand was not an outgoing person, but he did express welcome to people, regardless of class, who seemed sensible, down to earth, and ready to fulfill their duty in life.

Robert had returned from his extraordinary experience in Compostela with a warmth in his person that granted a sense of value to others as his brothers and sisters. He and the earl saw in the other an extended vision of those who had travelled in their world but also maintained a graceful pride in being English.

"So, Master Kenwood, Polly tells me that you have seen a great number of foreign countries. Yet, you return to our West Country home despite its lack of miracles."

"Indeed, my lord, I confess to exploring the world in search of meaning and have visited many of the great pilgrimage sites, but in the end, I found that God is present with me here. I need not search for him. You, my lord, have travelled as defender of our kingdom, in battle for our king."

"Service to our realm has been the goal of my life, Master Kenwood, but I, too, am always glad to return home."

"My Lady Apollonia tells me that you are recently returned from the court. Can you share with us news of the health of our King Henry?"

"Praise God, he seems to be somewhat improved. He was able to attend Parliament and is now travelling to the north. Thankfully, he travels with a highly regarded court physician at his side who has been able to bring relief to his reoccurring discomfort with sickness."

"That is truly good to hear, my lord, especially as you bring it directly from the court. Gramercy for sharing welcome news."

Apollonia could see that Ferdinand warmed to this new acquaintance who spoke so well and expressed no subservience or discomfort in the class differences between them.

"In a sense, Master Kenwood," Ferdinand said suddenly, "it was when I returned to Marshfield that I found myself facing a phenomenon for which I am truly unprepared."

Robert's face expressed question, but he said nothing.

"I told Polly that I could not share this with anyone, largely because they will think I have grown senile and doddering in my years, but she is right. You are a man of faith as well as good sense. I shall be grateful to have your opinion, Master Robert."

"Gramercy, my lord. Having faced several unexplainable happenings in my life, I shall be grateful to share the disturbing puzzle you have encountered in Marshfield."

"Then, it will be best if we travel together to my home," the earl told him. "You and Polly must see this to grant me your honest opinion of it. Can you spare the time for a visit to Marshfield?"

"I shall be honoured, my lord. If the Lady is ready, let us away at dawn."

* * *

The ride to Marshfield seemed to pass quickly while they continued to enjoy their conversation as well as the late springtime beauty of their West Country homeland. Apollonia, accompanied by her maid, Nan, and Waldef, was pleased to have this opportunity to be with her former page, young Owen, now feeling very grown up, having progressed to Ferdinand's squire on his own road to knighthood. Owen knew well how much the Lady loved riding and never missed an opportunity to point out places of interest along their way.

It was nearly noon when they arrived at the earl's manor in Marshfield, and Apollonia could feel a distinct change in her brother's demeanour. It was as if the tension in her brother's person increased, even as they shared a meal.

"Will you be ready for a short walk on the morrow, Master Kenwood?" the earl asked across the table. "I fear I am an early riser and would like you to see with me the bizarre happening at sun's first light."

"I shall be glad to be at your side, my lord. As you may imagine, my curiosity is burning."

"Will you come with us, Polly?"

"Dear brother, I can think of nothing that would keep me away."

"My lord, Waldef and I, too, will walk with my Lady," Nan added hopefully.

Ferdinand smiled for the first time since his return home. "Of course, Nan. You are a sensible woman, and I shall be grateful for your opinions of what we shall see, as well."

* * *

As they gathered in the hall the following morning before breaking their fast, Ferdinand announced, "The first light has brought the promise of August sunshine, but clouds in the east could bring rain. We shall leave through the kitchen as that will be closest door towards the back garden."

His guests were obviously ready to go with him, so the earl led them through the busy kitchen. Ferdinand greeted members of his staff, but Apollonia could sense anxiety in their reactions to him. Everyone seemed to know what it was they were going out to see. The gossip among the earl's affinity had infected even Owen, a well-educated young squire who prided himself as being fearless in his lord's service. Yet he, too, felt something threatening about this sudden bizarre disturbance in the earl's pond. No one in Ferdinand's household had any explanation for it except the likelihood of some divine displeasure with the earl.

The Lady offered her hand to Squire Owen as she walked through the door into the early morning's sunshine. She was pleased to see how tall and gallant her former page had grown and took a moment to say to him quietly, "I dare say we shall find some realistic explanation to this mystery, Owen, but would it not be good to have Alwan here with his forester's insight into woodland mysteries?"

"Aye, my Lady, no one has better understanding of earth's mysteries than Alwan."

Chapter Ten

Blood Red Spring

This path was a personal favourite walkabout in Ferdinand's manor for Apollonia. She knew it to be a quiet woodland stroll leading to a lovely pond, which the Lady enjoyed visiting in every season of the year. Today, however, as they approached its waters, she was shocked. She, Nan, Robert, Ferdinand, and Owen saw immediately that the pond's waters had turned into a rippling soup of red fluid.

"Dear God," Robert gasped, "how can this be, my lord? What in the world would cause such an intimidating disaster?"

Nan made no comment, but as she stepped back from the pond, the Lady could tell that she was terrified by what she considered a hellish apparition. Waldef obviously wished to see the apparition more closely.

They walked straight to its banks as Ferdinand answered, "You can see, Master Kenwood, why the people of my affinity and nearby farmers on my lands are terrified by this sudden unnatural happening. I can understand that they are frightened by it. I, too, am distressed, but how am I to correct it?"

Robert walked around the ponds banks and could see the red water bubbling up from its spring, deep in the pool. He looked steadily at its unbelievable colour and asked the earl once again what the local folk attributed this to?

"Their story has come to me in bits and pieces, Master Kenwood, but my steward tells me that the people of the manor whisper that this is meant as God's judgement against me as a faithful subject to our King Henry. No one will say so, but some put it about that our king is not only a usurper but also the murderer of King Richard. Of course, they will never speak such words in my presence."

"When did this begin, brother?" the Lady asked him.

"It was first seen the day after I returned from my stay in London, Polly, as if it were waiting for me," Ferdinand said in his most irritated voice.

Robert walked around the banks of the pond, looking at the red colour flowing upward with the spring and spreading outward to its banks. As they watched, he reached down into the pool and put his hand into the water to bring some to his tongue to taste. The Lady and her brother were dumbfounded when Robert stepped back from the bank of the pool and began to smile broadly.

"My Lord Ferdinand, this is not a punishment from God. It appears to me that someone who has contacts with the dyers of Bristol is more likely the cause. That same someone, who likely has a grudge against you, has continually added pots full of concentrated red dyes into the spring-fed depths to keep its blood-like colour bubbling up. If you have one of your servant's swim into the deepest part where the spring bubbles forth, I believe he will find a sizable pot of concentrated red dye slowly leaking colour into your waters."

"Red dye!" Ferdinand blustered. "Why should anyone wish to do this? Surely no member of my affinity would cause such a foolish thing."

"Yet, brother, is there not someone outside your personal household and village who might have a grudge against you?" Apollonia asked. "When you were at Lambeth with our recovering King Henry, who had been refused access to him?"

"I care not, Polly. I was asked personally by our Archbishop Arundel to give my time to visit with the king during his recovery. I did so and, praise God, King Henry has achieved some signs of improvement after the return of the Physician Marimon."

"Then, brother, let me tell you of a malicious foreigner named Dravini whom I have learned was able to worm his way into the court and oust the excellent care of Doctor Marimon to insert his own healer as head of the king's physicians. It is also my suspicion that this

Dravini is empowered by some member of the aristocracy of England who seeks the increased sickness to emphasise King Henry's inability to rule."

"Your suspicions have little to do with me, Polly. Why would a foreigner to England want to come to Marshfield just to turn my pond's waters blood red? I do not know this man."

"Perhaps it is because you are one English nobleman against whom he felt he could take revenge by terrifying your affinity. As the Sheriff of Gloucestershire, Ferdinand, you must be on guard against this evil man who seeks to do you ill."

"Where am I to begin, Polly, and what charge am I to bring against this foreigner if I should find him?"

"If it is he who has done this, putting red dye into your pond waters, begin looking for him here in Marshfield, and if you find him, demand to know which Englishman he serves."

"What is my charge against him?"

"He has entered your lands and damaged the waters of your pond, brother. Place a guard around your pond through the nights ahead. Have them watch to spy anyone who comes seeking to refill the dye. If so, arrest him."

* * *

Apollonia and Robert remained in Marshfield for two weeks, hoping that whoever was responsible for colouring the water of the pond would be caught. Ferdinand's men were instructed to hide themselves through the nights and maintain a vigilant watch. Though they insisted that they remained well out of sight, no one was seen trying to enter its waters and refill the supply of red dye. As days continued into a week, the colour slowly faded, and the earl's lovely pond began to return to its normal sparkling waters reflecting the colours of the sky.

Apollonia noticed that as his pond's waters returned to normal, her brother was more than ready to forget the bizarre occurrence and return to his interests in the daily jurisdiction of the manor. She and Robert decided that they could do little more now that her brother's great problem seemed to have been corrected, so the Lady announced to Ferdinand they would return to Aust.

"I shall be happy to escort the Lady's party home to Aust, my Lord Ferdinand," Robert told him, "and I thank you sincerely for the warmth and friendship of your hospitality to me whilst we have been in Marshfield. It is my honour to have been able to meet you."

"Gramercy, Master Kenwood, you must know that I shall always be glad to declare our friendship. Thank God for the chance to know you, for I vow that it was you alone able to correct a serious problem for which I had no solution."

"Still, brother, you must not forget what has happened here," Apollonia persisted. "I urge you, as sheriff of the county, be on the watch for this Dravini person. At least put about the word with your people to be watching for the appearance of any European foreigner seen in the area. It may amount to nothing, but be on your guard, in case it was he who blamed you for his dismissal from the court of King Henry. He may have tried to intimidate you in this way. Surely, if Dravini is near, he will be noticed, and if you find such a man, you must question him. We need to discover not only why he has attacked your manor in this way but whom he may be serving in England. There is murder to be solved, but I also fear, on-going threats to the life of our king."

* * *

Dravini sat with Buldoc at the inn in Marshfield. They were preparing to leave the village as the count could see that there was nothing more to be done here. The Sicilian was angry to learn from village gossip that their scheme had been so easily exposed and grew more aggravated because their attempt against the Earl of Marshfield had not turned out as damning as he had intended. Dravini had assumed that the simple people of the earl's manor and village would rebel, blaming their lord for what they thought was a betrayal of murderous blood flowing in his pond. The count had even paid several beggars in the village to put it about that the disaster occurred because of Marshfield's support of a murderous usurper.

During these weeks in the West Country, Dravini had given up his upper-class pretence in dress and manner and wore the clothes of a common labourer whose name, he now claimed, was Peter Declan. His beard had grown full, and because of his conspicuous foreign accent, he tended to let Buldoc speak for him. Of course, they were both regarded as foreigners here because they were unknown to locals, but Buldoc passed them off as travelling workers moving about the English countryside searching for jobs.

"What we do next, master? Any reason we stay? Are you waitin to ear from the baron?"

"No," Dravini said bitterly, "when I was no longer able to serve him at court, he told me to stay away and never reveal my services for him. He said when he needs my help, he will contact me."

"Then, why we be stayin ere in the west?"

"I have not yet completed my revenge, Buldoc. If I can not leave the earl with a nasty revolt on his hands, we will travel on. I have learned, however, that the Earl of Marshfield has a sister who is a vulnerable old widow. Let us pause in Aust. As simple labourers intending to use the ferry crossing there, help me think of ways to cause pain and distress to the Lady of Aust."

"There be many ways to kill er, master. Ow much pain does you wish to cause?"

"We shall travel on to Aust and study the daily pattern of life there. If the earl's sister is well guarded by her household, we will find ways to cause serious trouble in the village. I will be sure to let the earl know that what happens to his sister is his fault for having thwarted me."

* * *

Apollonia, Nan, and Robert left Marshfield, and the Lady could see that her brother had returned to his normal, in-charge self. When she kissed him goodbye, she whispered into his ear, "Remember what you must do, Ferdinand—continue the search for this Dravini. I am convinced that he has come to the West Country to cause you harm. It is your duty as sheriff to take him into custody."

"Yes, yes," Ferdinand growled. Though he knew his sister was correct, he so wanted to put the entire incident behind him.

"It is your duty," she repeated as they left the manorhouse to mount up.

Ferdinand nodded but said nothing more, just waved a hearty goodbye, more than ready to see them gone and concentrate on something else.

* * *

The ride back to Aust was a pleasant one for the Lady and Robert, but their conversation was more limited. Each was obviously preoccupied in many ways. Apollonia continued to think of what she might be able to do next in behalf of young Waldef. Robert was convinced by the Lady's reasoning that there was, indeed, a possible threat to the life of their king but could think of nothing that he could do to expose it. Smiling, Nan was simply looking forward to returning to the Falcon Farm and being with the precious baby, Arild, newly part of her adopted family.

When they all rode through the manor gate towards the barn, Gareth came to take their horses. He welcomed them home but could not help but add, "There be somethin amiss in Aust, m'Lady. Everbody in the Boars Ead be talkin bout it."

"I must retire to my solar for a bit of a sit-down, Gareth, but will you come to speak with us straightaway?"

"Master Giles will tell you, m'Lady."

"What a welcome home, Robert," she said turning towards her friend. "I dare not think what is coming next."

"Well, my Lady, if it be red dye in the Severn, we shall know how to deal with that."

* * *

They were all happily returned to Aust, but the Lady and her friend were now forced to concentrate on a disturbance in her home village. Apollonia called for her steward, Giles Digby, to meet with her, and when he entered the solar where she sat with Robert, she could see that his mind was troubled.

"Greetings, my Lady, Master Robert. It is good to have you with us again."

"God's peace, Giles," Apollonia said with a smile. "I am glad to be returned, but when we left our horses with Gareth, he told us that something was amiss in the village. Will you kindly bring us up to date? What is happening that everyone is talking about at the Boars Head?"

"I can not be entirely specific, my Lady, but it appears that many families of the village are struggling with illness, a serious stomach upset, which strikes suddenly. It has been especially severe for the children and two of the elderly."

"Will you please have the village warden call upon me as soon as possible. I must learn more of this."

"Yes, my Lady, Warden Godfrey will be grateful to speak with you. This mysterious illness has come upon us so quickly, and no one, including Physician James, knows what has caused it or what to do to prevent it."

"I shall look forward to the warden's visit to learn more of this, Giles, but it seems especially frightening if Physician James does not know what brings it on."

"He says its cause is unknown, yet its symptoms can be serious, my Lady."

The Lady turned to her friend after Giles left them. "Robert, I am unable to welcome you to a calm and peaceful residence. Truly sorry, dear friend. We seem to move from one difficult situation to another."

"My Lady, I hope you will always understand that your company is my joy. Surely, you must know that I am grateful to find any way to help you through a difficult time."

* * *

The village warden appeared at the Lady's door early the following morning, more than ready to leave his concerns with her. He announced that he was taking his family to stay with his son in Bristol until the cause of the recent sickness could be determined. Apollonia received him in the hall, and Nan introduced Robert Kenwood to him as the Lady's special friend from Worcester. As was her custom, Nan stood at Apollonia's side and spoke with the warden for her.

"Warden Godfrey my Lady of Aust has only recently returned to the village but has been told of re-occurring sickness afflicting many villagers. Can you tell us what has been happening?"

Godfrey knew that the Lady of Aust was a vowess who barely spoke publicly, preferring to have her people speak for her. However, he addressed his response directly to her.

"My Lady, children of the village began suffering some sort of severe stomach sickness. Now that summer is well on and we are near the end of August, the weather has been warmer, and the days are long. Physician James had not expected such a rash of affliction with our summer weather."

"What is the nature of this sickness, Warden Godfrey?" Nan asked.

"It seemed at first to affect the children with vomiting and the flux, my Lady, and later, two of the elderly grandparents in the village were struck. By now, nearly all of the boys in the village school have had this nausea, which makes them unable to keep food in their stomachs."

"Has someone spoken with the schoolmaster? Is he aware of anything which the children have been eating that might have sickened them?"

"He says he can think of nothing unusual, and the parents in the village assure him that their children are eating normally. Most troubling to all of us has been the speed with which this affliction has spread among us, and Physician James has been unable to protect us against it."

Apollonia listened carefully to the warden's description. Then, she spoke directly to him, "I will surely give my full attention to this problem, Warden Godfrey. I pray you will have Schoolmaster Luke come to speak with me."

As he prepared to leave, he assured the Lady that he would have the schoolmaster come to her that day. She could see that he was perspiring and obviously ready for her to deal with this problem.

"Gramercy Godfrey," she said warmly and directly to him. "I shall do my best to work toward some understanding of what we must do."

He bowed before her and left, truly grateful to leave this problem in her hands.

The Lady turned to Nan after the warden had gone. "Thank you, Nan, for speaking in my behalf, but it is important that I question the schoolmaster myself. Pray add your own questions of him whilst he is here and you as well, Robert, if you have questions to help us deal with this dilemma. Whatever is causing this sickness in the village must be dealt with. I have to agree with my brother, Ferdinand, who described his dilemma in Marshfield. This seems to have been waiting for our return. The timing is suspicious, and there is surely some human evil behind it. I shall not rest until we have found its cause."

* * *

Luke Winters, the schoolmaster of Aust, was a young man who had returned to his home village as an adult. He had been raised as a student/lay brother in Gloucester Abbey after the death of his parents. Apollonia knew that he had never chosen the religious life for himself but, as an orphan, had been placed in the abbey by his uncle. An excellent student, he was able to go on to university and had returned to Aust from Cambridge with a wife and infant son. Luke was not only pleased to be in his home, he enjoyed being able to use his education as teacher and head of the village school.

Master Winters knew the Lady to be an unusually well-read woman who always encouraged him to come to the manor and use her manuscript collection. Although she spoke little, she was welcoming and willing to consider any of his suggestions to improve the village school. Apollonia knew that Aust was fortunate to have its own village school, attached to the front of Luke's cottage, even more fortunate to have a devoted lay teacher to guide and instruct its students. Luke loved his job and living in his home village with his growing family.

"My Lady of Aust," Luke told Apollonia when he arrived, "I am sorry to bring this village problem to you, but we would all be grateful for your insights."

"Gramercy, Master Winters for your timely call. Can you describe just when these unexpected sicknesses began?"

"Not precisely, my Lady. One or two boys fell ill at first about two weeks ago, but their numbers grew suddenly. I have spoken with all the parents in the village, and none has suggested any unusual activities their children have done recently. Yet, the sickness multiplied suddenly, and Physician James has no explanation."

"Have there been any strangers in the village, recently?" Apollonia asked him.

"There are always travellers who come to use the Aust ferry, but no one has mentioned suspicious strangers in Aust, my Lady, not even folk who gather regularly at The Boars Head. The folk from elsewhere who come to Aust to take the ferry come and go but are not seen to remain in the village for long visits. I shall speak with some of the parents. Perhaps they can tell us if outsiders have been mentioned by their children."

"I pray you will pursue this for me, Master Winters. My friend from Worcester and I have just returned from my brother's manor in Marshfield where threatening events were happening on his lands. Now I fear that my village, too, is being afflicted by some nefarious person in revenge against me because of our family's loyalty to our king."

Chapter Eleven

Classmates' Secrets

Apollonia was obviously distressed, and Robert could see that, as lady of the manor, she could not relax until she had dealt with the puzzling outbreak of sickness in the village. Once she had completed her conversation with the schoolmaster, the Lady sent Garmon to the barn to bring Gareth and Waldef to her.

When her stablemaster and her young ward entered the hall, the Lady was impressed to see how confident Waldef had grown working under the well-informed, but down-to-earth guidance of Gareth. The lad obviously admired Apollonia's stablemaster and wanted to learn as much as he could from Gareth's extraordinary insight into horses and their care.

On this day, however, the Lady had a different assignment for Waldef and asked Gareth if he would be willing to grant the boy weekdays off from his work in the barn so that he could attend the village school now that classes were beginning.

"M'Lady, Waldef finishes all is jobs in the barn early. Surely ee can be off to school before is classes begin, then come back to finish when studies be done."

"I realise that you have been keeping up your studies with Friar Francis, Waldef, but I have need of your help and wish to express my household's trust in you. I wish to send you to the village school in Aust. Despite your advanced age beyond most of the students, you will learn from an excellent teacher in the village school, as well as gather information for me that I have no other access to," the Lady told him.

"I will serve you in any way that I can, my Lady," Waldef said earnestly. "Pray tell me what you would have me do."

"First, I want you to spend time becoming acquainted with the village boys. Learn to know them by name, tell them a bit about yourself, and find out what sorts of things they enjoy doing in their free time. You are older and more experienced of the world, so their curiosity will draw them to you. Be sure you note anything that the boys enjoy, especially if they might be keeping it secret from their parents." Then, the Lady paused, "I am not asking you to spy on them, Waldef. Regard this as an important quest to help me learn the true nature of a serious problem in my beloved village."

"I shall begin on the morrow, my Lady."

"Gramercy, Waldef. Friar Francis, as my chaplain, will accompany you in the morning and introduce you as a member of my household to Schoolmaster Winters. Then, I shall wait until you have anything helpful to share with me."

After Waldef and Gareth left the hall, Apollonia sent for her chaplain and almoner to meet in her solar. As she and Nan stood to walk upstairs to her private space, she asked Robert to collect her steward, Giles, and her Almoner William, and bring him to join her there, as well.

Robert and Giles soon made their way to the Lady's presence where she welcomed them with a worried smile. "It must seem that I am drawing together my own council of war, and in some ways I am. I fear that someone is attacking the people of my village, and I am determined that it shall be stopped."

"My Lady, you are wise to be preparing your household while collecting more information," Robert told her. "I thought your assignment for Waldef was ingenious. The lad is mature for his years and has a strong sense of devotion to you."

"Waldef has sought ways to prove himself to me every day since his coming under my protection. I could not find a more devoted servant to place among the lads of the village, and I must confess, though I know their parents, I know very few of them."

"Everyone is aware of the sickness, my Lady, and worried that it will spread," Giles told her.

"As am I, Giles. We must discover its cause."

They were not long until Friar Francis and Brother William joined them. Apollonia introduced her chaplain and almoner to Robert and then went straight to the point of their meeting. "Francis, William," she began, "has either of you learned anything about this sudden illness in the village? What can you tell me?"

Francis did not have the daily contacts with villagers that William maintained in his ministry, and her almoner did not hesitate. William told her that he was not only aware of it as a growing problem, he had seen its symptoms and was grateful that the sickness had not spread to the Lady's affinity.

"Since its beginning, the illness has stayed in the village, my Lady, and Physician Morewell is frustrated by his inability to determine whence this ailment comes. That frightens everyone, my Lady."

"Then, we must help him," she said with conviction.

"My Lady," Nan insisted, "I can assure you that this sickness is limited to the village. Joshua and Jeanne have seen no expanse of it to their farm near Aust, praise God. They and their children, including precious infant, Arild Marie, are flourishing during the long days of summer. Is it not strange that it is only happening in Aust?"

Robert knew Nan as the Lady's maid from his earlier visits. He could only shake his head in response to her question. When the Lady answered her, however, Nan could see that Apollonia was angry as she looked directly into her maid's eyes.

"I am convinced that the answer to your question lies in some sort of revenge against me, dearheart. My brother found his manor in Marshfield attacked by a mysterious phenomenon, and now Aust is being assaulted by unexplained sickness."

"Who would seek revenge against you, and for what reason, my Lady?"

"I can only guess, Nan, but it is a person, not an act of God. We must first discover the means being used to inflict such sickness, and then, I pray, we will be led to some answers. In the days ahead, William, as you go about the village calling on various folk, will you make a special effort to watch as Waldef walks to and from school. I ask this as a favour to me for I wish to keep someone from our household always near at hand for him should he need help."

"Indeed, my Lady, it will become part of my routine, William said obviously ready to be of service in this way."

* * *

The days seemed to move slowly, and the illness continued in the village. Apollonia became worried about what she might be exposing her friend Robert to.

"Robert, I do hate to say goodbye, but I am convinced that you should escape from any possibility of contagion here. Please return to Worcester until I can be certain that it is safe for you to be in Aust."

"Dear Lady, I am an old man but relatively hearty. I could never forgive myself for abandoning you at this time. With your permission, I shall remain, taking full advantage of your hospitality until we have some understanding of what must be done."

"Accept my heartfelt thanks for your companionship, especially now, Robert," Apollonia smiled, "and know that my welcome is always extended to you."

Robert could see that the Lady was being worn down by the frustration and worry, so he suggested that they should think on other things for a few hours and take one of their favourite rides along the Severn.

At first, the Lady could not allow herself to consider doing something pleasant, but Robert insisted. "It is a lovely, sunny day, and we shall be gone for only a few hours. Nan will be here to deal with any news and will know where to send someone to find us should anything important happen. I pray you, my Lady, let us away."

Before Apollonia could change Robert's mind, Nan hurried off to collect her riding cape. "Just remember to go carefully, and stop regularly to enjoy the view," the maid insisted to them as they went out towards the barn. "I shall be here whilst you are gone," she said as she walked with them to the door.

* * *

The banks of the River Severn were blooming, and the sunlit river offered a gigantic, sparkling stream flowing for miles. Apollonia could see why Robert had insisted on this ride today and found it to be a renewing experience for her. She could allow her mind to simply receive and thrill to the beauty of the day as they rode along a familiar path, took time to dismount, and sit for a while on a fallen tree trunk while entertained by the birdsongs celebrating the brilliant sunshine. The sun was beginning to set in the West when they rode back to the manor house, tired but refreshed.

It was when they entered the hall, Nan rushed to the Lady's side. "My Lady, Waldef has come to speak with you. He says he brings news and awaits you in your solar."

Apollonia threw off her cape as she rushed up the stairs to her private chamber with Robert close behind.

The lad stood as the Lady entered, and she could see that Waldef was pleased. He obviously had something to tell her, and she was more than ready to know what he had learned.

"What is it, Waldef? Have you discovered anything from the village boys?"

"Indeed, my Lady, I have discovered this," he said as he held up a fig in a gloved hand.

Apollonia was nearly breathless from her hurried ascent, but she reached out to take the fruit from him while urging Waldef and Robert to sit with her while she tried to understand its meaning.

"I pray you will not touch this fig, my Lady," Waldef told her as he put the fruit behind his back. "Something is dreadfully wrong with it, and I believe these figs are the cause of the re-occurring sickness in the village. The children of the village find them as special treats regularly left in a small space next to the base of the tower inside the church. When they find them, they love to gobble them up or take them home and hide them to eat later."

"When the children eat these figs, does that cause their stomach problems?" Robert asked.

"Yes, Master Kenwood, I believe so. The boys say that they wipe them clean before they eat them, but they are such a treat they tend to eat them immediately whenever they find them. On one occasion, two of the boys shared them with their grandparents who also became ill."

Apollonia laid out a handkerchief on her table. "Please leave it on this, Waldef, so that I may have our Physician James examine it. Have you pointed out to the priest of the church the place where the children found the figs? This treachery must be exposed."

"Yes, my Lady. Father Michael was truly upset to see how the church was being used as a place of distribution for such things, but he has assured me that he will burn any others he may find and will wait for further instructions from you."

"Quickly, Giles," Apollonia said as she wrapped the fig in her handkerchief, "take this to Physician James in the village. I pray he will be very careful when examining it because this fig must be poisoned in some way. Ask him to report to me if he is able to determine what has been done to it."

"I shall go straightaway, my Lady, and bring the doctor back to speak with you after he has completed his examination."

* * *

The doctor of physic was at home when Giles arrived. He took the handkerchief from Apollonia's steward as soon as he realised what it held, then opening the handkerchief carefully, he laid it upon his table. He removed a pair of tweezers from his bag of instruments and lifted the fig to examine it closely. Finally, he put the fruit back on the handkerchief and scraped some substance from it. When his examination was complete, he looked to Giles with a smile of triumph.

"Let us return to the manor, Giles. I can now tell the Lady the cause of the reoccurring illnesses in Aust. These have been infected by a natural substance but a deadly one put in place by human hands."

"Can you tell my Lady what has been done, Physician James?"

"Indeed, I can tell what, but I have no idea why."

* * *

Nan went to collect the Lady and Robert from her solar when Giles returned with the doctor. Apollonia came down the stairs from the upper chamber immediately, anxious to hear what Physician

Morewell could tell them. She was excited to see a rather triumphant smile on his face as he continued to hold the fig that Waldef had brought in her handkerchief.

"Welcome, what is your news, Physician James?" she asked immediately while indicating that they should all gather round the table dormant in the hall.

"My Lady, this fig has been infected with poisonous herbs."

"How has this been possible?"

"Someone has used sundried foxglove leaves ground into a powder. That powder was layered onto the flesh of the fig and left to soak into the juice of the fruit. When such figs are eaten, no one would notice change in their taste, but that is what brought on sickness in the stomach with nausea and vomiting."

"Oh, gramercy, Physician James," the Lady said in obvious relief. "Call the village together and explain these things to them. Everyone will know how to protect themselves once your discovery is understood by the people. Waldef has told me that the priest of the church has been shown where the children found such figs hidden, and aware of the fruit's insidious nature, he has promised to burn any more of them that he might find."

"My Lady, there is some person who has created this serious threat against your entire village. Who would do such a thing and why?"

"I can only suspect at this point, James, but I shall not rest until this creature has been exposed and punished, God help me," Apollonia promised. "For the moment, I depend on you and all of my household to spread the news of your discovery to every cottage in the village. Everyone must be told the cause of the sickness and how to protect against it."

* * *

Late in the day after Waldef had finished his chores in the barn, Apollonia sent Nan to bring him to meet with her and Robert. The Lady was so proud of the lad and grateful for the information he had gained for her. She was convinced that he alone had provided the avenue of understanding how to stop the sicknesses that had plagued Aust, and she was determined to express her personal gratitude to him.

When Waldef entered the hall, he was invited to come and sit by the fire with the Lady, Nan, Robert, and Giles. He was a little nervous to be called into their adult presence but relaxed considerably when the Lady spoke directly to him.

"I want you to join us at the head table for our meal, Waldef. Thanks to you, we discovered the cause of the persistent illnesses in the village and how to stop them. I am eternally grateful," the Lady said as she extended her hand to him.

It was as if a miracle had occurred. Waldef suddenly realised that he, who had come to this manor as an accused murderer, was now being recognised as a local hero. "My Lady of Aust, I can only thank you with all my heart," he said as he moved to kiss her hand. "Being allowed to know your grace through your service has fulfilled the best hopes of chivalry in my life."

"Then, you will come to eat with us this evening and will sit between me and Robert as we sup at the head table."

"I should be honoured, my Lady," he hesitated, "but I fear I have no proper clothes for such an occasion."

"Come with me young man," Nan said as she stood to lead him from the hall.

Apollonia could not know precisely what was Nan's purpose, but it was obvious that her maid had something in mind. Nan led Waldef to her personal bedchamber and opened a trunk filled with her most treasured possessions. From it, she took a handsome multicoloured doublet with matching hose that she had saved since the days of Apollonia's youngest son David, always her favourite among the Aust sons. She made Waldef put them on and walk about the chamber in his transformed appearance.

"Not a bad fit, if a little roomy, lad. A few stitches here and there and you will be the well-dressed hero of this evening," she said as she collected her sewing basket and threaded her needle.

"Mistress Nan," Waldef said sitting next to her as she completed the repairs on his borrowed clothes, "you have restored me. I have not been able to feel whole since leaving my home in Bristol."

"What do you mean, whole, Waldef?" Nan asked.

"I left my home and family there to serve a knight, for I was convinced that chivalry offered achievement of the highest goals of my life even though I was not born to knighthood. When I observed Sir Hardulph's ridicule of chivalry, he made the code of knighthood seem a sham. Here in Aust, I have been able to be myself, make good friends in the village school, be encouraged by an excellent teacher to stretch my mind, and be granted value and respect by a gracious noblewoman. These are treasured gifts which sustain me."

Nan smiled at him. "We can only recognise such gifts if we value them in others, Waldef," Nan said in her very practical manner. "Now stand up and finish dressing yourself with these fashionable shoes of Master Davey's. If they are a bit large, we shall stuff the long toes a bit further."

* * *

The celebration that evening seemed more grand than the usual meal. Nan's extended family joined the gathering, and Gareth brought his wife, Lucy. The Lady Apollonia felt comfort in having the families of her affinity together. MaryLizbet was pleased to be allowed to join this adult occasion, especially when she realised that it was Waldef, the Lady's ward, who was being celebrated. Taller than she and far more experienced in the world, Waldef was a young man whom she personally admired, now more than ever.

When the Lady's steward proposed a toast in honour of Waldef, the entire company stood to raise their goblets and shouted, "To Waldef, the discoverer of our healing!" MaryLizbet decided this lad had not only won the community's respect, he was hero of the moment.

The village fiddler began to play songs they all knew and loved to sing. The tables were dismantled, and the hall was cleared for dancing. Waldef did not hesitate. After bowing to the Lady at the head table, he walked to the place where MaryLizbet stood and asked her to dance with him. She was pleased to be honoured in this way and took his hand gladly. They joined in a round dance, encouraging others to enlarge the circle.

Apollonia, seated next to Robert, was especially pleased when he stood to take Nan's hand to join the dance. The Lady's heart was full. This had become a perfect celebration. As a vowess, she would never again take part in the dance, but she would always be excited by the sheer joy of sharing celebration with her family, her affinity, and dear friends in her home in Aust.

*   *   *

Late that evening after everyone had gone home or to their beds, Apollonia invited Robert to her solar for a brief private conversation near the fire. The Lady could see that Nan was exhausted and urged her to retire.

"Robert and I have several things yet to discuss, dearheart. We shan't be long before we, too, will find our beds."

As Nan happily bid each of them a good night, Robert could see that the Lady was not at all ready to end the day. She walked to her great chair and asked her friend to join her by the fire.

"It was such a beautiful celebration of Waldef at dinner, Robert, and he was happy. Did you see how much he enjoyed the company of MaryLizbet?"

"Indeed, my Lady, and how much she enjoyed his company. They danced together as long as the fiddler continued to play."

Though the Lady was obviously pleased, he could see that she continued to be distracted. Her on-going thoughts were troubled.

"My Lady, how may I help you? It is clear to me that you are more than grateful for the evening's celebration of Waldef, but your mind is not at peace."

"Robert, I hate to bring us back to the main problem at hand, but I am unable to forget that, as Physician James said, some person caused this evil attack upon the village. So, I must ask myself, why was it done? I have to believe that this was a kind of vengeance against me."

"And whom do you suspect seeks such vengeance?"

"I do not know the man, but there is one person who may think he has a motive against my family, and that is this insidious Count Dravini."

"If he is near enough to cause this upset in Aust, should we not, as you insisted with your brother, increase our guard against him here?"

"Of course, Robert, that is my next move. If he is nearby, I shall not rest until I find him, and Waldef is my chief witness, my means of identifying him. A man like Dravini will not be unnoticed. Aust is small, and folk of the village are immediately aware of the presence of foreigners in our midst."

"But, how can we use Waldef's eyes yet keep him out of sight? Surely, we can not allow Dravini to see him as part of your household, my Lady."

"Dear God, no. We must protect him at all costs. Will you bring Gareth from the barn in the morning so that we might speak with him, Robert? My stablemaster has been my first line of defence for Waldef, and he must be aware of a present danger that may threaten the lad."

"First thing on the morrow, I shall go to the barn and bring Gareth to speak with you here in your solar, my Lady," Robert told her. "Gareth and all the men of your household must be made aware of the possibility of threat against the manor and their need to protect Waldef. I beg you, do not try to minimise this as merely your suspicion. If Dravini is anywhere near to Aust, all your defences must be raised straightaway."

Chapter Twelve

MaryLizbet's Tale

The Lady was waiting in her solar when Robert arrived with Gareth. The stablemaster knew something must be of concern to the Lady; otherwise, she would have come to speak with him in the barn. Their friendship was decades old, as was hers with Nan, having begun at the time of the Lady's first marriage. Gareth and Nan had both served her since their childhoods, yet Apollonia had never regarded either of them as mere servants.

When they were seated, the Lady expressed her appreciation for Gareth's willingness to guard Waldef since he had been brought to her. "I never asked if you would take charge of Waldef when he arrived so unexpectedly, but you have proven more than a guard, Gareth. You have been an excellent guide to the lad. He is convinced that no other person could have taught him more about the care of horses. Gramercy, Gareth, I am truly grateful for all you have done."

Always a shy person, Gareth blushed at her compliment but surprised her by responding enthusiastically. "Ee be a good lad, m'Lady, and as elped me every day. Ee learns well and remembers too. Oi ave been grateful to ave is elp."

"This morning I have called you here to ask for your advice, Gareth," the Lady went on. "I fear that Waldef needs special protection. It is possible that an evil man has come to Aust recently trying to avenge himself upon me. I have never met him, but Waldef knows who he is, a foreigner from Europe whose name is Dravini. This man poses a threat against the lad because Waldef is the only one in Aust who can identify him and his criminal past. How can we best protect Waldef and our household should this creature be skulking anywhere near the village?"

Gareth did not answer at first but carefully considered what she was asking. When he did speak, he said immediately, "Though Oi ate to give up is stayin in the barn, m'Lady, would you consider taken im into the manor to serve you? If ee be sleepin with the other men in the servants' quarters and workin inside the manor, ee will be better protected cause Oi goes ome to Ingst every night."

"Gramercy, Gareth, a good beginning. I shall see that it is done, but I have one more service to ask of you. Will you gather all the men and boys of my affinity together so that Giles can speak with them of how best to ready ourselves against a possible threat?"

"Having seen the foiled attack upon the village, Gareth," Robert told him, "the Lady fears that the manor may be next."

"Aye, Master Robert, when do you wish for us to gather?"

"Ask everyone to come to the hall late this afternoon. We can do little but anticipate, yet everyone in the household must be alert and aware of the threat. Will you send Waldef to us now? I shall assign him new duties."

* * *

When Waldef entered the hall, the Lady received him with Robert. She indicated to the lad that she wished to take advantage of his service inside her household as her page. He was pleased, for he knew that a page could mean one in training for knighthood. It was a step before squire, and if he could convince this noble lady of his dedication to chivalry, she would better understand his goals in life.

"My Lady," he said very earnestly, "whatever you require of me, I shall be proud to serve you."

"Well, the first thing you must do is move your things to the manor servants' quarter where you will sleep. Then you will ride out to the Falcon Farm with Gareth and bring Nan home to me. We shall have to design new apparel for you as my page, bearing the arms of Aust."

* * *

Apollonia was already seated in the hall when the men of her household gathered. Quietly greeting each of them, she remained silent as Giles told them of her suspicion that a threat was being made against her and asked for their awareness of a need for defence of the manor. "Unfortunately," Giles said, "the Lady is unable to tell us anything more specific."

Every man of her household made a point to assure her of his loyalty, and each promised to keep his eyes and ears open to anything unusual, especially watching for the appearance of foreigners in the village. Garmon made a heartfelt declaration that he and the others were grateful for her gracious lordship of the manor, and he with the other men would devote themselves to her protection. In closing the gathering, Giles issued a gentle but serious reminder that each of them must remain on the alert, every day.

"If any person, foreigner from wherever, should come to Aust to avenge themselves upon our Lady Apollonia, each of us must see ourselves as her first line of protection,"

The Lady remained in the hall after the meeting to receive Waldef who returned with Nan later that day. Apollonia was not entirely surprised to see that they brought MaryLizbet with them. After welcoming everyone, the Lady told Nan that she had a new assignment for her, to create for Waldef an appropriate tunic for him bearing her heraldry.

"Waldef is to begin his service in my household, Nan, but he must be given suitable clothes to wear marked by the heraldry of my affinity," the Lady said with a great smile.

Nan made no comment, but taking him by the arm, she led the lad back towards her chamber. "Perhaps I can use more of Master Davey's things, my Lady. Waldef is about the right size."

When Apollonia was alone with MaryLizbet, she could tell that the girl shyly enjoyed being in Waldef's company but at this moment seemed anxious to share some news with her. "What is it, MaryLizbet," she asked gently, "do you have something to tell me?"

"My Lady, I pray you will not find my concerns childish, but little gifts have appeared on our doorstep for baby Arild. They are thoughtful things, a tiny hand-carved toy rattle and a lovely little carved dog, the proper size for her to hold."

"Who brings these things, MaryLizbet?"

"That is the mystery, my Lady; we never know. They simply appear with Arild Marie's name on them."

"Is it correct that these are left as gifts specifically for the child?"

"Yes, my Lady, each has been marked with her name, but we have no idea from whom they come."

"Well, if they offer no danger to Arild, someone obviously wishes to give little gifts to the infant anonymously. I dare say your parents should examine them carefully and then let baby Arild play with them."

"Yes, my Lady, I have not meant to say that there has been ill will intended, but does it not seem possible that Arild's real parents may be seeking a way to express their love for the child? She was a founding, after all."

"Ah, I follow your meaning, but how can we know?"

"I am an early riser," MaryLizbet said, "and will keep careful watch during the mornings ahead. Perhaps I will discover who is doing this."

* * *

When the household gathered for dinner, Waldef appeared in his new apparel. He wore a tunic of dark blue over his hose, and upon his sleeve, he proudly displayed the badge of the Lady of Aust, a swirl of English ivy entwined about a dark red heart. Though he now sat in his regular place at the lower table, next to Garmon, everyone in the household who also wore such heraldry, recognised his change in status and made a point to welcome him.

Waldef especially wanted to get to know Garmon better. He hoped the older servant, a young man in his early twenties, would teach him more about the Lady's affinity, how it worked, and how to understand his duties as her page. Garmon was precise and meticulous about the performance of each of his responsibilities, always seeking to impress the Lady's steward, Giles, because Giles had been in her affinity for years. Waldef had been told that Garmon, too, was recently come to Aust, but he was somewhat distant and not easy to get to know. He was not resentful against Waldef yet felt a need to maintain his superior station in the household. Waldef assumed that he was cautious or perhaps still adjusting to his role in the household of a noblewoman. It was when Waldef mentioned archery that he saw the elder Garmon's interest really perk up.

"I know nothing of weapons," Waldef said earnestly, "but I have always wished to gain skills with the bow."

"Well, as an Englishman you must, lad," Garmon said quietly, as if just between the two of them. "It is the law of the king that every Englishman equip himself with a bow and arrows." Then, he added, "If you have any time to slip away later in the afternoon, meet me behind the barn, and I can help you."

"How is it that you have learned such a manly skill?"

"All men of my age are required by law not only to learn how to shoot but to practise regularly and be ready to serve our king in time of war."

"Do you have a bow?"

"Of course, and I practise daily to keep my eye sharp. It is required by law on every Sunday and holiday for all men to be at the butts for practice."

* * *

Later that day, Waldef did not hesitate. When the Lady dismissed him in the afternoon while she rested, he ran outdoors and found his way behind the barn where Garmon had brought his bow and already set up his target.

Waldef was amazed to see the size of Garmon's bow. He was tall as a young man, but his bow was even taller than he. Waldef walked next to him and asked if he might hold it.

"Aye, lad, take a good look—it be a grand weapon, made of the finest yew, and with it, my arrows can penetrate a knight's armour."

"Really?" Waldef exclaimed unbelieving. "I did not think anything could pierce armour."

"I have never been in warfare, but my grandfather told me that at Crecy in France, we killed thousands of French knights and soldiers with our arrows whilst the English lost just fifty men."

"Will you teach me how to use the bow?"

"I would welcome your company at practice, Waldef. Whenever I can, I slip away to this place to improve my skill. I think I will soon be able to release eight arrows in a minute, but my hope is to do twelve!"

* * *

Every afternoon, when Garmon and Waldef could be excused from their duties, they would meet behind the barn, set up the target while Garmon took a special pleasure in demonstrating to Waldef the basics of shooting. Gareth noticed the two of them at practice one evening when he was preparing to ride home to Ingst. The stablemaster was getting on in years but remained a sturdy, well-built man whose strength was never questioned nor tested by the lads of the household. Gareth noticed that Garmon was the proud owner of a longbow who was using his ability to demonstrate his skills to Waldef. Turning back into the barn, Gareth dismounted and went to the upper storage level to bring down one of his bows stored there.

Then, walking around to the back of the barn, Gareth handed his bow to Waldef. "Here lad, use this to work with Garmon. It not be as mighty as Garmon's weapon, but you shall get better if you ave a bow of your own for practice."

"Gramercy, Master Gareth," Waldef said as he very respectfully took the bow in hand. "It is good of you to share this with me. I know not how to thank you enough."

"Tomorrow when we ave a bit of spare time, Oi shall show you ow to care for it, lad, and will depend on you to keep it well."

Waldef was stunned and could think of nothing to say except to express his thanks several more times. The stablemaster smiled as he turned to walk back to his mount. "Remember lad, Oi will expect you to care for it well."

Garmon, as witness to this exchange, said little to Gareth except to wish him a pleasant evening. "Master Gareth, you have the best of days for your ride to Ingst as the sun has not yet set." Then, turning back to Waldef, he added, "Come along then, Waldef, let us practise. You will learn little by staring at it."

Waldef smiled and responded by holding the bow properly, "Yea, Garmon, as you say, I have much to learn."

* * *

The days of summer were long and warm as August brought a glorious time of harvest, the celebration of new fruit, glorious sunrises, and setting suns. Late summer always seemed an especially welcome season to the Lady Apollonia. She and Robert spent many afternoons riding along the River Severn, pausing to enjoy the green and growing beauty of each day but also to observe the wild creatures who hunted and fished along its banks. On this ride, however, Apollonia noticed that Robert appeared more than usually distracted, and the Lady felt she must find some way for them to talk. Their friendship had grown to feel as close as family, and they had regularly shared personal thoughts on many subjects, whether concerns of their faith or the rule of their king.

When they came to one of their favourite overviews of the Severn, Apollonia suggested that they dismount to sit together and watch the glorious setting sun. Once seated, she said to him, "I fear you are troubled by something, dear friend. May I offer my concern and seek to share your thoughts?"

"In a few words, my Lady, I must leave Aust. I have received a message from my son who tells me that he needs my help in Worcester."

Though taken aback by his announcement, Apollonia looked directly into his eyes and with one of her encouraging smiles said frankly, "I am not pleased that you must go, Robert. You are surely aware how I am grateful for your friendship. Yet, you know where I will be in the months ahead, and if there is any possibility of your return to Aust, I shall look forward to it."

"You know that I treasure our time spent together, my Lady. I have never experienced a more meaningful friendship with anyone, man or woman, as we have shared. I do feel some guilt at leaving you just now, and I surely would not unless the needs of my son's family were not urgent."

"Robert," Apollonia said with grandmotherly concern in her voice, "of course you must be there for your family, and my prayers will return to Worcester with you. I hope you will continue to send word of developments after you are home," she said as she extended her hand to him.

Kenwood took her hand immediately and pressed it to his lips. "I must leave on the morrow, my Lady, but my thoughts remain here with you."

"Then let us return to the manor to help you prepare. A good meal this evening and I shall see you off after we break our fast in the morning." She knew as did Robert, that little more could be said, so they mounted up to return to the manor.

"If only all our problems in life could be as simply solved as your diagnosis of the red dye," she said with a sigh.

* * *

The Lady was up at the break of dawn and found Robert waiting for her when she descended to join him in breaking their fast. He lingered a matter of minutes, after they had finished their meal, to say goodbye to her household and offer his sincere thanks to each of them. Apollonia knew she could not hold him back, and Robert obviously did not wish to draw out the leaving process. He was packed and ready to begin his journey, so when Gareth brought his horse to the manor entrance, the entire household gathered round the Lady to wish him Godspeed.

After Robert was gone, Apollonia asked Francis to offer special prayers for him and his family during that morning's chapel. Her friend had offered no explanation for his need to return home so speedily, but she could see that something important required his personal attention in Worcester.

* * *

Later in the day, MaryLizbet came to the manor from her family farm and asked to speak with the Lady. Apollonia could see that she had something special to tell her so led her up the stairs to her private solar. When they were seated together, the Lady asked, "What is it, child? I can tell that you have discovered something important, MaryLizbet."

"This was lying on our front step this morning, my Lady," she said as she produced a precious little hand carved pony. On the front of it was a small slip of parchment which said: "For Arild Marie."

"Baby Arild will love to play with this little toy as she grows," Apollonia said looking at it closely.

"This time I saw who left the toy, my Lady. As you know I have been watching most mornings to learn from whom such gifts come."

"Did you recognise the person, MaryLizbet?"

"Yes, my Lady and I was truly surprised. It was your butler, Garmon. He was wearing a broad brimmed hat to cover his face and moved silently to make no announcement of his presence. I am certain it was he, and I saw him lay his gift gently on the step, then slip away."

"There is probably a very simple explanation for his gift, MaryLizbet," the Lady told her. "I know he enjoys carving."

* * *

After MaryLizbet was gone, Apollonia asked Nan to bring Garmon to speak with her in her solar. As she began to walk up the stairs, she said, "I need to speak with Garmon privately, dearheart, so I hope you will take some time for yourself whilst he is with me."

When Garmon first came to the Lady's private chamber, she thought that he seemed on edge. He could not think of anything that he had done to displease the Lady, but this sort of summons was unusual. Apollonia sensed his unease, especially as the Lady rarely spoke with him personally and certainly never without Nan in their presence.

She asked him to sit with her for a brief chat because she said she wished to thank him for the time he had been giving to teach young Waldef how to use the bow. "You know that as a vowess of the church, I speak very little, but I must tell you, Garmon, your instruction with the bow has been a real gift to Waldef. He has spoken highly of your skill, and there is no way I would have been able to offer such training to him."

Garmon did relax a bit at her emphasis upon thanks, not complaint. "Waldef is making good progress, my Lady. He learns well, and Master Gareth lent him the use of one of his bows. Waldef joins me regularly behind the barn for practice whenever our household duties grant us free time."

"I, too, have been grateful for your excellent service, Garmon. My steward, Giles, recommended you to me as a young man he met at Bristol Fair. He said you were willing to come to Aust from your home in the city. Your diligence and dedication since joining my household have been impressive as well as your friendship and instruction to Waldef."

"Gramercy my Lady, I am pleased to have won a place in your household and will do all that I can to serve you well."

"Then be assured of your place here. You continue to impress my steward and have worked well with the rest of the household," she said encouragingly. "There is one more thing that I should ask of you, however. What more can you tell me of the infant who was abandoned upon my doorstep?"

At this question, the Lady could see Garmon's spine stiffen as he was caught completely off guard.

"I, I do not understand what you are asking me, my Lady?" he stuttered.

"I believe you do, Garmon. You have been seen leaving gifts for the child."

"Only little things that I carved, my Lady, nothing meaningful, I assure you."

"I do not seek to pressure you. If you prefer to tell me nothing, I shall ask nothing further of you. You are a good addition to my household here, and I have no desire to lose you."

"Oh, my Lady, this is the best position in life I have ever held. I have nowhere to go, and I can certainly do nothing for a motherless child," Garmon spoke out desperately.

"Whose motherless child is Arild Marie, Garmon? Can you tell me?"

Garmon went silent, dropped his head as if he had nothing further to say. Apollonia said nothing, and silence reigned between them.

Finally, he raised his head, looked straight into the Lady's eyes and said, "The infant was recently born to a young maid in Bristol where I last worked. We truly loved each other and had hoped to marry when I could establish myself, but my precious Lizzie died during the birth. I have struggled to find some way to care for the infant but could not manage. It was either abandon the child into an orphanage or bring her here where I prayed God you would see that she was baptised and find a loving family to cherish her."

Apollonia, listened quietly, then simply added, "You have been witness to your daughter's adoption by my Nan's family. Do you wish me to keep this truth between us, Garmon?"

"Yes, my Lady, I beg you will maintain my silence and allow me to remain in your household. The Falcon family offers the infant everything that I cannot. I vow to serve you faithfully and continue to offer my friendship and instruction with the bow to Waldef, but I pray you will let none other know the infant's true story. I left my little gifts to her in memory of my love for her mother who should never have died. Lizzie was barely into her teens, and I can not help but feel some blame for her death. You have given Arild Marie a beautiful name, seen that she is baptised and is welcomed into a good home with excellent parents, twin brothers, and a devoted elder sister. I remain unmarried, unprepared to be a father, and can offer her nothing. Being part of your household here in Aust, I have seen how beautifully she is loved and cared for. Please, only tell the Falcon family that I enjoy carving in my spare time and merely leave the little toys for their infant who is of an age to enjoy playing with them."

"Indeed, I shall do as you say, Garmon. But would it not be well for you to tell the Falcon Family that, as you enjoy carving, you have been leaving these small gifts for their adopted child? You could merely say that you did not wish to receive any remuneration, you simply did these little toys for your pleasure. The Falcons are a beautiful family whom I know well and respect. They have much to offer little Arild. Why not reach out to them as well and be welcomed into their home, not as the child's father but as a neighbour and a friend?"

Chapter Thirteen

The Druid Returns to Aust

The Lady Apollonia was pleased to receive in late September another guest to her manor. When he had first visited England in 1397 from his home in Ireland, he introduced himself to Englishmen as Maurice of Tyrconnell, but as his friendship with the Lady grew, he had revealed his Celtic identity as Cunomorus Amairogen, Seer and Brehon to the King O'Donnell of Tyrconnell. Apollonia had been especially pleased to maintain a correspondence with this Irish scholar through the past decade, not only because of his official position in the household of a king, but also because he had told her he was of the Druidic caste. She admired him for many reasons but especially as a highly-educated, studious man who had shared with her his interest in astronomy and the study of the stars.

When they finished the evening meal, the Lady invited Cunomorus to join her and Nan in the solar so that their conversation might continue. Seated in the great chairs near the fire, Apollonia began by telling the Druid again how surprised she was that he had returned to England.

"It is a special pleasure to be with you, Cunomorus," Apollonia told him sincerely, "for I feared we might not meet again. I dare say you probably will not be able to tell me why you have come to England, but I am truly curious."

"Indeed, my Lady, my reason for being here is to study a grand phenomenon, which will happen soon and be best observed from the West of England."

"May I ask what sort of phenomenon we are to witness?"

"I hope you will grant me the privilege of viewing it with me," he said. "There will occur in three days an *eiclips* as we say in my home country. You know that we, as Druids, study the heavens, and I faithfully report to my king the results of my study. Therefore, I have been sent to be here in Aust where you will have an excellent view of the darkening of the sun."

At that, Nan who was sitting next to the Lady dropped her embroidery and gasped. The Lady, too, was shocked. "Dear God, what will be the cause of such a frightful thing, Cunomorus? What will happen to our sun? Will its light cease?" The Lady was obviously concerned. She had no idea what an *eiclips* was, but she knew well how dependent all people are upon the sun's heavenly light.

"No, dear Lady, the darkening will be temporary. It will only happen for a brief while as our moon will cast its shadow passing across the face of the sun. The shadow will continue to move slowly away, and our sun's brilliance will return."

Apollonia was grateful for this assurance that such a darkening of the sun would be a passing shadow, but she thought immediately that her people must be told of this thing that was soon to happen. She decided that with Cunomorus' help, her people and local folk could be granted some understanding so that they would not be terrified when it occurred.

"My friend," she said anxiously, "I will call my household together and invite the village warden of Aust, our schoolmaster, the local physician, and the priest of our church to a meeting tomorrow morning. Will you be kind enough to explain to them what they will witness? I fear people in the village, as well as my household, will be frightened when witnessing such a phenomenon."

"Of course, my Lady, I shall do my best, but first will you allow me to speak with the men of your household, especially those of the church, your almoner and chaplain? The local people will be best calmed by their reassurance of nothing to fear if they have the instructions from men whom they know and trust, not foreigners."

Immediately, Apollonia sent Nan to collect Giles and to bring William, Francis, and Gareth, the stablemaster, as quickly as she could. When the men joined her, she introduced Cunomorus to them as her friend from Ireland, a servant of his king, and a great scholar of the heavens who had come to Aust for an extraordinary natural event, which was to take place three days from now.

The Lady could see that Francis did have some memory of this Irishman's visit years earlier. Nan said nothing but continued to be uneasy about this Irish gentleman whom she remembered as having declared himself to the Lady as not only a foreigner but a Druid—a pagan Celtic priest. Nan listened carefully when Cunomorus began to speak, and soon even the Lady's maid found his voice reassuring in its very well-educated, though slightly accented, English.

The Druid spoke directly to the men of the household while standing next to the Lady's chair. They accepted him as an important friend of the Lady from Ireland, and as he spoke, they too listened carefully to all he had to tell them.

"I have come to Aust to see an extraordinary phenomenon that will happen in three days and be best viewed here from Aust Cliff. As we all know, the wheel of the sun moves around our world, rising in the east, setting in the west. In three days, the sun will continue its journey, but on the third day, its surface will be covered briefly by a shadow from the moon. I wish to witness this and then report to my king details of the experience. However, my hostess, the Lady Apollonia, has asked me to explain what will be happening so that her people will not be frightened by it. Will you all prepare yourselves to speak with the people of the village and nearby farms? The Lady has arranged for a meeting in the parish church tomorrow morning. I ask you especially to be there to help me calm people's fears through understanding. We must never look directly at the sun, but we will all see the day darken as the shadow of the moon moves in front of the sun to block its light from us for a brief while."

Everyone remained silent at first, trying to take in what had just been told them. The first question came from Francis. "I have never seen such a thing in my lifetime, sir. How do we know that the shadow will go away? Does this thing happen very often?"

"More often than we realise," Cunomorus said, "and we all know that our sun and our moon move daily. The earth is a very large place, and this phenomenon, when it occurs, is seen differently in different places in our world."

"My lord, how can we reassure our people that it is temporary?" Giles asked.

"We must tell them that such things have been studied by scholars who have written of seeing them since the time of Christ."

"What are folk to do when it happens?" William said as he thought of the number of uneducated people in the village who would be unable to comprehend and terrified by the darkening of midday.

"There is always comfort in being near to God in prayer," Apollonia's chaplain, Friar Francis, said gently. "I suggest that we encourage everyone gather to pray. We shall tell folk that we will meet in the church and offer heartfelt prayers of thanks for all the blessings of our sun. As Saint Francis taught us, I shall help everyone repeat his Canticle of the Sun, and we shall all offer our thanks to Brother Sun. I will remain in the church with you and our parish priest, and we will lead in prayer throughout the period of darkness, however long it may be. As soon as the sun's light returns to full brightness, we shall lead in prayers of praise and thanks."

* * *

Apollonia was especially excited on the morning of the day when Cunomorus said the shadow over the sun would happen. It was an unusually bright late September day, and when he invited her to accompany him to the top of Aust Cliff to make his observation of this great event, she was more than ready. Nan, however, begged to be excused as she said nervously that she preferred to join the others who were gathering in the church for prayer.

Apollonia was by now convinced of Waldef's innocence of the faked murder charge against her young servant, so she asked him to accompany them, and the lad was thrilled. She and Waldef rode with Cunomorus to the base of Aust Cliff where they left their mounts and climbed to its ridge. Apollonia noticed that the Druid carried with him two large sheets of white parchment. It was a calm day with little breeze, and Cunomorus watched the heavens carefully. At a certain point he laid one of the sheets on the ground, stabilised it against any unexpected breeze by placing rocks at each corner and told Apollonia and Waldef to watch its surface. Waldef moved closer to the Lady and positioned himself to listen carefully to all the Druid's comments. As they watched the sheet on the ground where it lay, Apollonia could see that the sheet of parchment which Cunomorus held in his hand had a small hole in it. He held that sheet above the one lying on the ground so the sunlight shone through the hole and cast a small circle of light upon the lower sheet.

Slowly, as she and Waldef watched, the small circle of light began to be covered by a small round dark shadow. What a wondrous thing she was seeing, the Lady gasped to herself, too amazed to add any comments. She could see the shadow on the sheet move to cover the face of the sun. As she and Waldef watched, wide-eyed, they could not help but notice how dark the day around them became. She looked to Cunomorus who nodded encouragement to her and directed her view back towards the circle of light, now around the circle of shadow on the parchment below.

Apollonia felt somewhat frightened. In all her years, she had never observed such a thing, and her heart seemed to be pounding within her silent body.

Slowly the darkening of the day began to lighten as they watched the shadow across the sun continue to move until the sun's full light beamed down once again upon them.

The Lady and Waldef stood silently watching the Druid whose lips moved in silent prayer and careful mental recounting of the unbelievable event they had just witnessed.

* * *

Waldef seemed to be the only one of them with words as they rode home to the manor. "Gramercy, my Lord Cunomorus, for sharing your knowledge of this extraordinary sight which we have witnessed today. I am certain that our Schoolmaster Winters will speak of it many times, and I shall be pleased to be able to add what I saw and how I saw it."

"It is a wondrous experience, young Waldef," Cunomorus said, "and one which will stay with you throughout your life. Always remember that study of the heavens can be done by everyone and study in general builds our understanding of the world about us. We need not remain in school endlessly, but we can continue to read, to explore, to experiment, and continue to learn as long as we live."

* * *

Nan met them at the door when at last they returned to the manor late in the afternoon. She seemed composed to her usual in-charge practicality. "My Lady," she announced happily, "have you noticed how beautifully the sun's setting this afternoon has filled the western skies with glorious colour? I must say, things seem returned to balance where they ought to be. As we were all praying in the church, we could see the dark world slowly brighten as our prayers of thanks rose."

"God is gracious, Nan," the Lady said. "We have all been witness to a marvelous event this day, but I am eternally grateful to have been granted some understanding of its wonder," she added as she smiled at the Druid.

"My Lord Cunomorus, I pray you will spend some time with us in my solar," she suggested, "so that we might continue to ask our questions and share your thoughts."

"Indeed, my Lady it will be my pleasure, but I must be ready to begin my journey home on the morrow."

* * *

On the following morning, the Lady took several private minutes with her guest after breaking their fast. She told him that she hoped that he would send her word of his safe return to Tyreconnell and share with her his report to the king of the phenomenal occurrence they had witnessed together.

"I hope to read your description of the *eiclips,* but I shall also be grateful for your continued correspondence, Cunomorus. You, as no one else could, helped us understand the heavenly vision we have seen together."

The Druid thanked her for her hospitality and promised that he, too, was grateful that they would continue their correspondence. Then, he added something rather surprising to her, "In recent months, I have been talking with King O'Donnell's personal chaplain, a truly godly man, and have begun to understand that you Christians worship one God, but a triune God--Father, Son, and Holy Spirit--whom you say created all the earth and the heavens. We Celts also worship gods in triune form. I shall study your holy word to learn more of your God and how you seek to communicate with Him through His Son."

"If I can be helpful in sharing my faith with you in any way, Cunomorus," the Lady said, "I shall be glad for the opportunity. Your wisdom and study have brought balance and understanding of our world to my life and my belief."

"Dear Lady, he said as he bowed over her extended hand, "I admire your inquisitive mind, which I have witnessed seeking answers to the most challenging of questions." She could see that he was not anxious to be gone and seemed to linger. Slowly, he turned to leave her. "I shall write when I am home," he said. "Farewell, gracious Lady."

Her household was gathered outside where Gareth held the Druid's horse for him to mount. Cunomorus was grateful for the Lady's continuing gestures of friendship to him and waved a hearty salute to all her household as he rode away towards the ferry.

When he was gone, Waldef looked to the Lady, saying quietly, "I have never met such a wise man, my Lady. I should love to learn from him."

"It is not likely that we shall see him again, Waldef, but every time I have been in his presence, it has been truly memorable for me. He is a great source of wisdom, and I will seek to continue our correspondence after he is home again in Ireland. I shall let you know when I have received word of his safe return and will share his letters with you."

* * *

Apollonia was more than prepared to understand the distress in her next message from her brother, Ferdinand. The earl's community had experienced a brief period of the sun's darkening and had dissolved into a panic. Ferdinand told her that a known troublemaker in Marshfield had stood in the middle of the village square stirring up the people who had been drawn out from their homes by the midday's darkening. Ferdinand said that the villain continued to shout judgements upon everyone for their sin, insisting that they were the cause of God's vengeance upon the earth. The villain threatened a permanent darkening of the sun unless people of the village paid him to reverse it. The credulous folk poured whatever coins they had into his hat until Ferdinand and two of his men walked into the square and arrested him, restoring calm, ordering the folk to reclaim their coins, and return to their homes.

> I told them that the sun was God's creation and would never be responsive to such a mean-spirited peasant. You know I do not think of myself as any kind of preacher, Polly, but I had to restore order and would not allow such a creature to take advantage of my people. Thank God, as we watched, the shadow did move from the face of the sun, so I simply shouted to them all to get on with their day. "The Lord God has restored balance in His world," I told them. "Now, you, too, must get back to your daily chores."

Smiling to herself as she read her brother's message, Apollonia could understand the fear and chaos his people faced trying to understand the mysteries of an *eiclips*. What a blessing Cunomorous' visit in Aust had been for her and her people. She knew she would share her brother's story with the Druid when next she wrote to him.

* * *

It was late in the autumn when the Lady received yet another returned guest to Aust Manor. Sir Julian Thurston arrived alone and asked to be received by the Lady. Apollonia was glad to see him because she knew that he was coming from the court of King Henry.

"I pray you will stay with us, Julian, and will also plan to be my guest in the days ahead. We have been hearing conflicting rumours regarding King Henry's health and will be grateful for your news."

The knight was pleased by her invitation but insisted his visit must be brief. He said he had to continue back to Bristol to be with his friend John Purvey, but he knew that being in Aust would be especially restful. In truth, he felt that a few days in Aust Manor afforded him the pleasant opportunity to visit with this elderly noblewoman whom he admired, not only for her achieved independence but her well-read intelligence. It was good to be here again; the knight knew that he and the Lady would pick up their friendship where they had left it at their last visit. The Lady Apollonia was decades older than he, but her brilliant smile always brightened his life, as if his loving parents were still with him.

"His Grace, King Henry is truly struggling, my Lady. Parliament, which met in March, continues in session, and our king is frequently unable to attend due to his sickness. His royal power has been severely curtailed, subjected to the supervision of a council. The skin ailment of our king continues to worsen, my Lady. His rapid heartbeat has often been worrisome, and our friend Physician Mark remains at his side constantly. In confidence, I shall tell you that Mark fears that King Henry has some sort of wasting disease, which at times totally incapacitates him, but his mind remains sharp and alert. I only share this with you, because I know you to be a loyal subject who does not promote gossip. Our monarch physically struggles to rule on some days and is aided in every way by his devoted friend, the Archbishop Arundel. Since the Percy rebellion, King Henry has retaken all of the castles of Northumberland, and he has been seen by his people at the head of his armies, which is the way he wishes to be remembered."

"Does Mark feel that healing is possible for our king?" the Lady asked gently.

"Again, I share this with you alone, my Lady. Our king is alert and fulfills his responsibilities, but his body strives with crippling illness. It appears that his grace has come to the realisation that he will never be well again."

"Gracious Father in Heaven," Nan pleaded, "there must be something done to bring full healing to him."

"We must pray, Mistress Nan," the knight said quietly. "Mark tells me in utter privacy that there is no cure, yet the king does seem to have some days better than others."

"You bring tragic news, Julian, but Nan and we shall keep all that you have said concealed in our heart," Apollonia said quietly. "If prayer is our only recourse, then my household will offer constant requests for God's healing presence with King Henry throughout the days ahead."

* * *

The next morning, after breaking their fast, Apollonia invited Sir Julian to ride with her along the Severn. It was a bright, late autumn day, full of sunshine and blue skies reflecting their glorious colour in the river. The Lady led Julian to a favourite spot along the bank where they dismounted and sat together on a fallen log.

Unexpectedly, Julian asked her a surprising question. "Are you acquainted with a man in service to Archbishop Arundel whose name is Brandon Landow, my Lady?"

Apollonia's eyes widened in recognition, but her voice was tinged with irritation. "My acquaintance with Brandon goes back many years, Julian, but it has never been a cordial one. I have known him since he was a member of my household as a deceitful boy, and I have followed his career in the church where he began as a young pardoner whose motives were driven only by greed. I did not know he had risen to the heights of service to the archbishop. Why do you ask?"

"I encountered him in Lambeth as part of the household of the now Chancellor of England, Archbishop Arundel."

"If you encounter him again, Julian, always be on your guard. He will use anything that he sees as a weakness to take advantage of you and promote himself. Does he know anything of your sympathies with Wycliffe?"

"Some people associated with the court of King Henry have called me a Lollard Knight, not in my presence, but I am aware of their suspicions, my Lady. Gramercy for telling me these things of Landow. I suspected that he might be driven by self-promotion, and I am well aware of Archbishop Arundel's actions against the Lollards. Therefore, Mark and I tread very carefully, thanks to the personal warnings of your gracious brother, the earl."

Apollonia decided to redirect their conversation to pursue one of her concerns. "I must confess to you that I am about to ask a favour of you as a knight, Julian, though I have no right to do so."

"How may I serve you, my Lady. Pray, tell me what favour I may grant to you—it is yours."

"I fear that my household may be in need of protection. Can you remain with us in the days ahead while I search to discover the whereabouts of an evil man who may be intending some sort of threat to me?"

"Who is this man, and what has he done to threaten you?"

"I confess I have never seen nor met the man, but I suspect him of having made a poisonous attack against the people of the village and having misused the village children to spread figs, a great treat laced with ground foxglove leaves. At first, the children of Aust were sickened, then two grandparents grew seriously ill, and our doctor of physic was baffled by the sudden outbreak of sickness that plagued the village."

"If you do not know this villain, how are we to identify him, my Lady?" Julian pressed.

"He is known by my page, Waldef, who says that his former master served him. This man calls himself Dravini and at one time served our king as a visiting foreign dignitary. Not long ago, Dravini was thrown out of the palace by Archbishop Arundel as a foreigner. He claims to be a count from the Kingdom of Sicily."

"If you believe this creature may be here in Aust to threaten you, my Lady, why would he seek revenge upon you?"

"He does not know me, but he does know my brother, the Earl Ferdinand, whom he has also managed to threaten by malevolent means against his people in Marshfield. I suspect that Dravini is driven to seek revenge against us because of our support to King Henry. Forgive my lack of specific information, but I know that there are members of the English nobility who might use such a villain to cause unrest and rebellion against King Henry whom they insist is a usurper."

"If you do not know this Dravini, how shall we find him if he is here in Aust?"

"As I have said, I have in my household a witness to identify him, Julian. My page, Waldef, not only knows what he looks like, he heard him give instructions to murder."

* * *

When the Lady and Julian returned to the manor house, she called for Waldef to come to her and be introduced to her friend, Sir Julian Thurston, a mature knight who served their King Henry. Waldef was obviously glad to become acquainted with the knight. He said little at first but then timidly asked the knight his opinion of the code of chivalry.

Sir Julian did not take time for thought. He answered Waldef immediately, "Chivalry is the code that governs my life, young man. Courage, honour, courtesy, justice, and a readiness to help the weak grant direction and purpose to my daily life and to sustain my Christianity."

Apollonia could see Waldef's eyes glow as he expelled a great breath of air, as if to say, "I knew it must be so."

Julian asked Waldef why he was interested in chivalry? The boy responded without hesitating, "As a merchant's son, I have no hope of becoming a knight, Sir Julian, but I seek to fulfill the goals of chivalry and have them govern my life as you have done."

"I hope, Julian, you will wander out to the back of the barn where Waldef and my servant Garmon regularly work to perfect their skills in archery," the Lady added. "Garmon tells me that Waldef is showing significant signs of improvement with the bow."

"I shall, my Lady, and with your permission, I will take time to move about the manor now to observe its layout. Will you allow your page to accompany me?"

"Indeed, Waldef," the Lady said, "I pray you will spend the days ahead with Sir Julian and be his daily guide. Thanks to Gareth's instruction, you already know as much about Aust Manor and the village as many in my household."

"Gramercy, my Lady," Waldef said enthusiastically. "I shall be glad to serve you, Sir Julian."

"Then, let us begin today, lad," Julian smiled. "I have much to learn."

Chapter Fourteen

Sir Julian Prepares

Waldef began by riding with Sir Julian into the village and then turning down toward the banks of the Severn River. He took the knight to the ferry point, and they watched together as the ferryman returned from his first crossing of that morning. Waldef wanted Sir Julian to meet the ferryman because he knew him to be a special source of information who quietly noted every person who used the ferry services coming into and leaving the village of Aust.

"I can not give you his name, Sir Julian. No one seems to know him as anyone but 'the ferryman'. He seems to be a crusty fellow and not at all welcoming, but I know him to have a good heart."

Waldef felt very grown up as they dismounted, and he walked with Sir Julian. When they reached the ferry dock, Waldef asked if he could introduce the knight to the ferryman. Instantly suspicious, the ferryman scowled and seemed to turn away. Waldef refused to be put off and simply walked closer to the ferry, not to board but to continue speaking.

"This is Sir Julian Thurston, ferryman, who has come to Aust to protect our Lady of the manor against attacks that have been threatened in the village."

Julian did not hesitate but began to speak immediately, "You provide a unique service to the village, ferryman, and I am glad to know you. You have seen endless numbers of folk travelling both ways, some good and some more questionable in their purpose. May I come to you with any questions as I seek to learn more of Aust?"

The squat old ferryman was taken aback at first by the knight's respectful approach to him, but he did respond. "Aye, Oi do see much goins on the village folk know nothin of," he said, looking down toward the ground.

"That is precisely why I ask you to be my first source of information as I seek to protect the Lady of the manor. She fears that some foreigners may be coming to Aust to threaten her."

"Aye, there be foreigners comin reglar, but usually they goes back reglar."

"The Lady believes this particular foreigner who seeks to threaten her is not an Englishman. I will be grateful if you alert me to anyone of suspicious nature whom you notice coming 'regular' to Aust."

"Oi stays on me ferry, Oi not be comin to find you."

"Of course," Julian said, "but if you will allow, I shall check with you 'reglar'."

Turning to Waldef, the knight said, "Let us return to the village, lad. I should like to meet the parish priest, the doctor of physic, the village school master, and the warden. Gramercy for your help, ferryman," he said waving goodbye as they left.

Waldef was pleased to continue with this assignment. He was especially proud to be able to introduce Sir Julian to these leading men of the village community. They, in turn, were obviously impressed by this gentle and respectful knight who had personally assumed some degree of protection for the Lady Apollonia.

The knight's message was the same for each of the village leaders: "Should they encounter any unusual visitors to Aust who stayed on with no apparent purpose, he would like to know of them." Having just experienced an obvious attack against the village through its children and the poisoned figs, all of the leaders in the community were aware of possible threats by some unknown strangers who sought to do them harm.

"The Lady of Aust fears that she was the cause of the attack," Sir Julian told them, "because of her loyal support of King Henry. She seeks to guard herself against any further threat." Sir Julian also told his new acquaintances that she would be grateful to use their eyes and ears to learn of anything suspicious or unusual happening in the village. They must not hesitate to contact him at the manor. He would look into it.

* * *

Dravini and Buldoc were staying in Wales where Dravini had found a pleasant accommodation not far from the ferry back to Aust. The Sicilian had also sent word of his change in location to the Baron Wenlock Paine, and within days of settling in, Dravini was surprised to be summoned to meet the baron for new instructions. Paine announced that he would be in Gloucester for several days and told him of their meeting place. Dravini travelled with Buldoc on the day that Paine had indicated, but when they arrived in Gloucester, Dravini went alone to his conference with the baron.

Dravini knew well that the baron did not hide from him his bitter, frustrated anger, driven by personal revenge against King Henry. Paine was rude and aggressive towards this foreigner but would not be identified as any part of an ongoing rebellion. Though Dravini thought him a disgusting person, he paid well and promptly, and the so-called count was greedy.

"I learned that you managed to irritate the Lord of Marshfield," Paine told him brusquely, "and made him the object of suspicion by his people, but can you not do something more serious than poisoned figs to frighten his sister? She seems vulnerable, widowed, and obviously alone here in the West Country. Can you not make her feel that her life is in danger? When she cries out to Marshfield for protection, we shall see to it that he knows his family's support for the Usurper is unpardonable."

"My lord, I have scouted out the Lady's situation in Aust and found that she is extremely well protected by an intensely loyal household affinity," Dravini told him.

"Still, she must have occasions to emerge from her household and go about the village unguarded. Why can you not target her when she is visiting the village on a holiday, for example? You have made her aware of a threat against her village, but now I wish you will create a far greater sense of personal danger to her."

"I shall do as you say, my Lord Paine, and will let you know when Buldoc and I have completed the task after we have returned to our refuge in Wales."

"Hesitate not. I wish to return to the north and will want to report that the Usurper's faithful subjects suffer because of their loyalty to him. Get it done."

* * *

When Dravini, who now called himself Peter Declan, and Buldoc arrived in Aust, they made note of an upcoming saint's day celebration, which would bring the Lady onto the streets of the village. Buldoc also made a special point to show Declan that he had created a miniature, but lethal, weapon, which he could easily conceal in his sleeve. He demonstrated how he could shoot a small dart into the heart of his target and never be observed. It was his own concept, he said proudly, especially designed to make painful wounding or assassinations far easier.

"When Oi shoots someone in a crowd," he told Dravini, "folk start rushin around to aid the victim. With this, Oi walks away midst the confusion with me weapon idden in me sleeve."

"Our opportunity will come soon," Declan told him. "Michaelmas Day will happen on the 29th September, and I learned from our visit to the Boars Head in Aust that the folk of the village are planning an autumn festival in the church yard. After rents are paid, the Lady is said to be providing a feast to serve Michaelmas goose for the village. Surely, that will be our best time to strike her. Keep your weapon concealed, my friend, for I believe we can achieve the baron's will and wound the Lady seriously, slipping back across the river in the chaos, unnoticed. Then, we shall receive our largest payment ever," he said as he rubbed his hands together in avaricious glee.

* * *

The Lady Apollonia and Nan were looking forward to this year's celebration of Michaelmas Day. It was always a favourite saint's day because Apollonia would be with the people in her village as they came to pay their quarterly rents after the harvests were complete and everyone would be ready for a holiday. It gave her an opportunity to speak with them, not only share their greetings but also learn their family news, their losses, and their hopes for the year ahead. She was also grateful that Sir Julian would remain at her side throughout the celebration, alert to any possible appearance of Dravini.

Waldef would remain at her side as her servant, especially because he was the one person able to spot Dravini and provide witness to his crimes. The Lady was willing to take these personal risks because Sir Julian agreed to be present to guard them. She was convinced that if Dravini was captured, he might be pressured to reveal the names of the Englishmen enabling him. Apollonia could not give up her conviction that behind all the troubles of the past year, someone of the nobility was using these foreigners to thwart King Henry whom they insisted was a usurper.

The Lady Apollonia also looked forward to the celebration of Michaelmas Day because she loved to think of the church's teachings that angels were capable of interceding for believers in their time of need. Regarding herself now as facing a time of personal need, the Lady offered daily prayers to the archangel, begging for his protection and guidance when the folk of the village gathered in honour of his special day.

She made a personal visit to the kitchen in preparation for the holiday to speak with her Norman cook Guise, a prickly, effeminate man, yet a well-respected artist within his kitchen realm. Guise had been overseeing preparations for the special holiday meal the Lady was planning for the village on Michaelmas Day, and she knew that his ego was spurred by the significance of his role in this holiday celebration. He would do his very best for her. He had selected ten geese from the Lady's farms, which he had been fattening for the past months. Guise wanted to create an especially grand meal for the Lady this year so that his name, as her cook, would be legendary in the West Country.

She walked with him to the goose pens where he displayed for her the plump, waddling birds whose wings had been clipped so that they could no longer fly.

"You can see, Madame, zeese birds will be perfect for Michaelmas feast," he told her proudly.

Apollonia made a point of leaning down to look at each of the fowl, nodding her head and complimenting her cook on his excellent forethought. "In every way, Guise, these are perfect birds," she told him. "Surely folk in the village will remember this holiday or be told of its glory should they happen to miss it."

For a brief moment, Guise seemed to grow taller as he pulled up his shoulders and bowed very elegantly to her compliment.

"Guise, I am aware that you will be especially busy on the day of the feast, but I must ask one further favour," the Lady said to him quietly. "I am asking every one of my household to be especially sensitive to the appearance of strangers here in Aust at our celebration. There is a man, at least one, perhaps two, who may be near Aust to threaten me. I know not what they look like, but my page, Waldef, will recognise them should they appear. You have a very sharp eye, and if you should notice any unusual European foreigner at the village feast, I pray you will call his attention to Sir Julian straightaway."

"Your servant, Madame," the cook nodded importantly as he, too, assumed the Lady's protection was also part of his role in her household.

* * *

As September came to its latter days, everyone in the village was involved in the preparations for Michaelmas. Apollonia knew that the villagers were also looking forward to the special feast that she, as Lady of the manor, offered them. On Michaelmas Day, a few travellers staying at the inn came to join the village celebration. Having introduced themselves, they, too, as guests to Aust found themselves invited to join the feast. On this saint's day, the church was filled.

Sir Julian was constant with the Lady, Nan, and Waldef. The knight's eyes were zealously on guard, as was every member of her household, keen to fulfill their responsibility for the Lady's safety.

* * *

Peter Declan and Buldoc had stayed away from the village and waited till the saint's day before taking the morning ferry across the Severn to Aust. Dravini, now Declan, and his henchman Buldoc had each grown a full beard. With their long hair and wearing the clothes of common labourers, they were convinced that they were unrecognisable to anyone who might have known them earlier. They walked into the village from the ferry and found a growing crowd of people gathering in the church yard. As they wandered about from booth to booth, they pretended interest in the variety of hand work that some of the village folk had on display for sale. Then, they purposely moved toward the table where the Lady sat with Nan and her steward, Giles Digby, receiving the rents from a line of her tenants. The Lady could not be missed, and Declan gestured to Buldoc that they should remove themselves from the centre of activity and merely observe for the moment. Buldoc suggested that they could wander down to The Boars Head for a drink, and Declan could see no problem with that.

After some time, they left The Boars Head and walked back toward the church. Declan and Buldoc saw that the Lady remained among her people who were glad for their opportunity to speak with her. The assassins had their horses tethered near the church, and now, bolstered by drink, Declan went to collect their mounts as he gestured to Buldoc to complete the task. The assassin quietly joined the villagers standing near the Lady and slid his dart gun forward under his sleeve into his hand. With several people still ahead of him in the line, he quietly lifted his armed hand towards the Lady, aiming the weapon towards her chest.

Suddenly, coming unawares from behind him, the Lady's stablemaster, Gareth, brought a massive club crashing down upon Buldoc's arm, breaking his grip and hurling the dart gun to the ground. At the same time, Sir Julian pressed the blade of his dagger into the neck of Declan whom he captured, having been sighted by Waldef. Calling him by his name, Sir Julian shouted midst the gathered people. "Pietro Dravini, I arrest you and your partner for the attempted murder of our Lady Apollonia of Aust. These folk gathered here are witnesses to your crime!"

Dravini drew himself up to his full height and declared his innocence. "I have nothing to do with him," he said pointing to Buldoc. "My name is Peter Declan, and I am a visitor from Europe to the festival of Saint Michael, currently residing in Wales," he said in his heavily accented English." You will allow me to return to the ferry."

Holding his wounded wrist in one hand, Buldoc suddenly realised that Dravini was accusing him of the attack. Buldoc shouted back, "Ee be a liar! Ee be the leader. Ee be paid to do this! Oi just used me skills accordin to is commands."

Apollonia, now standing between Gareth and Sir Julian, told the knight to take them both into custody. As everyone watched, they were taken to a small cell in the village and pushed inside its bars, glaring at each other, each ready to kill the other. Once alone, however, Dravini began to speak quietly to Buldoc. "Our best defence is silence. Say nothing. This woman does not know us, Buldoc, and she has no charge against us. Nothing happened; you simply raised your hand and was struck down. I shall demand that I be allowed to return to my country and will take you with me as my henchman if you cooperate. No matter what she says, she has no charge against us. Be silent. Nothing happened."

* * *

As soon as the Lady returned to the manor, she sent a message to her brother: "Ferdinand, You must come to Aust. We have the foreign villains in custody, charged with an attempt to injure me. A."

After her message was on its way, the Lady called Waldef to her.

"My sincere thanks for your services this day, Waldef, and now you must positively identify the men taken into Sir Julian's custody."

"Of course, my Lady. When shall we do this?"

"Let us go into the village now, Waldef. Sir Julian will accompany us and will be my witness to your identification."

When Nan brought the Lady's cloak, she was accompanied by Sir Julian. Their little group left the manor to walk into the village. As soon as Waldef saw the men sitting sullenly inside the cell, he said quietly to the Lady but in a voice positive with accusation, "He now has a beard and long hair, my Lady, but I recognise him," he said pointing. That is the foreigner who says he is from Sicily, for whom my lord Sir Hardulph served."

Then, pointing toward Buldoc, he told her, "That creature is the frightening man whom I believe drugged my ale whilst I waited for my master at the whorehouse. He is the last person I remember seeing before I woke up on the bed where Sir Hardulph and his mistress lay murdered."

"And you were witness to Dravini's orders to Hardulph to kill the king's physician, Doctor Marimon, were you not, Waldef?"

"Yes, my Lady, as a mere servant, he paid me no mind, but I heard his evil words against the physician."

"When my brother, the Earl of Marshfield arrives, you must tell him everything that you have told us, Waldef. As sheriff, he will use your witness to see that these creatures are hanged."

Suddenly realising what was happening when he saw Waldef pointing him out and speaking quietly to the Lady, Dravini stood up and began shouting. "My name is Peter Declan, and I have come to Aust from Wales with my henchman. We are here simply as visitors to the celebration of Michaelmas in the village. We do not know this lad, and he does not know us."

"Aye, this lad be lyin," Buldoc shouted. "Master Declan and Oi not be who Ee says."

Then, Sir Julian produced the weapon which had been struck from Buldoc's hand. "We are all witness to your attack against the Lady of Aust, Buldoc, but before you hang, you will tell us who sent you to Aust with instructions to kill or maim."

At that, Buldoc went silent, but Dravini moved toward the bars beyond which the Lady stood and suddenly began to speak with her in Latin, a language unknown to Buldoc.

"My Lady of Aust," he said in the language of the church, "I declare that you can do nothing to me, for I claim benefit of clergy." At that point, he went on to quote Holy Scripture, reciting for her words from Psalm 100.

"Shall I continue, my Lady?" he asked. "I am able to complete this Psalm for you and several others, if you wish. You must turn me over to the church, for I am an ordained priest in my home country. I claim benefit of clergy and demand that I can only be tried by canon law, in ecclesiastical courts. Regardless of your charges against me, you must transfer me to the courts of the bishop."

Apollonia refused to respond to him, but she was completely unprepared for this declaration. The Lady was fluent in Latin though she could tell that others in the room did not understand. Certainly, Buldoc had no idea what Dravini had said. Sir Julian knew what had been told her, and he looked at the Lady with real concern in his eyes because he knew the church would require them to turn Dravini over to church law as he demanded.

Without any further comment, Apollonia nodded to Nan, Sir Julian, and Waldef to return with her to Aust Manor. This was a quandary no one had anticipated, and the Lady knew they must take time to consider their options. As her party walked away, Dravini kept shouting at her in Latin, "I will be tried by canon law, woman! Send the priest to me!"

Chapter Fifteen

Ferdinand's Vindication

When Apollonia's brother arrived in Aust, the Lady could see that Ferdinand was ready to hang Dravini and Buldoc and be done with the humiliating attacks against their family. He was not prepared to acknowledge the revelation, which she shared with him as believable, and he insisted that he would never believe Dravini's claim.

"Polly, Dravini is evil, and I refuse to accept the possibility of his being a priest. We both know that if we turn him over to the church courts, he will be given less rigourous punishment. He has no proof that he is anything more than a foreign worker from abroad, and we know certainly that he was part of an attack upon your life as well as an attempt to inspire rebellion in Marshfield. He deserves to die."

"But, brother, hear me out. You know I am convinced that someone among England's aristocracy is funding and directing Dravini's attacks, and that person probably represents one of the families who remain hateful against King Henry as a usurper. Therefore, before we lose our access through Dravini, we must learn the identity of those who are employing his services."

"I will speak with the churl—you stay away, Polly. Keep your knowledge of Latin to yourself. I speak no Latin and will insist upon Dravini's responses to me in plain English in front of Buldoc."

"I shall do whatever you say, brother, but pressure him to reveal the name. I have some sense of where the Kingdom of Sicily is in the Mediterranean world and can not imagine why any Sicilian would have motive to do damage against you or me or our monarch."

* * *

Ferdinand had Dravini and Buldoc brought to him chained hand and foot. As soon as they entered the chamber where Ferdinand waited, Dravini began to speak in Latin to insist that he was being held illegally. "I am subject only to canon law, my lord."

The earl simply looked at him in disgust and said aggressively, "Silence! Respond to me in English when I address you. I do not understand anything more than a few words of the language of the church. I am an Englishman, and you will speak in my native tongue."

"You must understand the uniqueness of my situation in England, my Lord of Marshfield," Dravini began to protest in his most cringing tones.

"You and your partner in crime were witnessed attempting to cause rebellion in my home parish of Marshfield. I have learned that posing as foreign labourers, you invaded a peaceful saint's celebration in my sister's parish and attempted to wound her. For that you will hang."

"My Lord of Marshfield," Dravini whined, "I have explained to your sister that you can not try me within your manorial court because I claim benefit of clergy. In my native Sicily, I was ordained a priest and am eligible to be tried only by canon law in church courts."

Hearing this, Buldoc scoffed aloud. "What you be sayin, Dravini? You ne'er told me such a lie. In all your phony claims of life that I ave knowed you to play, you ne'er played the priest."

"No, no my lord, do not listen to him. I confess that I have not been faithful to the church, but I can repeat for you endless passages from Holy Scripture. Psalm 100 says," and he madly quoted several verses from memory. When he finished, he said. "And I can go on, my Lord Ferdinand."

"As Sheriff of Gloucestershire, Dravini, I acknowledge your statement is, as Buldoc says, a lie. I have witnesses to the attempt made by you and your henchman to attack my sister. In the courts, you will be judged and be hanged, drawn, and quartered for your crimes."

"My Lord of Marshfield, surely there is something I can do to save myself from such a death," Dravini wailed.

"You will tell me for whom you have been working," Ferdinand said coldly. "There can be little doubt that you have been set upon my family by some Englishman. Give me his name."

"My lord, I am a foreigner, one of noble lineage from the Kingdom of Sicily. I have not come to England as a criminal."

"Then, why are you involved in criminal activity? Perhaps you must stew awhile," Ferdinand growled, "and think on what you face at the end of a rope."

"If ee tells you a name, can we live?" Buldoc asked. "The Lady were not injured; nothin appened to urt er."

"The intent of your attack was witnessed by many. I promise nothing until you tell me that which I can prove to be the truth. For whom are you working?"

Ferdinand waited for a bit, and as neither of them said anything, he simply announced, "You both deserve your punishment, and I shall see it done." As their silence continued, he had them taken back into the cell.

* * *

Sir Julian made a special trip back to the ferry landing, but this time rode with the Earl of Marshfield. They dismounted and waited until the ferryman arrived with his most recent travellers from Wales. After everyone else had disembarked, the knight and Ferdinand climbed aboard the ferry to speak with him.

"You played an important role in protecting the life of our Lady of Aust," the knight told him. "This is her brother, the Earl of Marshfield. We have both come to thank you for the timely warning you had brought to us by the young lad of the strangers from Wales."

"Gramercy for your news of suspicious foreigners coming for the feast of Saint Michaelmas from Wales to Aust," Ferdinand said sincerely. "It is thanks to you that her household was prepared and watching for their attack as the festival continued."

The ferryman merely grunted and looked down, but his face blushed with pride as the earl extended his hand to him. The ferryman shook it enthusiastically, then turned away. As Julian and Ferdinand left his vessel, he shouted after them: "Oi be glad to know she be safe."

"It is due to your help," Sir Julian shouted back.

Ferdinand asked the knight, as they were returning to the manor house, if he had any idea how they could force more out of Dravini and Buldoc. "Polly is convinced that these evil-doers are in the pay of some Englishman. I have rejected all their claims of innocence and keep the weapon that was knocked from Buldoc's hand as my chief evidence against him. We have more than enough to hang them, but my sister insists that we must use them to gain information."

"Perhaps it would be best if you would separate them and question them individually," Julian said. "I can not think that either of those men have any sense of loyalty to or protection for the other. If one thought he could make a kind of deal with you, could you not insist that he tell you a name of someone who is responsible for putting them up to this attack?"

"Indeed, you are to the point. I will question them separately and let the other stew a bit while I am in process. What say you? Which should I approach first?"

"Well, my Lord, it appears to me that Buldoc is the weaker of the two and probably Dravini's hired assassin. Dravini was obviously in charge, and Buldoc might not have specific information. Yet, perhaps, he will tell you anything he knows in the hope of achieving a less painful death sentence."

"Excellent, but I pray you will join me in this, Julian. If two well-armed gentlemen are standing over him chained to a chair, it may well enhance his terrour."

"I will do whatever I can, my lord," Sir Julian said sincerely. "If the Lady's suspicion is correct, we must use these creatures to learn more."

"Then, Julian, let us begin. I shall have Buldoc brought to us now.

* * *

The day was cool, but Ferdinand could see that Buldoc was sweating as he was pushed into the room and chained to a chair. The earl purposefully stood over him with the knight at his side, each of them armed with daggers and swords at their waists.

Buldoc began to protest immediately, "Oi done nothing; none was urt; let me go and Oi shall ne'er come ere again."

"You shall not leave here alive, Buldoc," Ferdinand said to him with threat in his voice as he held Buldoc's weapon in his hand. "You were seen threatening my sister with this in your hand, and you will hang for your crime."

"Nothin appened, she not be urt!"

"Silence, churl! If you wish to be heard, tell me who sent you here?"

"Oi only come ere with Dravini. Ee be telling me what we must do."

"You attempted to start a rebellion on my lands in Marshfield and came as assassins to Aust. Who sent you?"

"Oi don know—Dravini gets the orders and tells me."

"From whom does he get his orders? Let me tell you the nature of your death, villain. You will be drawn to the place of execution and there hanged by the neck but cut down while still alive. Then, your privy members will be sliced off, and your bowels cut out to be burnt before your eyes whilst you live."

"Wait, wait, Oi can tell you somethin. Can Oi just be anged if I tells you?" Buldoc was trembling to such an extent that the chains on his wrists were rattling.

"I make no promises, Buldoc," the earl told him.

"You tell us nothing," Julian said aggressively, "you can expect nothing."

"No, no, listen, there were some gentleman called Paine."

"That is nothing, Buldoc, it means nothing."

"But, m'lord, Ee were the knight Dravini said brought messages from is lord."

"I know no one by such a name," Ferdinand said, "it means nothing. Who was his lord?"

"Ee were a knight," Buldoc whined, "Oi only know ee were the messenger from Dravini's lord."

"Who did he serve, Buldoc?"

"Oi know not, m'lord. Oi can only tell ya, the messenger be called Paine."

"Take him away!" Ferdinand shouted at the jailer. "Put him back into the cell."

When Buldoc was gone, Sir Julian suggested to the earl that they have Dravini brought to them immediately. "Let one of them be alone speculating whilst we have the other here in our custody. We have a name, my lord, so why not suggest to Dravini that we know a knight named Paine came to him with instructions and suggest that we can now pursue him to discover whom he serves."

* * *

When Dravini was brought in by himself, he assumed a proud stance, pretending that he should be given special attention. He had thrown off his workman's posture and sat grandly on the chair despite his chains.

"I take it that my Lady of Aust has explained to you that I was a priest in my native land," he said defiantly to Ferdinand, "and can only be tried by canon law. I have nothing to do with Buldoc. He is a known murderer who has controlled and abused me since my coming to the West Country. You can easily check this in Bristol. Buldoc is an assassin for hire, and you can trust nothing he says. It was he who murdered the knight, Hardulph, and his mistress and left the drugged servant lad lying on the bed beside the bodies."

"Ferdinand's eyes widened as he took note of that accusation, but his next question completely changed the subject, "Then, you are saying that the knight, Paine, was coming to give him instructions?"

"Oh, he told you about the baron, did he? I had nothing to do with their scheming. Do what you must with Buldoc, but I insist that you release me to return to my home country."

Ferdinand looked at Sir Julian, and they both realised immediately that Dravini had unwittingly revealed the rank of the man who served as messenger.

"No, you will remain here while we continue to search for the truth. Tell me why have you come to England, Dravini, and from whom do you take orders?"

"I serve the church, my lord earl, and if you have charges against me, I demand to be given over to the local bishop. I can only be tried by church law."

"Take him back to his cell," Ferdinand ordered the jailer, "but keep an eye on the prisoners. Both accuse the other of the evil they have done."

Dravini was especially aware of the earl's last sentence. "What has Buldoc accused me of?" he demanded.

"I suggest that you ask him," Ferdinand shot back.

* * *

The earl and Sir Julian returned to the manor where Apollonia waited anxiously for them. From the hall, Ferdinand signalled to his sister that they must retire to her solar where they could speak privately.

"Sir Julian and I have much to tell you, Polly."

When they were seated, Ferdinand and Julian shared with her the multiple accusations between Dravini and Buldoc. "There is no loyalty between these two thieves, Polly. Each accuses the other of overseeing the crimes they have committed together, but you must know first that Dravini accuses Buldoc of being the murderer of the knight, Hardulph, and his mistress, who left the boy's drugged body lying at the scene."

"Waldef is innocent. I knew it must be so," Apollonia smiled at her brother, clasping her hands together. "Gramercy, brother, my heartfelt thanks for clarifying this in the eyes of the law. Ferdinand, will you send this information to your friend in London whose son is the sheriff who released Waldef to my protection? I have believed the lad's pleas, but Waldef will be so relieved to know that he is cleared of all charges."

"Now we must work together on the other revelation that Julian and I received from Dravini, Polly. It was inadvertent, we think, but Dravini revealed a name of the contact with whomever he has served. You have consistently maintained that a Sicilian would not likely set upon us because of our support of King Henry, but some English nobleman may well be paying for Dravini's wickedness. Now, we must discover who is the Baron Paine, and whom he does serve."

At that, Ferdinand abruptly announced his departure. "I shall return to Marshfield, Polly, but I beg you, Julian, remain in Aust whilst I am away. I will not be long, Julian, but if you can stay in protection of my sister's household, I will be eternally grateful. When I return, I hope to bring news."

* * *

Sir Julian was true to his word and remained in Aust after the Earl of Marshfield departed. He had no precise idea of how he was protecting her or from whom, with Dravini and Buldoc in the gaol, but he respected the earl's request of him and saw to it that he accompanied her with Nan wherever she went. In truth, he was pleased by this assignment because they rode together on good days and found time to read together on days of unpleasant weather. Julian loved listening to the Lady as she read aloud to him from various works in her collection. He especially enjoyed listening as she read from *Piers Plowman's Protest*. They both found William Langland's writing enjoyable, as he addressed many concerns of their day. It stimulated endless conversations between them.

It was during these days while Sir Julian was visiting the manor when the Lady received a long letter from her friend Robert Kenwood. She was glad to hear from him but sincerely concerned when he described the reasons for his sudden departure from Aust to return to Worcester.

To my dear friend, the Lady Apollonia of Aust,

I truly apologise for my abrupt departure from our visit together. It was my pleasure to be with you, come to know your august brother, the Earl Ferdinand, and pursue many of our favourite topics of conversation. However, it was critical that I return home to be here with my son, Geoffrey, and his wife, Evelyn. They have three sons and a late-in-life daughter, my precious granddaughter, Carrie. Geoffrey's family have been forced to deal with a most disturbing event. You know that I am a man of faith and one who respects our church and its teachings. Tragically, a member of the clergy here in Worcester has committed a heinous sin against our family that must be dealt with.

The past year, Geoffrey and Evelyn welcomed into their home a friar to serve as teacher and chaplain to their family. His name is Friar Bathan who claimed to have come to them from Scotland, having been trained in the north by the Franciscans off the coast on Shetland. He appeared to be a truly devout servant of the Lord, constant in his prayer life and an excellent preacher but has revealed himself to be one who has sinned mightily against an innocent young girl.

When my son wrote to me, he and Evelyn had just discovered that Carrie had been impregnated. The name of the man responsible for this evil abuse was Friar Bathan. He had offered himself to their household as a devoted Franciscan, dedicated, he said, to a life of service, when in truth my son discovered him to be a wanton perpetrator of abuse.

We have learned that Friar Bathan not only took advantage of Carrie's innocence, he made her believe that it was God's will that she must do whatever he asked of her. He continually declared to my son that during the time he frequently spent away from their home he was ministering to the poor and destitute of the town. In truth, he was spending his spare time in the local tavern, cavorting with the prostitutes of the town, and bringing their diseases into my son's home. He used his position as friar to gain money by selling pardons through hearing confessions and offering easy penance for a price. Eventually, it could be seen that Bathan began to wear expensive robes ordered from a local tailor, lined with fur.

When confronted with his sin against Carrie, Bathan's only

words were that he could not change her condition but would see to it that she was married to a respectable Christian who would care for her. It was the best he could do, he said, because he is dedicated to a life of celibacy.

My son and I complained to our local priest against the friar, but he told us quite frankly that he could do nothing to control him, as a Franciscan, but would take our complaint to the bishop.

I confess to you, my Lady, that I believe I would willingly beat this scurvy creature senseless, despite the Commandments of our Lord, but my first concern must be for Carrie and the safe delivery of her child, my great grandchild. She is frightened, overwhelmed by the changes in her body, and unable to understand that she will deliver an infant from the growing bulge in her stomach. Evelyn continues to speak with her daily of the joys of parenthood, but Carrie has been told by her friends of the pain and suffering of childbirth. She spends most of her days in tears, and my daughter-in-law has told me that the girl has been infected with a cruel disease of her private parts. Will you keep us in your prayers, my Lady? Our family is struggling and desperately needs to feel the healing presence of the Holy Spirit with us.

Your respectful and admiring friend, Robert

* * *

Apollonia was angry, disturbed, and truly worried for Robert's granddaughter yet fully aware of the real human struggle they were facing. She also knew it was not the first time she had heard of such evil committed by men of the church. Worse yet, the Lady could not help but remember her first terrifying encounter with sexual intercourse when she was newly married in her early teen years. She knew she must respond to her friend's letter with whatever encouragement she could offer. The Lady called Friar Francis to her to read Robert's letter with him and beg his counsel.

She told Francis that she could never express any sense of judgement against Robert or his granddaughter. "I want to offer my sincerest sympathies with Robert, but what sort of consolation can we offer. I can not condemn young Carrie, for I can personally understand her overwhelming innocence. At thirteen, I was ignorant of any understanding of sexual interaction between men and women. But, what can I say of this wicked friar? In truth, I can understand Robert's desire to brutalise him, though that will do nothing to help his granddaughter."

Francis' eyes closed, his head fell, and he remained silent for several minutes. Finally, he said to her, "My family dedicated my life to the Franciscans when I was born and named me for the humble founder of our order. I have tried to live according to his instructions, to embrace personal poverty, and maintain a life of service, my Lady, to you and to the poor of our community as well. Saint Francis named us Frati Minori, lesser brothers, and before he died, he was known to have received the physical wounds of Christ, the stigmata. Saint Francis is the model for my life, but I can think of nothing positive to say about this Friar Bathan. He has broken every vow that we take. His abuse of Master Robert's granddaughter goes beyond evil. He has made fraudulent any claims he may have to serving God. I pray you will tell Master Robert that this Bathan is not a brother, pastor, or teacher. He is fraudulent, disobedient, and a humiliation to everything that we friars represent. Please tell him that I shall see that this Bathan's behaviour is reported in detail to the head of our order."

"Gramercy, Francis. You know I am grateful for your service and will always be thankful for your preaching and counsel, but what can I suggest to Robert when dealing with the struggle he and his family face?"

"I pray you will tell Master Robert that as a friar, I can only beg his pardon for this evil done against his family by one whose life is a lie. Assure him that I shall honour his granddaughter in my daily prayers and ask God to protect her and deliver her safely of a precious new life. Remind him that God loves her innocence, and His Grace blesses her always."

"I shall write to him straightaway, Francis, and quote your words." Apollonia sat quietly and simply shook her head. "I have known many good people among the friars and the Poor Clares, but those who abuse their role are capable of evil beyond description."

Chapter Sixteen

Clash of Allegiances

It was less than two weeks before Ferdinand returned to Aust, and after a brief rest, he announced to his sister that he had much to share with her. "This adventure of yours has revealed itself to be more complicated than I thought, Polly," he said shaking his head.

They were seated with Sir Julian in the Lady's solar, and Apollonia could tell that her brother was more than troubled by what he had learned. "I never anticipated that this attack upon us would be initiated, and I certainly had no idea of the extent of the bitterness and anger I would encounter. It appears that those who consider us their enemies reach all the way to the north of England."

Apollonia's tone remained calm, but Julian could hear the tension in her voice. "What have we done to create such powerful enemies, brother, and how can we make peace with them?"

"I have heard that we have fallen afoul of one of the most important border lords in England, Henry Percy, the Earl of Northumberland."

"Holy Mother," the Lady started. "How can this be so?"

Julian sat forward in his chair in an attitude of disbelief. "My Lord Ferdinand, surely, the Lady has done nothing to encourage any sort of argument with Northumberland or anyone else."

"It is not mine nor our family's aggression, Julian. My sister and I are known in the kingdom to be loyal supporters of King Henry, and that is our sin."

"I was aware of the influence of Henry Percy within the court of King Richard," Julian told them, "but I also had heard that he and his son played an important role in the support of Bolingbroke to depose Richard and enable Bolingbroke to ascend the throne as King Henry. What happened to bring about the dramatic change in the Percys' loyalties?"

"King Henry rewarded them well, but they did not anticipate the strength that the Scots would hurl against them in the north as a reaction to Henry's insecure rule. Further, they did not benefit financially nearly as much as they had anticipated, and when they sought reimbursement from King Henry, it did not come due to the impoverishment of the royal treasury. It appears that they soon began to regret helping him. Henry Percy insisted that Bolingbroke had made a vow to him, declaring that he only returned to England to regain his lost inheritances, not to take the throne."

"Do we have any idea of what specifically brought on the Percys' actual rebellion against King Henry after he had taken the throne, Ferdinand?" Apollonia pressed her brother.

"In part, it had to do with their defence of the border against the Scots' raids, which King Henry expects of them. After the Percy family's significant victory over the Scots at Humbleton Hill four years ago, King Henry was impressed with their victory and praised them for it, but then he expected the Percys to hand over the Earl of Douglas whom they had taken prisoner. Northumberland handed over his hostages to the king, but his son, Hotspur, insisted upon keeping the Earl of Douglas for ransom. King Henry was angered by this and threatened the Percy family that there would be steps taken against them if the most important prisoner was not surrendered to him."

"As you both know, the bloody battle at Shrewsbury between royal forces and the Percys was a decisive victory for the king. However, the earl's favourite son, Hotspur, was killed at Shrewsbury, and Henry Percy is said not to have recovered from that loss. After the battle, he was pursued by Henry's army and forced into submission. Northumberland was required to swear allegiance to the king and stripped of a large portion of his lands. For some time, he lived quietly on his remaining lands, but later he joined Glendower and Mortimer and again rebelled. Since then, he is on the run, has a price on his head, and is wanted for treason. God knows how this conflict will finally end, but I fear that you and I have been drawn into the midst of it, Polly."

Apollonia sat quietly, attempting to digest all that her brother had told them. Sir Julian was unable to stay silent, however, and announced that the Lady must forgive him, but he could no longer remain in Aust for her protection.

"Do you not see, my Lady, if the now outlawed Percy is behind these disturbing attacks against you and your people, they may well continue, and I can no longer offer my protection. By my word, I am committed to return to Bristol."

"Sir Julian is correct, Polly. You will have to be prepared to deal with continuing episodes of evil disturbances committed against you here. Therefore, I insist that you and Nan will come home with me to Marshfield and remain under my protection until we know it is safe for you to return to Aust."

The Lady remained deep in thought until finally she announced to both men that she was grateful to be able to better understand what she was facing, but she would stay in her home. "We have two agents of Percy's evil intent against me in a cell here, Ferdinand. In my mind, Buldoc is a hired assassin and an ignorant man. Dravini has the crafty intelligence to plan their schemes, but he does his evil for hire. Both are under lock and key and will hang. As an old woman with malicious intent against no one, I see no need to abandon my household. Instead, let us put continued pressure on both prisoners. Repeat to them that they are soon to be tried for their attempt against my life and can only be given some positive consideration if they confess who paid for their service. If Percy is positively identified as being behind this, I believe we can make King Henry's case against the Earl of Northumberland complete."

"My Lady, do think of your safety," Julian insisted. "If you remain here alone, strange attacks may well continue in varying forms of danger against you personally."

"Yes, Polly, listen to Sir Julian. Come with me to Marshfield."

"I am grateful for your loving concern, brother, and I would be glad to spend more time with you, but I will not abandon Aust, the village, nor the folk of my manor. I shall stay here and see what the future brings. As a woman alone, perhaps I can challenge the true nature of the chivalry of the Percys. Let us see if they possess the devotion to protect the weak that my young servant Waldef declares."

"Forgive me, sister," Ferdinand said as he shook his head, "but you seem to be making a bloody life and death quarrel of our time into some sort of test of chivalry. Do not play risky games against forces you obviously do not understand. I can not remain in Aust; come home with me."

"Dear brother, and you Julian, there is no need for you to remain to protect me. I pray you will both see that I am not fearful. Those directly responsible for the attack against me are in the gaol, and all the men of my household have declared their devotion to me. I remain a faithful subject of King Henry and devoted in my service to the church as a vowess. However, I too have lost a dear son and can share with the earl the bodily pain of such a loss. If Northumberland has a complaint against me, Ferdinand, I submit to his chivalry."

"You are a stubborn woman, Polly," her brother said in a state of obvious frustration with her, "but I must return to protect Marshfield."

* * *

Garmon and Waldef looked forward late each afternoon to their meeting behind the barn for practice with the bow. Since turning sixteen recently, the young page had grown. He was taller, well-muscled from his exercise, and was displaying significant improvement with the bow. Though Garmon made little comment, he felt some pride in Waldef's increasing skill. Yet, on this afternoon, Waldef displayed a lack of focus, and Garmon called him out.

"You must not let your attention drift about, lad. Keep your mind on what you are doing. The weapon that you hold is lethal, and you want to be in control of it."

"Truly sorry, Master Garmon. I desperately seek to note all that you are telling me, and I am grateful for every minute of our time spent together. I have been unable to cease worrying about the safety of the manor and the protection of the Lady since the recent attacks against her. I have come to know her as more than a woman of faith. She is loving, trusting, and grants grace to all."

"Well, you know, lad, the villains are in the gaol, and the Lady receives constant protection from those of us who serve her. What more do you think we could do?"

"What would you think of creating a kind of watch through the night?" Waldef asked him. "Indeed, Aust household remains on the alert daily, especially since Sir Julian was required to leave and return to Bristol, but once the household sleeps, do you not think it wise to post a guard during the night?"

"I am not certain of precisely what we are to watch for, Waldef, but perhaps during the nights ahead, you and I might take turns doing a careful walk about the manor after everyone has retired. I shall take the first one this evening."

"I will be grateful for us to work together, Master Garmon, watching against any strangers who might come to Aust to threaten our Lady Apollonia again. If, as time passes, no suspicious stranger is seen, we shall cease, but for a while, let us post a nighttime guard."

* * *

The days began to shorten into the autumn, and Apollonia noticed that her page seemed keenly alert to every moment of free time granted to him. She assumed that Waldef was grateful to have additional hours to spend with Garmon in practice behind the barn, and she could see their friendship growing significantly as the time they spent together increased.

The Lady was grateful for the companionship they shared. She could tell that it was a very positive experience for Waldef, but she knew that Garmon, the elder of the two, was also benefiting. He seemed to be relaxing in his position in her household and was less rigid and distant when working with other staff. As she privately knew him to be a young man who had lost one nearly his wife, she could see that the admiration and respect that Waldef expressed to him was in many ways healing for Garmon.

What she did not fully realise was that the admiration and respect Waldef felt for her had grown to be as sincere as any family sense of devotion could be. The Lady had no idea what responsibilities her young servant and his friend had taken on her behalf. Each night, after she and her household had gone to their beds, Waldef or Garmon would remain awake and walk the grounds of Aust Manor on watch.

Weeks went by and all remained quiet through their evenings on guard; nothing seemed amiss. The evenings grew cooler, and the winds from the Severn made their time outdoors significantly more uncomfortable. Garmon and Waldef both began to wonder if this nighttime watch was necessary. Garmon finally told Waldef, "I am not seeing any value in this, lad, and we are both losing sleep which badly affects our daytime duties."

"Will you check out one thing with me," Waldef said. "I can not be certain, Master Garmon, but there may have been some unknown person prowling about the manor last night. The only evidence I found of alien presence was a pile of fresh horse shit. It may amount to nothing other than a late-night rider on his way to the ferry, but would you be willing to stand watch with me, one more night?"

"Show me where you discovered the horse's leavings, and we will begin there this night, but let us both carry some sort of weapon just in case you have really encountered a person of threat."

* * *

That evening, Apollonia's servant guard walked silently about her manor, watching in the light of the moon for any movement. They carefully remained within the darkness of the trees and walked quietly from Alwan's cottage back to the manor gate. When they approached the place where Waldef had found piles of fresh horse droppings the night before, they remained quietly watching behind the trees.

The moon was nearly full and the evening bright, making it easy to move about this very familiar ground. Time passed slowly, and finally Garmon signalled to Waldef that, as nothing was happening, he was ready to return to his bed. Yet, as he began to turn towards the house, Waldef suddenly put up his hand and pointed towards a light burning in the woods, some distance toward the river. Garmon signalled to Waldef to wait for him while he continued into the rear of the manor house where he woke four other young men of the lady's household. Returning in force to where Waldef stood, they walked into the woods till they came to the place where a small fire was burning, and two well-dressed men were leaning towards it to warm themselves.

Garmon assumed command of the men of the Lady's household and signalled one of them to go and take charge of the fine horses of these men, obviously of the knightly class. Then, with bows drawn, Waldef, Garmon, and their friends walked into the firelight, and in a voice expressing command, Garmon shouted that the men were trespassing and must surrender to him.

The two men stood up and looked about rapidly, only to see that their horses had been taken and they were surrounded. The less distinguished of the gentlemen seemed to smirk at them.

"Put your weapons down, lads, you have no idea with whom you are speaking."

"We know that you are strangers here and are trespassing on the lands of the Lady of Aust Manor," Garmon shouted at them.

"Take us to whomever is in charge here. I demand to have our horses returned and to be respected as members of England's nobility."

Garmon and Waldef had lowered their bows and went to disarm the gentlemen whom they were obviously taking in custody while the other men of the household remained on guard. They led the way back to the manor house as the sun was rising and put their captives into the locked space in the barn until the Lady Apollonia could be told what had happened during the night.

The Lady and Nan were up with the rising sun and had already gone to the chapel for morning prayers. Waldef joined them in the chapel but waited to tell the Lady of their adventures during the night until Friar Francis had completed his service.

When they could speak with her, Garmon and Waldef began by telling the Lady of their efforts to protect her manor through the night. "Waldef and I have thought it our duty to patrol the manor grounds during recent nights, my Lady, and last night we discovered two gentlemen sleeping rough near a campfire on your lands. As we did not recognise them nor were we aware of any purpose for their being here, we collected the men of your household, captured them and locked them into custody in the barn. The surprising thing is that these are gentlemen, my Lady, obvious from their speech and their clothes, but they would offer us no explanation for their behaviour."

Apollonia was concerned by their unexpected nighttime encounter, but she could not be unhappy with her young men's worry for unknown strangers appearing on her lands. "Have you learned their names?"

"One of them, the younger knight, will not speak with us at all. He simply insists that we must release him and his lord."

"And who is his lord?"

"That gentleman refuses to speak with anyone but the head of our household."

"Have Gareth with you and bring him to me. I shall want you all to remain whilst I question him."

* * *

Apollonia was sitting by the great fireplace in the hall with Giles at her side when her young men escorted their captives into her presence. The Lady noticed immediately that the elder of the two men was probably older than she and needed some assistance because of his limited eyesight. As soon as he was standing before her, Giles announced that they had been taken while on the lands of the Lady Apollonia of Aust, sister to Ferdinand, Earl of Marshfield.

"My Lady of Aust is a vowess who speaks only when necessary. She asks you to tell her why you were sleeping rough on her lands without informing her of your presence?"

The elder man said nothing at first, but his companion announced, "We are English gentlemen unaccustomed to being thwarted while peaceably travelling within our country."

"My Lady recently has suffered a murderous attack against her, as well as attacks against the village and her manor. Her household has been required to remain on guard."

"My lord and I have come to take the ferry. There is no threat in that. Therefore, you will release us, return our horses and weapons to us, and we shall be on our way."

"My Lady of Aust asks you once again to state your names and position. During these dangerous days of rebellion frequently coming out from Wales, she asks you to understand her purpose in defence against serious threats already made upon her."

At this point, the elder gentleman spoke directly to Apollonia. "My Lady, I am an English gentleman but one who desires to remain anonymous whilst travelling. Release us and we shall be gone."

The Lady made a gesture to the men of her household. She told them the younger man was to be taken back to the locked space in the barn. The elder was to remain with her. Then, the Lady dismissed everyone else. Apollonia could see that no one of her household, especially Nan, was ready to leave her unguarded, but she insisted. Without going far from the hall, everyone left her but stayed guard outside each door leading to the hall.

When the others had gone, and Apollonia was by herself with the elder gentleman, she spoke directly to him. "Pray be seated here by the fire with me, English gentleman. As you can see, I am now alone and relying upon your personal code of chivalry as my protection. I suspect that you know who I am, and you are aware of my family's loyalty to King Henry. I require to know your name and your station in life."

The elder gentleman was obviously relieved to be able to sit down. He turned closer to the fireplace holding his hands out for warmth and smiled gently to her, pleased to see the pleasant smile that she returned to him. "This is a gracious gesture, my Lady. I am an old man and one suffering from the length of my years."

"Why are you sleeping rough, sir?" she asked him? "It would seem to be somewhat beyond what is expected of a man of your years, as well as your station."

"I do not wish to describe my situation nor its present purpose, but to you alone, my Lady of Aust, I will reveal my name. I ask you to honour my request to keep that revelation just between the two of us. I am Henry Percy."

Apollonia's eyes opened wider with recognition. She knew immediately that this was not only a nobleman, he is the Earl of Northumberland, a fugitive from King Henry. Head of a powerful noble family, Percy was thought by many to be ruler of the north of the kingdom. Even more, she knew why he would not state his present purpose to her. He was being searched for by all the forces of King Henry's law because he and his son had led rebellions against the king and, when defeated, had been forced to declare his allegiance to the crown. Many of his castles and possessions had been seized by the king, but of all that he had suffered from his rebellions, Apollonia knew that the death of his favourite son, Hotspur, at the Battle of Shrewsbury had left him as she saw: aged, scarred by deep wrinkles, and personally wounded for life.

The Earl of Northumberland that she faced was a tall, stately gentleman, but one who had grown thin and bent. Worse yet, Apollonia could see that his eyes seemed to express a dull hopelessness and lack of interest in life.

After sitting in silence for several moments, the Lady looked directly into his face and said quietly, "I can not agree with your actions, my lord, but I, too, have suffered the loss of a precious son, and I know the painful wound of your loss."

At this, she could see Percy's head drop and his eyes close. For several minutes, nothing more was said between them until he finally looked up, straightened his shoulders, and said, "I have reached a point where I have no reason to live, my Lady. Worse yet, I can feel no reason to do any noble service with my life. I am empty, purposeless, and without goals, though many still rely upon me. I will not support the rule of Bolingbroke as King Henry."

Apollonia nodded her understanding but added, "As you find yourself granted life, my lord, whether you wish it or not, can you not see that God may well have purpose for you? I have found that I still have family to love who return their love to me. I am blessed by an affinity of people who express their devotion to me through their service and for whom I am responsible in this life. Surely, Lord Percy, you are needed to provide for your family, to protect your loyal people of Northumberland, and serve our church as well?"

The Lady asked her last statement in the form of a question, suggesting that the nobleman in her presence should think again about his lack of interest in life leading him to rebellion. He continued in silence and made no response to her.

When he finally did, he said, "I respect your losses in life, my Lady, and I acknowledge that you comprehend my pain, but I am a wanted criminal and on the run from the king's law. I have no reason to go on living. Without purpose, without a sense of desire, what can be the point?"

Apollonia bent towards him, and though she did not touch him, she extended a hand toward him. "My point is your need to be faithful to all those who depend upon you, all those whom Christ commands that we extend love to, to God and to our neighbours as ourselves."

Percy would not answer this declaration of her faith, instead he said to her, "I promise you that I shall see that no harm will come to your manor." Then, he simply changed the subject of their conversation and asked if he and his faithful friend Paine still locked in her barn, might be allowed to have a meal.

The Lady nodded to him and then called for Giles and Nan. They re-entered the hall quickly, and she asked Giles to bring the gentleman's companion from the barn. Next, she sent Nan into the kitchen to have a meal prepared for them. She offered no explanations to either of her people and did not indicate that she meant to partake of the meal in their company.

Eventually food was brought, hot from the kitchen, and the Lady could see that their hunger drove them to eat rapidly, not from mere enjoyment of the excellent preparations by Guise, the Lady's cook, but from sheer hunger.

When both men had finished eating, Apollonia asked Gareth to bring their horses to the front entrance of the manor. She had Garmon return their weapons to them, then bid them farewell.

Percy could be seen to have been emotionally moved by the time he had spent in the Lady's company. Paine merely offered his thanks. Percy walked to her chair and said humbly, "Gramercy, my Lady of Aust, I shall not forget the meaningful pleasure of your company."

"Your courtesy and chivalry speak to your honour, English gentleman. Though I can not agree with your expressed disloyalties, as a vowess of the church, I shall pray for you."

Everyone in the Lady's household could see that she did not offer her hand to them or rise to wish the men Godspeed. The manner of her behaviour toward the two gentlemen was so unlike her. Nan and Giles looked towards each other and could not believe this abrupt dismissal in the hall was her only gesture of farewell.

When both of the men were gone, Apollonia called Garmon and Waldef to her and expressed her sincere appreciation to each of them for their willingness to take upon themselves guarding the manor through the night.

"You have proven to be excellent servants to me, and I will always remember the extent of your concern and willingness to offer protection on my behalf. However, I am now convinced that there is no further threat to the manor, so I beg you both to remain in your beds through the nights ahead.

Chapter Seventeen

Landow's Meddling, Lady's Grief

L ater that week, as Nan sat with the Lady in her solar working on her embroidery, the maid's curiosity concerning the recent visitors was nearly bursting. Apollonia had been silent since the two gentlemen departed from the manor and had seemed distant, as if she was deep in her personal thoughts. At last, Nan could bear it no longer; she turned to the Lady and said, "How strange that both of those gentlemen did not wish to introduce themselves that you might acknowledge their rank as well as their persons, my Lady."

"Oh, the elder of them did so to me, Nan, but asked to remain anonymous as travellers on their journey into Wales."

"One would think as travellers, they would have sought accommodations at the inn rather than be found sleeping rough on your lands."

"It turns out that they had reason, dearheart."

"If the elder gentleman shared his name with you, my Lady, surely he also revealed something of his purpose?"

"There was no reason, Nan," the Lady told her. "I knew what he was about." At that, Apollonia returned to the manuscript she was reading and said nothing more. The maid could see that she may as well put her curiosity aside, for the Lady's silence pronounced all that would be discussed.

* * *

Days continued to grow colder with less length of daylight. A surprising visitor was announced to the Lady as she sat near the fireplace in the great hall. Giles came to her and asked if she would consent to receive him.

"It is that disreputable churchman whom we once knew as a pardoner, Brandon Landow, my Lady. He assures me that he is now considerably advanced in the church and is part of the household of the Archbishop of Canterbury, Arundel. He says he requires a place to stay while he prepares to complete a mission for his lord. Will you receive him?"

Apollonia looked at Nan who immediately objected. "My Lady, from long experience you have known the character of Brandon Landow and all that he truly represents. If he is travelling in the West Country, he can stay at the inn."

"I can not be true to my calling as a vowess if I refuse hospitality to one seeking it from me, dearheart. Of course, Giles, I shall receive Brandon but here in the hall, not in my solar. You will inform the staff of whom he is and warn them of our past experiences of his presence. I must offer hospitality for the night if he asks for it."

When Giles returned, Landow entered the hall behind him, walking grandiosely with a great jewelled stick and dressed far more expensively than the Lady had ever seen him. It was almost as if the once pardoner was not only wealthier, he wished to be seen as moving up in class.

"My Lady of Aust," he greeted her with a grand bow.

The Lady however responded to his pretentious appearance by addressing him with his boyhood name. "You have no doubt come for a purpose, Brandon. For what have you come to ask me?"

"Always straight to business, my Lady," Landow said with his usual counterfeit smile, "but on this occasion, I have come to Aust to renew our friendship. I am pleased to tell folk that I have known you since the days of serving your household in my youth."

"And from those earliest days, my household has known you to be untrustworthy, deceitful, and deceptive. Indeed, I do know you, Brandon. What is it that you wish from me?"

"Ah, to business then, my Lady. It has come to my attention that you have in your local gaol a foreign nobleman of some significance who has been wrongly accused. He is not only a man of high birth from the Kingdom of Sicily, he is also an ordained priest, subject only to canon law and must be returned to his home country. I have come to Aust to take him back to London with me."

Apollonia listened carefully and could see immediately that, somehow, Count Dravini had gotten a message to Landow in the archbishop's household. She knew that Brandon often asserted himself as her friend and must have committed himself to come to Aust for the archbishop to sort out what he had been told was a rather messy, possibly international problem.

"You know that an attempt was made on my life in public view here in Aust by Dravini's henchman. He was returned to Bristol where he was hanged as a known assassin."

"That is the essence of the case, my Lady," Landow lied. "Count Dravini had no idea of the evil character Buldoc was. He has told me that he merely took him on as a sturdy manservant whilst he was here in the West Country."

"Why then did Dravini assume a false identity when he came to the West Country with Buldoc?" Apollonia said as she lifted her eyebrows. "I am told that he grew a beard whilst he was here and insisted that his name was Peter Declan, a commoner who was wandering about the West Country searching for work."

Landow simply shrugged his shoulders. "I know nothing of such things, my Lady," he said nervously.

"Do you know his manservant, Buldoc, killed Dravini's henchman, Sir Hardulph of Leicester, and his mistress whose murders remain unsolved?" The Lady continued, "I have a source within my household who once served Sir Hardulph and who knew that Dravini used Hardulph's questionable skills to pursue his own evil purposes."

"Who might this source be, my Lady? Can you be certain that this person is trustworthy?"

"Brandon," the Lady said quietly but looking directly into his eyes, "you know my sources are indeed reliable in every sense."

"Well, dear Lady, you must first acknowledge this order from the Archbishop of Canterbury. I shall take the count back with me to Lambeth where he will be examined according to canon law."

Apollonia took the document from Landow's hand and examined it carefully. Finally, she put it into Giles's hand and instructed him to do as Landow wished, first thing on the morrow. "You will be responsible for this release, Brandon, and you must send me word of your arrival at Lambeth as well as how Dravini is judged. In my mind, there is no doubt that he was part of an attempt to harm me and probably do ill to my brother of Marshfield, as well as to the manor of Aust."

"Ah, gracious Lady, I knew our friendship would prevail."

"It is not our friendship at work here, Brandon. It is the document you brought ordering the release of Dravini into your hands that I must respond to. However, I pray that you will do everything possible to protect yourself when alone in his company. Dravini is an evil man who will grant you no value as a human, much less as a churchman."

"Perhaps we are not speaking of the same gracious gentleman, my Lady?" Landow smiled snidely.

* * *

The days were growing colder, and Apollonia encouraged her household to settle in for winter. Somewhat surprisingly, the Lady felt that most everyone in her household was ready for the change of seasons. It had been a good year; frightening things had been solved, and important things had been accomplished. Although the days could be seen to be growing significantly shorter, Giles was especially pleased with what he knew to have been another financially successful year for the Lady.

Apollonia and Nan were settled into her solar, close to the fire and reminiscing. Suddenly, Giles came to her with a very worried expression. "This message has just come from Marshfield, my Lady."

The Lady put her lenses to her eyes and opened the seal. When she read its contents, she dropped the folded sheet into her lap and collapsed into tears.

Nan rushed to take the Lady into her arms as Apollonia sobbed. Finally, she was able to say, "It is Ferdinand, Nan. My brother is dead."

"What brought this on, my Lady? Has he been ill?" Nan asked as her eyes filled with tears. The maid had never been close to Apollonia's brother, but her heart rushed out to the Lady whom she knew was devastated at the loss of her only brother.

"Ferdinand would never admit to his increasing years and the rheumatic pains he regularly suffered, but he fell when dismounting from his horse and struck his head against a rock. They say his death was instantaneous. Oh Nan, dearheart, remain close to me. Let me take your hand," she said as she continued to sob.

* * *

By that evening, Apollonia had calmed enough to send the tragic news to each of her surviving sons and tell them that she was preparing to go to Marshfield. She especially sought Sir Hugh, her eldest son, to join her there for he was next in line to inherit the earldom from his deceased Uncle Ferdinand.

When Hugh's response finally reached his mother, he offered his sincerest sympathy but told her that having just gone to London, he would be unable to get to Marshfield for a matter of days. By this news, Apollonia was further distressed to realise that she would have to go alone at first to arrange her brother's funeral and burial. Her son, Thomas, was head priest in his parish and sent word that he would join her as soon as he could. Chad, second eldest of her sons, was in Cornwall and would take days to reach Marchfield, much less be able to arrive in time for his uncle's funeral.

She called Nan, Giles, Friar Francis, Brother William, and Gareth to her. Each of them had displayed their loving service for her, and she said quietly that she especially needed their help. By this time everyone in her household knew that the Lady's brother had died suddenly. Apollonia told them that she was struggling to deal with a difficult personal loss.

Nan assured her mistress immediately that they would travel with her to Marshfield and help in every way possible. Giles and Gareth individually expressed their sympathies to their mistress while Friar Francis and Brother William remained in prayer at her side. Apollonia seemed to sink into a state of numbness as she tried to deal with the full extent of her loss. Friar Francis stayed by the Lady's side constantly praying with the Lady and for her whenever she turned to him. Brother William left her presence to move about Aust Manor and see that the Lady's loss was understood by her affinity and whatever could be done to keep things in good running order must continue.

The Lady's brother Ferdinand had been a widower for several years and during those years had come more frequently to Aust to spend time with his sister or take her home with him to Marshfield. In many ways, these later years of Apollonia's life had been spent in Ferdinand's company. Their friendship and respect for each other as brother and sister had not only grown closer but more loving. He was eight years older than she, already in her elderly years, but Apollonia had always regarded her brother as indestructible.

Everyone could see her pain and loss but Nan, especially, was keenly aware that Apollonia withdrew for longer hours alone in her private chamber or to the household chapel with Friar Francis. Once Giles and Gareth had prepared for their journey to Marshfield, however, Giles came to speak with her.

He found her kneeling at her prie-dieu with her chaplain at her side and waited quietly until she had risen and walked to her seat near the fire. Then he said quietly, "When you feel prepared to make the journey, my Lady, all is ready."

Apollonia did not look into his face, but he could see her painful demeanour and tear-reddened eyes. Eventually, she said, "Francis will accompany Waldef and me. Brother William will remain here in charge of the manor until we return. Let us leave first thing in the morning, Giles. There will be much to do, and I must have you and Gareth with me in Marshfield to work with Ferdinand's steward, Godric Smithson."

"Yes, my Lady, we shall be ready at first light.

* * *

That evening, Apollonia seemed to have little to say to Nan when the maid came to her chamber to prepare her for bed. Nan had not seen the Lady in such an emotional state since learning of the death of her son, Alban, years before. At that time, however, the Lady was married to a loving partner, merchant Richard Windemere, who not only treasured her as his wife, but also willingly tried to share her suffering.

The maid could understand the cause of Apollonia's grief, yet she now seemed unable to find a way to comfort her. She remembered that when the first news had come, Apollonia had begged to hold her hand, but since then, the Lady had begun to distance herself from everyone—even her devoted Nan.

After saying good night, Nan returned to her own chamber, privileged as she was to have a small personal bedchamber. The maid felt especially lonely for the first time in her life. She had given herself to Apollonia's service since their earliest days together. The maid knew privately that she had refused Gareth's offer of marriage to her because of her devotion to the Lady. Now, suddenly Nan felt abandoned. She knelt by her bedside, begging for some direction to her thoughts to bring comfort to the Lady during the difficult days ahead.

It proved to be an arduous night for Apollonia and her maid. Nan could find no way to ease their painful estrangement. The Lady seemed unable to reach out to her.

* * *

Nan was up before dawn and prepared the necessary items for the Lady to have on their journey. Apollonia, too, was up before sunrise and descended to the kitchen to break her fast. Though the Lady greeted everyone in her household kindly, she was withdrawn and unusually quiet. She ate very little and seemed ready to be on the road immediately.

Nan insisted that her mistress wear a warm, woollen cloak with hood against the chill of the day, and although Apollonia followed her maid's instructions before departing, the Lady said nothing. As their party rode out from Aust, Francis was constant in his prayers, and as no one else wished to speak, their journey was spent largely in silence.

* * *

Late in the day, Godric Smithson was watching for the Lady when her party rode into Ferdinand's manor. The steward stood quietly next to the dismount to offer his hand to the Lady and then walked behind her into the manor house. But, before Apollonia could sit and rest after her journey, she insisted that she and Francis must be taken to Ferdinand's coffin in the chapel. Once there, she dropped to her knees beside her brother and remained in tearful prayer with her chaplain for nearly an hour.

The rest of the members of Apollonia's household simply waited. Nan seemed unable to anticipate the Lady's needs or her next move, but each of her household tried to be readily available should their mistress call.

* * *

When Apollonia and Francis finally left the chapel, they went to the great hall where everyone of significance was gathered from both households. The Lady asked to be shown to Ferdinand's private space where he conducted the business of the manor. She remained there with Nan, Waldef, Giles, Friar Francis, and Ferdinand's Steward Smithson until her brother's will was read aloud to her. There was little new to Apollonia of her brother's final wishes, but throughout her discussion with his steward, the Lady acknowledged Ferdinand's preferences for his funeral in the parish church and his burial next to his wife's grave in the Marshfield parish churchyard.

Afternoon finally arrived, and the two households began to gather in the great hall for dinner. The Lady begged to be excused from their company and withdrew with Nan to a quiet meal in her chamber where she and her maid remained until evening for private prayers led by Friar Francis. When Francis had bid them goodnight, the Lady allowed Nan to prepare her for bed. Then, she asked Nan to sit with her briefly.

"I pray you will forgive my abrupt behaviour, Nan, but I confess that I have been struggling to maintain my composure since the moment I learned of my brother's death. I am aware that you of all my people have constantly sought to bring me comfort, but now and for the days ahead, I have too much to be responsible for and to manage until dear Hugh arrives. I have few tears left, dearheart, but I know I must control my emotions to fulfill my duty."

Nan said, as she smiled with her eyes at Apollonia, "I am here for you, my Lady. As you are able, allow me to help you deal with your loss."

* * *

Apollonia and Nan were up and about early the following morning to make their way to the chapel where Francis began their day with morning prayers for Ferdinand's soul. After chapel, the Lady specifically asked Nan to remain with her and Giles while Gareth was sent to the barns, with Ferdinand's squire, to oversee the day-to-day workings of the manor.

Apollonia could not help but be grateful for the way in which everything continued to run very smoothly in Marshfield. Her brother's household was small but well trained and very loyal. Several of them had been with her brother for years, and there could be no doubt that they grieved for him. Even Flora, the ancient cook, could be seen wiping her eyes as she went about her morning preparations in the kitchen.

"Give it your best, Polly," the Lady seemed to hear Ferdinand say with his elder brother's pushiness, as if he were still beside her. "I will never be far away."

Ferdinand's household had not had a resident chaplain since the most recent had died of old age just after the death of Ferdinand's wife. Ferdinand always insisted to his sister that the parish church of Marshfield was well served by Father Farthing, and he would regularly attend there with his people. The good father had been with his Lord Ferdinand soon after his death and came to call upon the Lady Apollonia when he realised she had arrived in Marshfield.

"My gracious Lady of Aust," he said quietly as he walked into the hall, "it is always my pleasure to see you once again, but I beg pardon for the tragic circumstances of this visit. All of Marshfield are in mourning at the loss of your dear brother, the earl, and we remember you daily in our prayers as we rejoice to give thanks for the blessings of his lordship."

Apollonia could see the honest sadness in the face of this old friend of her brother, and she could tell from his voice that his words were deeply felt. Father Farthing, too, was feeling her brother's loss. Pinching herself against losing control, she reminded herself that she was not the only person in mourning here. She reached out to take the priest's hand and thank him sincerely for his expressions of sympathy.

"I will be so grateful to you, Father Farthing, for officiating with my son Thomas at Ferdinand's service in the parish church. I know that it is my brother's wish to be buried in the churchyard next to his wife. When my son, Father Thomas, comes, will you help him with all the arrangements?"

"Indeed, my Lady, when do you wish to have the service?"

"My sons will not be with us until later in the week. May we prepare to have the funeral on Sunday week?"

"As you wish, my Lady," the priest said while lifting one eyebrow as if questioning the days already passed since her brother's death.

"Indeed, Father, that will be eight days, but I have seen to it that a specialist from Bristol will be here on the morrow to bring strips of fabric impregnated with wax to wrap snugly around Ferdinand's body to exclude air. Maintaining this wrap will preserve his body until my sons can say their last goodbyes to their uncle. Sir Hugh and Father Thomas will be here by Sunday next."

* * *

Before the Lady left the hall for the night, Ferdinand's Steward, Smithson, came to speak with her at the high table.

"My Lady," he said with a bit of question in his voice, "there is a group of minstrels resting for the night in the forecourt. My Lord, the earl, regularly invited them to use this place as a stopover on their journey and looked forward to their return performances. They have begged to be allowed to entertain you. This is a travelling group who have come to Marshfield regularly and have always been welcomed by my Lord Ferdinand. However, I have told them that we have suffered a terrible loss at the recent death of the earl, and no one in the village will be ready for entertainment of any kind."

"Thank you, Smithson, you are correct in your instructions to them, but I would like to have them speak with my steward, Giles, before they consider moving on."

After Smithson had gone, the Lady sent Nan to bring Giles to her. When her steward came, she told him she had a very different kind of assignment for him at this moment.

"Will you kindly go out and speak with the leader of the minstrels who are gathered within the forecourt to rest for the night, Giles?"

"Of course, my Lady, but what would you have me say to them?"

"First, make a point to get to know something about this troop and who is in charge? You have insight into the various kinds of players and performers who might form the troop, Giles, and I want you to find out whatever you can about their performances as well as the route they will travel as they continue on from Marshfield. If they seem worthy performers to you, I should like to be certain that they will include Aust on their route this year."

Chapter Eighteen

Players' Gifts

The Lady Apollonia was especially grateful when two of her sons, Sir Hugh and his younger brother, the priest Father Thomas, finally arrived together in Marshfield to be with her. The Lady knew that her son Chad would not be able to be with them. He was in distant Cornwall, and by the time her message reached him, the burial would be over. She also knew that there was no hope of release for her youngest son, David, from his monastic home at Tintern Abbey in Wales. Tintern was not only one of the first Cistercian houses in Britain, it was also one of the most strict and rigid in its rule. After she sent news of his uncle's death to him, she received a very brief note from David expressing his love and devotion to her and his constancy in prayer for the soul of his Uncle Ferdinand, but it contained no personal news from her precious Davie.

In the days since the shock of her brother's death, Apollonia knew herself to have become an unfamiliar person to everyone in her affinity. Her alienation from Nan epitomised this strangeness. Surely, the Lady told herself, she would find some sense of restoration, having two of her sons with her once again. Each of them was now a grown man in his mature years and contributing significantly to his own community. Still, the Lady could not help feeling live memories of their boyhoods with their father, Edward Aust, and her second husband's boyish love of roughhousing with all five sons at once.

"Oh, my precious, Edward," Apollonia wept to herself. "How I miss you, our Alban, our Davie, my dear Robert, and now Ferdinand."

Nan could tell that her mistress was relieved to have Sir Hugh and Father Thomas join her in Marshfield, yet the maid could not help but be aware of the Lady's silence. Her thoughts seemed distant, continuously sinking into her personal mourning.

"Having her sons with her will help." Nan assured herself. "My Lady is truly struggling with this loss, but pray God, she will find it better endured through time shared with her remaining family."

Once in the village, Sir Hugh took charge of the transfer of the Marshfield property to himself by working with their stewards and Ferdinand's man of law. Father Thomas went first to speak with the Marshfield village priest and prepare for the funeral mass to be held for his uncle in the parish church.

Thomas, immediately sensitive to his mother's state, hoped the mass would help her in dealing with the shock of Ferdinand's sudden death. Nan made a point to speak with him the moment he arrived, emphasising that she had not seen his mother so spiritually depleted by loss. Finally, after making arrangements with Father Farthing, Thomas returned to their uncle's manor to be with his mother.

"Mamam," he said, hoping to encourage the return of her usual take-charge attitude in times of family struggle, "I need your help in selecting the scripture for Uncle Ferdinand's service." He had his own copy of an English translation of the Bible, and with the scriptures in hand, he began searching for meaningful passages. At the very first, it appeared that his request was painful to her, and as they began to read passages together, Thomas thought he could feel his mother grow more tense.

"Shall we begin in this way, mamam?" the priest addressed her gently, using his boyhood pronunciation of mama, boyishly confused with madame.

"I am the resurrection and the life, saith the Lord: he that believeth in me, though he were dead, yet shall he live; and whosoever liveth and believeth in me, shall never die."

"Yes, Thomas, that is an uplifting way to begin," Apollonia quietly nodded.

"Then shall we continue: 'Lord, thou hast been our refuge from one generation to another. Before the mountains were brought forth, or ever the earth and the world were made, thou are God from everlasting and world without end.'''

"Gramercy, Thomas," she sighed, "Yes, that passage inspires a possibility of hope."

"But Mamam, I think that we should express thanks for God's gifts to the lives of men. What do you think if we continue: 'The Lord is my light and my salvation; whom then shall I fear? The Lord is the strength of my life, of whom then shall I be afraid?'"

At this, Thomas could feel his mother start. "I am not afraid." she turned on him abruptly. "I am alone again. I have lost my only brother, Thomas. I do not fear dying, but how often must I lose a loved one? I have been widowed three times. The only remains that I have of one son is his heart in a crystal vase. Another son is taken away from me by his devotion to his monastery. Again, and again, it seems as if a part of me, of my heart, has been torn from me." Her eyes were full of pain, and Thomas moved to take his mother into his arms.

As a priest but also as her devoted middle son, Thomas simply said quietly into her ear: "God is here mamam: 'Truly a very present help in trouble.' "

As he continued to hold his mother, Father Thomas looked to Nan and sent her into the kitchen to bring glasses of wine.

"Rest with me, precious mamam. You are not alone. You have been horribly wounded by shock and loss, and now you must open your heart to the healing presence of God. Hugh and I are here; Nan and Waldef are here, Giles, Friar Francis, and Gareth as well. We are all gathered with you to mourn the loss of your brother but also to remember his life and to share with you our love for him, a man of signal meaning in our lives."

Nan brought the wine, and Thomas poured a glass for each of them. Together they sipped in silence as Thomas held his mother's hand. Slowly Nan and the priest could sense the Lady's person beginning to relax. It was as if Thomas' touch, as well as the words of his love and reassurance, began to restore balance to Apollonia. Nan was aware that the Lady had ceased to cry, yet she knew it would be many months before the Lady would return to a wholesome sense of equilibrium. Despite her grief, Apollonia was aware of her responsibilities and struggled to fulfill her duty.

* * *

When the day of Ferdinand's funeral mass took place, Marshfield's church was filled. The Lady Apollonia was greeted and quietly offered condolences by many of the people of her brother's manor, not only because they knew her from her earlier visits to their village but because of their honest respect for her brother. It seemed to Apollonia that each of their kind expressions of remembrance gave her an extended appreciation of Ferdinand's lordship. Being with them, she could feel in her heart a sense of his presence. She knew he was gone, but it was as if she could hear him assure her, "We shall be together again, Polly."

* * *

Apollonia's eldest son, Sir Hugh, was busy following the rules of his inheritance as the new Earl of Marshfield and had begun the process of moving his family into the manor of his title. Thomas had already returned to his parish and she had received word from Chad that it would not be possible for him to return in time. When Apollonia felt she had done all that was required of her, she bade Hugh and his family goodbye and made ready to return to Aust.

The Lady and her household rode back to the village on the Severn with a slight sense of release after their stay in Marshfield. The funeral and burial services for Lord Ferdinand had been a real celebration of his life, presided over by the Lady's son Father Thomas, but everyone could see what a personal trial it had been for the Lady.

Once back in Aust, when Gareth took their horses to the barn, he seemed to be anxious to get to his home in Ingst. Apollonia made a point to thank him for his special service to her in Marshfield and encouraged him to return to his family. She was also aware that Nan, Giles, Waldef, and Friar Francis were pleased to be home--as was she.

"You know, dearheart," Apollonia said to Nan as they walked into the great hall of Aust Manor, "I believe I have grown too old to travel. How wonderful it is to be home."

"Yes, my Lady, I find long hours on horseback very troubling to my old back," Nan said, returned to her usual in-charge self.

* * *

Later in the week, Giles entered the Lady's solar to ask for a moment to speak with her. "This is not a matter of business, my Lady, but whilst we were in Marshfield, you did ask me to meet with the leader of the minstrels who had served your brother. His name is Gero Hewyn, and his troop is made up of four other young men, one of whom, Reg, is married to Master Hewyn's daughter, Helen. Master Hewyn seemed to be a respectable man who maintains a high degree of performance within his troop. He assured me that they do not perform bawdy comedy but are bards and musicians whose poetry and music speak of distant lands, folk tales, and historical events."

Giles could see that the Lady was pleased by his description of the minstrel troop. "I can see why my brother especially appreciated having them return to Marshfield, Giles," she said. "Were you able to encourage them to bring their performance skills to Aust?"

"Indeed, my Lady, I have received word that they will be here later in this week, and I shall make arrangements for their accommodation."

"Excellent," the Lady said with honest anticipation. "I have been so distracted during recent weeks, I have done nothing to enhance entertainment for the village, and there can be no doubt that my household is ready for a bit of uplifting diversion. When the troop arrives, will you ask their leader, Gero Hewyn, is it, to come to the manor that I may speak with him?"

"Of course, my Lady, I dare say he will be pleased to have the opportunity to be introduced to you, the Earl Ferdinand's sister." As he turned to leave, Giles flashed a quick but meaningful grin towards Nan, sitting next to the Lady. Each of them hoped that the visit of the minstrels would bring diversion to the Lady and prove to lift her spirits after her recent depressing weeks.

* * *

Master Hewyn came to the manor to be presented to the Lady. She, with Nan, received him in the hall. Bowing elegantly to the Lady, he was obviously pleased that she invited him to sit with them near the fireplace.

Apollonia told him that she was grateful to be aware of his group of travelling minstrels and hoped they would, in future, include Aust on their annual route through the West Country's villages. "Though the village of Aust is small, it serves an important purpose, Master Hewyn, and brings many people to us. Aust is the Latin word for south, and our village is the southernmost ferry crossing point on the Severn Estuary. Many people pass through the village regularly on their journeys to and from Wales."

"Indeed, my Lady," he responded, "I am glad to learn of Aust and its access into Wales. We shall be glad to add it to our future travels, and I shall inform you of our coming. It is on our route towards Bristol."

"What instruments do you play Master Hewyn, and may I ask how my deceased brother, the Earl Ferdinand, became aware of your troop travelling about the West Country?"

"I play the psaltery, my Lady, my daughter's husband, Reg, plays the flute and the drum, his brother Tibur the shawm and the ocarina, and our youngest member, Kew, plays the viol masterfully. I must tell you that we met your brother through his dedication to chivalry. He was a knight and true nobleman, my Lady, but we met by accident, one from which grew our devoted respect for him."

"Can you tell me how you were introduced to him?" the Lady asked.

"Our troop was performing in Pucklechurch, not far from Marshfield, about three years ago. Unknown to us, one aggressively powerful village man, watching our performance, had become aware of my daughter, Helen, sitting by herself, hidden behind our performance wagon. Driven by his lust and her beauty, he brutally attacked her.

"We, the men of the company, were all performing on stage that day. Helen remained behind the scenes as always, providing our changes in silly hats and instruments. This man crept up behind her and, putting his hand over her mouth, dragged her away to a space behind the parish church where he sought to rape her. Thank God, the

Earl Ferdinand and several of his men were riding into Pucklechurch at that time and saw the monster drag her off. The earl could see Helen's struggle and rode to her side. He jumped from his horse and, with his men, forced the burley creature to release her. Once assured that Helen was unharmed, as sheriff of the county, he arrested her assaulter and took him off. We learned later that the villain had been following our troop on our route through the towns and villages, watching for his best chance to make his attack.

"As soon as Helen told Reg and me what had happened, we made inquiries about the earl as the knight who saved her and went to Marshfield to express our heartfelt thanks to him. The Lord Ferdinand met each of us in the troop and requested that we come regularly to Marshfield. He promised that we would receive his protection, and he hoped we would perform for him every year.

"To express our gratitude to him," Gero continued, "we have included Marshfield on our route every year since then. We are truly sorry that he is gone, my Lady, and offer you our sincere sympathy in your loss."

The Lady sat back in her chair and simply shook her head. "My brother never shared this story with me, Master Hewyn, and I can see that it is unlikely that he would. Ferdinand always regarded it his duty to protect the weak, but I must tell you that the more I learn of my brother, the more loving pride I cherish for him."

* * *

Apollonia never regretted having invited Master Hewyn's minstrels to come to Aust. This troop of entertainers travelled regularly from place to place throughout the West Country and was made up of excellent singers and musicians whose performances included no bawdy language or jokes. Their songs and poems spoke of the triumphs of King Arthur and told lovely tales of faraway lands. They were already skilled in the poetry of Geoffrey Chaucer, and everyone in the Lady's household was thrilled by the acrobatics of Reg, Tibur, and Kew who were also skilled jugglers.

Every afternoon that they were in Aust, the Lady saw to it that they were able to perform for her household and the folk of the village and then come to her manor for their evening meal. Nan showed Helen how to use the facilities of the manor to catch up with their laundry and use the manor kitchen to provide food to break their fasts each day.

When November began, however, Master Hewyn came to tell the Lady that they must move on to Devon where the short wintry days would be warmer than those of the Midlands. Apollonia was sorry to see them go, but she understood their concern and their need to move south. Before they left Aust, she paid them for what she described as their special gifts to her, as well their variety of performances for her and her household. As she handed a pouch filled with coins to Master Hewyn, she thanked him sincerely.

"You and your players have helped me return to some sense of normalcy, my friend. Though I continue to grieve for my brother, your songs, your celebration of life, and especially your excellence in performance have rewarded me with a heart-lifting balance that had gone. I am grateful to understand the meaningful, as well as entertaining, offerings of minstrels through poetry, song, and acrobatics. Please know that we shall look forward to seeing you all again next year."

* * *

Waldef had been well aware of the Lady's loss of her brother and had made a point to be at her side should she need anything throughout their journey to Marshfield, the weeks she spent there with her sons, and their preparations for the earl's funeral mass and burial. Waldef had grown very grateful for his role as the Lady's servant, even while she seemed to grow distant from those of her household who served her. He found himself largely alone in Marshfield, without a specific role. Mistress Nan made a point to assign him various tasks, but there was very little for him to do except spend his free time with Gareth. His respect and friendship for the Lady's stablemaster continued to grow.

When at last the Aust household returned to their home village, Waldef resumed his assigned duties within the household with Mistress Nan to direct him. He did not want to do anything that would trouble the Lady in any way, but for a long time he had wished to speak with her about a personal struggle he was having. She was the woman in his world whom he admired most, and this was a very personal struggle.

Sitting with the Lady in her solar, Waldef was trying to concentrate on his book, but Apollonia could see that his mind was on other things than his borrowed copy of *Mandeville's Travels.*

"I do hope you will forgive my distraction over the recent weeks whilst we were in Marshfield, Waldef. You have been an excellent page and have served me well, but I know my attention was solely on the needs of my family whilst we were there. Is there anything that you have wished to discuss with me?"

At first Waldef blushed a deep shade of rose, but he turned to her very seriously. "Yes, my Lady, I would be grateful to speak with you of a personal concern whenever you have a free moment. I promise it will not take a great deal of your time."

Nan looked up from her embroidery with a wondering smile but said nothing.

"Are you willing to share your concern with me in front of Mistress Nan?"

"Oh, yes, my Lady. Since I lost my mother, I regard you and Mistress Nan as the most important women in my life. I shall be very grateful for your help."

"Then, we shall hear your concern now, if you are ready to discuss it."

Waldef stood up, swallowed deeply and then began to address Apollonia, "My Lady, you know that I owe my life to you. It is only because of your willingness to take me under your protection that I was saved from accusations of murder. It is because of you that I have been elevated to the position of servant in a noble household. But, I am a merchant's son, and my father has sent word to me that he needs my help. He is struggling with ill health and wishes me to return to Bristol to master the basics of our business in the wholesale trade and help him through a difficult time."

Apollonia sat back in her chair, obviously surprised by his announcement. "Indeed, Waldef" she said, "you know that I was gratified when we were able to prove your innocence of the crime you were falsely accused of. I am truly sorry to learn that you are required by family problems to return home. We shall all miss you because you have made yourself a devoted member of my household here in Aust."

"Before I go, my Lady, would you allow me to bring up one more question that I have. There are no other people in my life that I respect more than you and Mistress Nan, and I would be grateful to have your perspective."

Nan looked up from her embroidery and nodded. The Lady responded to him with sincere interest. "Whatever your questions, Waldef, I pray you will share them with us. Nan and I will try to give you our heartfelt comments regardless of the nature of your concerns."

"My Lady, Mistress Nan, how can I express my love to a young woman whom I know I wish to marry?"

Apollonia was taken aback by his question, as was Nan, but after a brief pause, the Lady spoke first. "May we know the identity of the young woman who has captured your heart?" Apollonia asked with a gentle smile. "Is she someone nearby?"

Now, Waldef's face blushed again as he looked toward Nan. "It is MaryLizbet Falcon, Mistress Nan. She is not only the most beautiful girl I know, my Lady, but is intelligent, full of grace and goodness."

Nan did not seem completely surprised at this revelation but only asked, "Have you spoken to MaryLizbet of your love, Waldef?"

"I believe that she knows I care for her, and she has expressed some affection for me, as well, but I have not told her of my desire to marry her as I have told you."

"If you are to leave Aust soon, Waldef, should you not speak of your love to MaryLizbet? She is younger than you, but to ask for her hand in marriage, you must speak with your father as well as with Joshua and Jeanne Falcon. I dare say all of the parents will wish to know how you plan to support a wife and when you think you will be prepared to do so."

"That is just it, my Lady, Mistress Nan. I am returning to my home to follow in my father's footsteps. Hopefully, I shall become as successful as my father has been in the trade in Bristol. I am sixteen, ready to work as a man to support a family, but I am unable to offer anything until I have achieved success. I will tell my father that I plan to spend the months ahead building my own career but also trying to learn how to be a good husband. If MaryLizbet will wait for me, I offer her my heart but can offer little more just now."

This time, Nan was the first to respond. "It is obvious that you have given serious thought to what is required of you, Waldef, but if MaryLizbet must be willing to wait until you have achieved success, you must consider her position. She is of marriageable age, and I dare say will have other offers of marriage during those years of waiting for you."

"Mistress Nan, I can only tell her that I love her truly and will dedicate my life to become a good husband to her."

"Then," the Lady told him, "I suggest that before you return to your home in Bristol, you will ride out to the Falcon farm and make your proposal to MaryLizbet so that she may consider the full extent of your offer. If you are agreed, both of you must speak with her parents."

"With your permission, my Lady, Mistress Nan, may I be allowed to do that?"

"Waldef, you have served me well," Apollonia said with a loving smile. "My household and I respect you, and we will all miss you. But if you have decided that becoming a successful merchant is your goal in life, I can only encourage you. MaryLizbet is an excellent choice, but Nan is correct. You must first make your proposal to her. You not only have my permission, you have my blessing. Go with God. Nan and I shall pray for your father's return to good health and your success in all that you strive to do."

Chapter Nineteen

Seeking Forgiveness

It was later in the week after Waldef left Aust to return to his family's home in Bristol that Joshua Falcon rode to the manor and asked to speak with the Lady Apollonia. She and Nan were delighted to see him, and each knew in her heart the purpose of his visit. It was a chilly early November day with sharp winds, and the Lady bade him come with her and Nan to her solar where they could visit together near the fire.

They began their conversation with Nan and the Lady begging for news of the family, but after several assurances that all was well with Jeanne, MaryLizbet, and the twins, Joshua asked the Lady what she could tell him about her former servant, Waldef, who was leaving her service to return to his father's home.

Apollonia reminded him of the lovely meal that she had invited him and Jeanne to share with her affinity in Aust celebrating Waldef's remarkable success in helping the Lady learn the truth of the attacks of sickness in the village. No one else had been able to understand what caused the sudden outbreak, not even James Morewell, the local doctor of physic.

"As you remember, Joshua," she said, "Waldef was seated with me at the head table that afrenoon to honour him because of the extraordinary service he alone had been able to achieve for me."

"Indeed, my Lady, I do remember how you celebrated the lad on that day, but can you tell me more about him as a person? I have heard that he was an accused murderer. He is the only commoner I know who makes such a fuss about chivalry. What are the real truths of his life?"

"Joshua," the Lady responded immediately, "Waldef was, as you say, accused but proven innocent of murder. As a young man who had no hope of becoming a knight, he adopted the code of chivalry as the guiding principles of his Christianity. He not only did a great service to me, at risk to himself on behalf of one living within my household, I have found him to be a devout believer always ready to go beyond the expected goals of service. Only recently, he worked with Garmon to spend their nights guarding the manor and discovered two questionable noblemen living rough on my property."

Before Joshua could ask another question, Nan spoke up, "And I, too, must join my Lady in endorsing Waldef's goodness, Joshua, and his extraordinary service to her. He has only been part of her household this year, and yet he has demonstrated a willing devotion to go beyond any limit to serve her."

"Do you think that Waldef is one who pushes himself beyond the limits of his class out of pride? Does he seek to present himself as someone better or more important than others?"

To this question, Apollonia answered him immediately, "Definitely not, Joshua. Waldef does push himself to achieve goals in his life, but those goals are guided by his faith and are within his reach."

"And I know, Joshua," added Nan, "that he is a hard worker, willing to stick to his objectives until he has achieved them."

"Well, my Lady, dear Nan, I will share all you have told me with Jeanne. We were both surprised when Waldef came to our home recently to visit with MaryLizbet. Later that day, they asked to speak with Jeanne and me. Waldef told us that he was leaving your service to return home because his father is ill and requires his help in the family business. However, he also declared his love for MaryLizbet and told us that he wished to ask for her hand in marriage."

"Do you know what MaryLizbet's answer will be?" Nan asked.

"Oh, she made it quite clear that her feelings of love for Waldef are very strong and that she would be glad to become his wife. I must confess to you both that Jeanne and I had given little thought to the possibility of marriage as MaryLizbet seems so young. Then, we remind ourselves that she is already of marriageable age."

"Yet, you are concerned about something more, are you not Joshua?" the Lady pressed him.

"His proposal to MaryLizbet is to be completed after he has returned to Bristol, having achieved success in his father's business when he is certain that he will be able to support MaryLizbet as his wife."

"Well, that seems well thought through, Joshua," Nan told him.

"But, dear Nan, how long might that be? MaryLizbet is young, but is she to remain single, refusing other offers for how many years? What if Waldef should require ten or fifteen years to achieve success or tire of her and abandon his promise to her? How can I allow such a tragic possibility for one as near to me as a daughter when she is not guaranteed a specific date?"

"Joshua," the Lady said gently, "how many guarantees are there in this life? I can understand your loving need to protect MaryLizbet, but I will speak on behalf of Waldef. He is a faithful young man who is truly in love with MaryLizbet, so much that he wishes to join with her in marriage. Is it not to his credit that he seeks to establish success in his father's business first to be able to support MaryLizbet as his wife? Waldef has proven his fidelity, his intelligence, his ability to learn, as well as his ability to deal with people of various classes. This has been endorsed by my special friends, Gareth, my stablemaster, and long-time member of my household, as well as Sir Julian Thurston, a gentleman of knightly honour. I am hopeful that you will trust in the words of Waldef and MaryLizbet and respect all that they have shared with you. Nan will speak for herself, but I know Waldef to be a young man of heroic intent in my service."

"And I am witness to his goodness, sensitivity to others' suffering, and hard-working willingness to serve faithfully," Nan said.

"I shall return home and share everything you have told me with Jeanne," Joshua said as he stood to leave, "but you can see that I am uneasy as the father of a lovely teenage daughter facing a proposal of marriage with no suggested date of its happening."

The Lady extended her hand to him with an encouraging smile. "Joshua, I remember you well as a young villager whom I took into my service when you were in your early teens. My son, David, especially respected you and enjoyed your company. You served me well as my courier, and I have always thought of you and Jeanne as near to me as family. If MaryLizbet loves Waldef enough to wait for him to establish himself, I believe we should all have faith in their declarations of love for each other."

"My Lady," he said sincerely, "Jeanne and I owe our marriage to you and from the very first days of my service within your household, as my noble patron, you have educated me and granted me a sense of value. Gramercy for sharing your opinions, especially now. All that you and Mistress Nan have said endorses Waldef in a way that no others could."

* * *

The days of November included some sunshine and were not bitterly wintry, but everyone was aware that each day had significantly shorter daylight. Apollonia saw that her household was well prepared for the winter and settling in for the long dark season ahead. An unexpected message was delivered to her door that Garmon brought. As soon as she opened it, the Lady realised it was from the former pardoner Brandon Landow:

> Dear Lady,
>
> Not far from Aust, I have been badly wounded here at Olveston and desperately need your help, for I have no way to care for myself. I confess that I have not been a respected churchman in your eyes, but I have nowhere else to turn for help. I pray you will grant me your aid. In desperation,
>
> Brandon Landow

Apollonia gave the note to Nan, and after reading it, the maid scoffed. "My Lady, you know better than anyone that Brandon Landow can not be trusted. It is likely that he only wishes to use you and your hospitality once again."

The Lady did not respond immediately, but she eventually said with caution in her voice, "I have never received correspondence from Brandon, certainly nothing that contained such a desperate plea, Nan. It is possible that he truly does need our help. I must at least send someone to him in response to his plea."

Nan simply raised her eyebrows as if to say, "We know he is not to be trusted."

"Call Giles and Gareth to me, Nan. Olveston is not far, but I shall not go. I will send two who have known the pardoner for years and will be able to judge for me what is the truth of his situation."

"If you insist, my Lady."

When Giles and Gareth entered her solar, the Lady gave her steward the letter and asked him to read it aloud for Gareth to hear. When both men realised who had sent this message to the Lady, they expressed the same dubious thoughts about him as had Nan.

Apollonia listened carefully to their words but finally told each of her men that as a vowess of the church, she must respond to his desperate plea for help.

"I want you both to go to Olveston as my agents, taking the wagon, Gareth, in case Landow is really too ill to ride. You are both insightful, experienced men whom I trust. Please, be my judges of Landow's condition. I rely on you. If you see that he is as seriously wounded as he says, bring him home to Aust that we may care for him."

The Lady could see that Giles, especially, was not ready to see anything but exaggeration in Landow's note, yet always a faithful servant, he and Gareth left her to prepare to make their journey to Olveston early the following morning.

* * *

Nan seemed more than usually irritated the morning after Giles and Gareth left Aust. Apollonia knew that Nan had not the slightest trust in Brandon Landow as a servant of the church or even as a human being. The Lady was sitting with her by the fire in her solar and told herself that she must respect the maid's feelings. Apollonia decided that they should speak openly of the responsibility they might be taking on if the pardoner's wounds were as serious as he described.

"Nan, dearheart, you know that I shall depend on your nursing skills to be chief caregiver to Brandon when he arrives in Aust. If he is as seriously wounded as he says, I shall call in Physician James, of course, but you will be my first agent of care with the help of our household staff."

Nan looked straight into the Lady's eyes as she was prone to do when she was expressing strong opinions. "I will do my best for him, my Lady, but first I shall see how seriously he really is wounded."

* * *

Giles and Gareth returned to Aust Manor very late in the day. The Lady and Nan were more than anxious to observe the truth of the condition of Brandon Landow. From the moment they watched Giles and Gareth nearly carrying Landow into the small chamber near the hall where a special bed had been placed and warmed to receive him, the women could see that his wounded condition was tragically real. The Lady looked at Giles, and he simply put his head down as if to say he did not believe much could be done. Regardless of the deceiving, abject churchman Giles always thought Landow to be, the Lady's steward could now be seen as feeling pity for the badly injured pardoner.

Everyone in Apollonia's household was on hand to offer help, but as Giles pointed out to Nan, little more could be done without the presence of a physician. "My Lady, Landow has been stabbed in the chest and has suffered a great loss of blood. I pray you will call for Physician Morewell to come straightaway."

The Lady did not hesitate. She told Nan to send Cassie from the kitchen to bring the physician from his home as quickly as she could. Nan ran into the kitchen and brought Cassie to her.

"It is late, Cassie, but if you find the doctor of physic at home, please tell him that we have an emergency here at the manor and need his help. If he is away from his home, do not return until you can bring him to us."

* * *

Apollonia remained at Landow's bedside with Giles. She thanked Gareth for his service but sent him home. "The physician will come soon, Gareth, and we shall do all we can, but this is far worse than I had imagined. Brandon has been cruelly attacked and his wound very primitively bandaged. You can do nothing more here. Please return to your family."

Bowing to her, Gareth seemed relieved to be excused and slipped away quietly just as Nan was returning from the kitchen. "Surely the physician will be here soon," Nan said, "but my Lady, should we cut away the filthy garments put upon him? It appears that his majestic outer garments as servant to the archbishop were stolen, and nothing covers him but this filthy peasant's tunic."

"We shall be ready to do whatever Physician James asks of us Nan, but at the moment, I fear to move Brandon because the bleeding may increase."

* * *

While the Lady and Nan waited for Morewell, they were seated on stools either side of Landow. The Lady and her maid listened as Landow began to moan, then cry out, "Why? I believed you to be my friend. I saved your life."

Neither could make sense of his words, but Apollonia thought that he was crying out against his attacker. Whose life had he saved? Who would have been so immoral to have turned on him in this way in Olveston? Was this the attack of a common thief? There could be no doubt that Brandon Landow had been struck in a murderous dagger attack. Words were muttered by Landow, but they continued to be beyond the understanding of the Lady and Nan.

The day was darkening when Cassie was able to bring the doctor of physic, and the Lady had the chamber lighted with as many candles as possible for Morewell's examination of Landow's wound. The physician quickly ordered water to be brought while he cut away the bloody tunic and underclothes from Landow's body. He said very little as he concentrated on cleaning the wounds and wrapping his body tightly in clean bandages. He was able to stem the flow of blood, and Landow's body slowly relaxed as he fell into a deep sleep.

The Lady left the chamber but gestured to Nan to remain should Physician James need anything. As she passed Nan, she said very quietly, "I pray you will have James come to me when he has finished."

* * *

It was not long before the doctor of physic came to her solar, anxious to speak with the Lady privately. From the look of his face, she knew he had little hope of recovery for Landow. Apollonia was waiting with Giles when the physician entered, and his words were not encouraging. "I have done all that I can, my Lady," he said, 'but the wound is vicious and deep. The patient has lost a great deal of blood. You must keep someone near his bedside constantly."

Answering him directly, the Lady wished to assure him, "I shall see that he receives all the care that my household can provide, Physician James, but I hope you will return to us on the morrow."

"I pray that he survives till the morrow, my Lady," Morewell said slowly, "but I shall return in the morning unless I receive differing instructions from you. Whoever it was who attacked your friend was surely intent upon killing him."

* * *

Apollonia went to the chamber where Landow lay after the physician left her. Nan was at his bedside placing cool damp cloths upon his forehead. "Landow's fever is high, my Lady," she said obviously worried, "but I shall remain through the night with him."

"Dearheart, if you can stay with him through the next four hours, I shall come and relieve you to stay with him till morning."

"My Lady," Nan said obviously concerned, "I shall remain until you come. There can be no doubt, Landow has been viciously attacked and left for dead."

* * *

The sun was just rising as the Lady sat at Landow's bedside. For much of the night, the Lady felt that the pardoner had seemed semi-conscious. Suddenly, his eyes opened, and he realised that the Lady herself sat with him at his bedside.

"My Lady of Aust," he whispered, "you are indeed a Christian woman."

"Say nothing, Brandon, you must rest," she said gently rebuking him.

"Forgive me, my Lady, but there are many things I should tell you. Will you allow me to make an honest confession for once in my life?"

"Later," she insisted, "at this moment, I require you to rest."

"My Lady simply know this," he said as he slipped back into sleep, "you warned me of his evil intent, but I did not listen. It was Dravini who stabbed me and left me for dead on the road."

For the first time in her life, the Lady reached out to Landow and touched his face. Her soft hands gently covered his eyes and made them close. "When you are better," she said very quietly, we shall talk and share all that you have to tell me."

In the midst of her effort to calm Landow, the Lady's mind was avidly aware of his words. He had just told her that Dravini had attempted to kill him in spite of Landow being his personal rescuer. Brandon Landow had personally achieved Dravini's release from the Aust gaol and saved him from hanging. She must get word of this revelation off to her son Hugh, now Earl of Marshfield. Dravini had not only ordered his henchmen, Sir Hardulph and Buldoc, to murder, he personally tried to kill the egotistical man who had enabled his release from the gaol in Aust through a fraudulent order of the Archbishop Arundel he had drawn up.

Landow slept soundly through the night and was only awakened when the doctor of physic returned to the manor as he had promised. Nan brought him to Landow's chamber and relieved the Lady of her watch at his bedside. Apollonia was ready to be replaced but once again asked the physician to speak with her before he left.

As soon as she could, the Lady went to her dovecote to send a message off to her son Hugh. It said simply: "So-called Count Dravini of Sicily is a vicious murderer. Anyone in law who finds him must arrest him!"

Then, the Lady went to her solar to wait quietly before speaking with Physician James. When he came to join her, she could see that the young doctor was grateful that his patient had survived the night, but he did not wish to raise the Lady's hopes.

"My Lady, I shall return on the morrow unless you call me for an emergency. Your friend, Master Landow, continues to be very weak, and I can promise you nothing. We must see how his condition develops day by day…if he lives."

"Gramercy for the excellent care you have brought to him, Physician James. Accept my personal thanks for your willingness to return each day."

"I do this not as a favour, my Lady, but as your physician truly concerned about the survival of my patient."

* * *

Apollonia went daily to Landow's bedside for brief visits. She stayed just long enough to tell the pardoner that she and her household were praying for him and urging him to continue to rest. On the third day of his recuperation, Landow begged her to remain for a bit longer so that he might get some things off his chest.

"I do need to speak with you, my Lady. In so many ways I have abused my role as pardoner and as servant of holy church. You alone have known me since I was a boy. I pray you will grant me time to share my truth with you?"

"Brandon, if you feel a need for confession, I shall send a priest to you," the Lady promised.

"No, I pray you, my Lady, allow me to speak with you in complete honesty."

Apollonia did not answer him immediately. Yet, she could see that Nan who was sitting at Landow's bedside seemed to be encouraging her.

"I shall come again on the morrow, Brandon," she finally said. "Rest now, and if you still wish to speak with me, we shall then talk together for a brief time."

Nan also left Landow's bedside when the Lady walked from his chamber. They were both in the hall beyond Landow's possibility of hearing their conversation when Nan said urgently to Apollonia, "Please take time to speak with him this day, my Lady. His body is weakening, and he seems to have a great need to win some sort of acknowledgement from you."

"I shall return, Nan. Pray tell me what it is that worries you? Brandon has never been your favourite person. Have you changed your mind about him?"

"My Lady, he is the changed person. This horrific attack against his life by one whom he thought he admired has crushed his sense of value. I think that the near possibility of death has brought him to make whatever changes he can to feel true forgiveness. He may have been a pardoner through much of his adult life, but he now seems unable to find pardon for his own sins."

When the Lady left Nan, she went directly to the chapel to speak with her household chaplain. Friar Francis was always glad to speak with the Lady. He admired her as the head of Aust household but also as an educated woman who had proven to be a devoted servant of Christ through her widow's choice of remaining in the world while serving God as a vowess.

"Francis, I have need of your counsel," the Lady said as she entered.

"Are we ready to begin our plans for Christmas, my Lady? I always look forward to the creation of our nativity scene."

"We shall work on that soon, dear friend, but as we must be gone for the actual day of Christmas, I was hoping you would work with our local parish priest to place our crèche near the door of the village church so that all of the villagers might enjoy it. Before that, I wish to speak with you on another matter altogether. I know that you have been visiting the chamber where Brandon Landow lies near death. You have prayed with him and over him daily. What has happened to him? Nan tells me that he has become a different person."

"My Lady, you and I have chosen our own roles of service to the church and as can happen, each of us has a real sense of the truth of our own sinfulness. Landow knows well that, as a pardoner, he used his connexion with the church for his own profit. Now, suddenly facing death, he realises his human need to experience God's pardon and forgiveness. Having lost so much blood, he is very weak but knows he must face up to the truth of his lies. His sales of fake relics and pardons to others in desperate need were evil. At this moment, he truly does not know where to turn."

"Gramercy, Francis," the Lady told him, thinking back over her years of experience with Landow, "I knew you would grant me insight."

Chapter Twenty

Affable Grace

On the first day of December, Apollonia's eldest son, Hugh, now the earl, sent a note to her, telling her he was preparing to celebrate Christmas, 1406, with his family in their new home in Marshfield, and he invited her, Nan, Francis, and Giles to join them. Apollonia happily accepted but asked to be allowed to come later, closer to the actual day. She told Hugh she and Nan were taking care of a former member of her household, badly wounded by a murderous attack. She asked Hugh, as Sheriff of Gloucestershire, if he had been able to learn of the whereabouts of the Sicilian Count Dravini who also went by the name of Peter Declan. The victim she was caring for had told her that it was Dravini who stabbed him, and Dravini was likely running away to London.

Hugh responded that he had sent word to his friend the Sheriff of London to be on the watch for Dravini who was wanted for murder in Gloucestershire. He added that whenever his mother and her household could join them for Christmas would be grand.

Early in the morning, Apollonia went to the chamber where Brandon Landow lay. Physician James had already visited him, and she sent Nan to take time to break her fast, saying that she would sit with Brandon. When they were alone, the pardoner said in a weak and trembling voice that he was grateful for the prayers of her household but especially for her presence now. He begged her to help him make his last arrangements.

"I have come to the end of my life, my Lady, and find that I not only have no family, I have no friends. May I turn to you as my friend?"

"You must rest, Brandon, and as your friend, I shall listen to everything that you wish to tell me."

"My Lady, you of all people know that I abused my role as pardoner to make money. I kept the larger amount of my sales and gave a pittance to the church. Cheating the church as I did, the monies I kept for myself grew significantly. I think I did believe in the church's doctrine of the Treasury of Merit, so what I was selling had its basis in truth. Yet, I knew in my heart, I was driven to abuse its teachings by my greed. When my parents died, I discovered that I had inherited land and money from them so that I could go to London, buy grandly tailored clothes, and be part of those who served the Archbishop of Canterbury.

"It is an extraordinary career, Brandon, but, I fear, not an admirable one in many ways."

"I am a hypocrite, my Lady. I have abused people's faith in the church's teachings to empower myself and make myself rich. Now, I know that I am dying. I feel a compelling need to make my confession and offer you a sincere apology for all the evil I have done."

"Brandon, your apology is accepted," the Lady said to him quietly, "but now you must accept that salvation has already been bought for you and *given* to you through Christ's sacrifice. You simply have to open your heart and receive it."

"How can I receive it when I know, my Lady, that I do not deserve it? I have sinned against the church, against believers of the church's teachings, and against those whom I knew to be sincere Christians. How can you not despise me? You know I am a liar, a fraud, and deceptive to my fellow beings."

"Brandon, you have been an irritation in my life. At your worst, I have sought to avoid you, but I acknowledge that I too am a sinner. I need forgiveness as do you, and Jesus' sacrifice enables me to overcome sin. My daily prayers begin with my constant thanks to Him."

"What price have you paid?" Brandon lifted his head and was becoming more feverishly disturbed.

Apollonia reached out and put her hands to his face to gently close his eyes. "We are loved, Brandon," she said as she caressed his cheeks. "You are loved, and no price is required of us. God has declared His love to us through His Son. I learned from our friend Wycliffe that the price of our sin is paid but we must acknowledge it. Rest now, Brandon, and we shall talk again when I come next."

Apollonia felt Landow flinch at the name of the Oxford scholar whose followers were still being persecuted by the archbishop's men, but he continued to reach out to her. "Come soon, I beg you, my Lady," Brandon pleaded.

Apollonia went into the hall where she found Nan seated by the fire. Nan looked up as she came. "I shall go back to Landow's bedside, my Lady. He has told me that he knows he is dying, and Physician James fears that his wound is corrupted."

"He is very weak, Nan, but I must spend some time working with Giles. I shall come back soon. Ask Francis to stay with you, hear Brandon's confession, and continue to pray with him."

* * *

When Apollonia returned to Landow's bedside, relieving Nan, Friar Francis was praying quietly on one side of his bed. The Lady made little noise because she thought Brandon was sleeping. She sat on the stool, which Nan had left, and suddenly he opened his eyes. Seeing she was with him, Landow said, "No one since my mother has touched me so tenderly. Will you take my hand, my Lady?"

She reached with both of her warm hands to hold both of his cold ones as Francis continued to pray over them. When she touched him, Apollonia could see that Landow closed his eyes once more. Slowly his hands went limp. The Lady thought his chest ceased to move; his breathing stopped. Francis bent over him, holding a small mirror near his nose.

"He is gone, my Lady."

Apollonia put Brandon's hands together on his chest and fell to her knees at his bedside. "Pray with me, Francis. Brandon Landow is gone, but Nan is correct. He sincerely sought to change his life at the last."

* * *

No one in the Lady's household knew whom to notify at the time of Landow's death. Apollonia was unaware of any of Brandon's surviving family, but the Lady sent off a message to the family's parish church in his home town of Cirencester. Apollonia also informed Archbishop Arundel's household that Landow had been murdered on his attempted return to Lambeth, and the murderer was a foreign man posing as a Sicilian Count Dravini who also went by the name of Peter Declan.

The Lady saw to it that Brandon Landow's life was celebrated with a funeral mass in the Aust parish church, and he was properly buried in the church cemetery. It was all accomplished before the Christmas holiday after which her affinity was encouraged to return home to the happy anticipation of Christmas and their usual celebratory mood. Nan noticed that the Lady remained calm, she was in control as ever, and had preserved the anticipation of Christmas for all of her household in Aust.

"I know your painful grief at having to deal with your brother's death so recently, my Lady, and yet, in spite of your personal loss, you not only cared for Landow at his bedside, you were the one person he wished to be with when he died. A difficult time for you, still, you have enabled those of us in your household to cope with it and look forward to the holiday celebration."

"Nan, you of all my friends and household have been closest to me through my long life. I will always be grateful to you. You have rejoiced with me, you have wept with me, you have been loved by my sons as part of our family, and you have offered your loving kindness to me even when I turned from you. Gramercy, dearheart," the Lady said as she reached out to pull the little maid into her arms.

"My Lady," Nan said, nearly weeping, "I have said many times before, but it is the truth of my life. You have granted me a sense of value; you have given me a soul."

* * *

While Nan was packing the Lady's garments to make the journey to her son's new home in Marshfield, Apollonia mentioned that she was looking forward to spending time with Hugh's wife, the Lady

Gwendolyn. Nan could not help but think back to an earlier time in her son's marriage when the Lady had not felt welcomed by her son's wife at all. In fact, during those earlier years, Apollonia had always felt restrained in Gwendolyn's company. Their relationship had changed dramatically in recent years, and the two women had not only become good friends but shared a special sense of mother/daughter love. Since Sir Hugh was now the Earl of Marshfield, Gwendolyn begged Apollonia to come to Marshfield and help her deal with her new role as a countess.

When the Lady with Nan, Francis, and Giles arrived in Marshfield on the day before Christmas, Gwendolyn was first among her household to rush out and welcome them. She took Apollonia into her arms after the Lady dismounted and continued to hold her hand as she welcomed the rest of her household.

"Welcome, dear ones; please come in by the fire where you may warm up," she said as she urged them into the hall. "Hugh and I are so pleased you are here. We will all go to the church tonight to celebrate the Angel's Mass at midnight. Then, at dawn, Friar Francis, will you join with our chaplain, Father Swithun, in the celebration of the Shepherd's Mass?"

"I should be happy to, Lady Gwendolyn," Francis told her, pleased to be included as an officiant.

"Then, after the Mass of the Divine Word in our chapel, we have a lovely surprise for our Christmas banquet, mamam," Gwendolyn told the Lady as happily as if she had returned to her own childhood. "I am so pleased. Our cook has been able to obtain a Yule boar. Our feast will have all the usual soups, stews, birds, and fish, mamam, but the kitchen will bring in the roasted boar with grand ceremony."

As they entered the hall of now her son's home in Marshfield, the Lady and her party found it decorated with ivy, mistletoe, and holly. Apollonia noticed immediately that Gwendolyn had worked hard to see that their new home was beautifully prepared for this family celebration. Nan was especially pleased to be taking part in it. She would celebrate with her adopted family when they had returned to Aust at the time of the New Year gift giving, but now the maid was gathering warm memories from Marshfield to share with Joshua, Jeanne, and their children.

* * *

The days of the Christmas celebration went by quickly, and Apollonia cherished each of them, especially this year. The Lady was so pleased to see how Hugh and Gwen found every aspect of the celebration a special kind of rejoicing for them as the new earl and his countess. Lady Gwendolyn created for them a grandly successful Christmas banquet in the great hall where all the Marshfield affinity gathered, and it was a sumptuous feast, nobly served. As Gwen had told the Lady, the high point of the meal was a grand presentation of the Yule boar, perfectly roasted and carried into the hall on a magnificent platter held between two muscular male servants.

The greatest surprise for the Lady was one that Hugh had planned for his household but especially for his mother. He had arranged for a group of travelling players to perform *The Shepherd's Play* and *The Wise Men's Play* from the Christmas Cycle of the mystery plays. He knew his mother was aware of these holiday entertainments but had never been able to see them. The new Earl of Marshfield saw that everyone in his extended household looked foreward to have these dramas presented in honour of the holiday. After each performance, the members of his affinity gathered round the stage to thank the players and learn more about their performances in different cities of the West Country.

Apollonia and her household also made an enthusiastic effort to personally thank the players, and Giles was once again instructed by the Lady to invite them to add Aust Manor to their route in the West Country in future.

* * *

Late that evening as Nan prepared the Lady for bed, Apollonia told her that though she was more than ready to return home, she was truly grateful that they had been able to spend a glorious family Christmas in Marshfield, thanks to Hugh and Gwen. The Lady had been especially happy to be in her son's new home for the holiday and see how he was maturing into his inheritance as an earl. She had been quietly thoughtful throughout their visit, but Nan had noticed the number of times Apollonia and Lady Gwendolyn spent time together. They shared their thoughts of many things as usual but especially dealt with Gwen's questions of how she should approach her new role.

"They are as close as mother and daughter," Nan thought to herself with a smile.

When the maid tucked the Lady into her bed and pulled out the truckle bed for herself from beneath, Apollonia said gently, "This has been a glorious time to be together, dearheart, yet I can not help but thank God for the chance to offer my friendship to Brandon Landow at the end of his life. You were especially good to him, and he made a point of thanking me for the extraordinary care you organised for him."

"I could see that Landow was a different man at the end of his life, my Lady. I believe he was truly sorry for the evil that he knew he had done as a churchman. His suffering and the great pain he endured came from the attack of a man whom he had believed to be a friend. I was glad to be one who could find any way to bring him comfort, my Lady."

* * *

The evening after the Lady and her party returned to Aust, Apollonia was happily sitting in her solar with Nan, "Grand to be with Hugh and Gwen, dearheart, but it seems we are all happy to be home once again. I have been pleased to learn how the rest of our household enjoyed their holiday here, thanks to Brother William's directing the celebration for our staff. Gareth has made a point to tell me what special times he and Lucy had with their children. Praise God, it was a happy Christmas."

"Indeed, it was, my Lady," Nan said. Then, quietly remembering her nursing care of Brandon Landow, she added, "But, what an endearing gift being part of a family is. I had no idea how alone in the world the pardoner was. He expressed that powerfully at the last when he reached out to you."

* * *

More than a week went by when the Lady received an unexpected visitor from Cirencester who asked to be introduced to the Lady of Aust as Matthew Trumwin, Brandon Landow's man of law.

Apollonia was grateful to receive him, largely because she wished to speak with a representative of Brandon about the arrangements that she had made after the pardoner's death.

Giles and Nan were with her as they sat round the table dormant in the hall. Giles began their conversation by explaining that as a vowess of the church, Lady Apollonia spoke little in public. Therefore, Giles said that he would describe for Master Trumwin what had been done under the Lady's direction: their collection of the wounded Landow, bringing him here to Aust in response to his plea for help, Landow's care by her household until his death, and finally a funeral mass and burial in the parish church yard.

"My Lady sought to notify any surviving members of the Landow Family, but we had no one to turn to other than the priest of his family's parish church."

The man of law took note of everything Giles was telling him, nodding his head as if approving of what had been done. When at last he spoke, he turned directly to the Lady. "Brandon Landow has no surviving family, my Lady. According to his instructions, I shall pay to have his body exhumed and transported back to Cirencester to be buried next to his parents."

At this point, the Lady decided to speak with Master Trumwin directly. "I take it that you have specific instructions from Brandon, and I shall see to it that the village pitmaker offers his services to you. Are there any other ways through which we may help you?"

"I have one more very important assignment which is to be brought to you, my Lady."

"Pray tell me, what more we can do?"

"Master Landow had become a very wealthy man. We have been able to sell the property acquired by his deceased parents at a very good price, but past that, as a pardoner, he had accumulated a great deal of money. My instructions are to bring the monies to you, my Lady, for Landow wished you to use it in his memory."

Apollonia was obviously startled and sat back in her chair as the man of law passed her a note indicating the amount of money he was instructed to bring her.

"This is a fortune," she said to him. "Why did he wish to give this to me?"

"I can explain nothing of his motives, my Lady. I am only here to carry out his final wishes."

"Then, you must allow me time to think on this, Master Trumwin. I am overwhelmed."

"I must be on my way back to Cirencester soon, my Lady. I shall call upon you in the morning to complete this transfer."

* * *

That evening Nan and Giles sat together in the Lady's solar after the rest of the household had gone to their beds. The Lady's maid could see that Apollonia continued feeling stunned by the announcement of the extraordinary bequest to her from Brandon Landow's last will and testament.

Giles made a point to comment on Landow's man of law. "I was impressed by Master Trumwin, my Lady."

"Yes, Giles, he seems a good man, very efficient and anxious to be true to Brandon's last requests, but why did Brandon leave all this money to me? I surely am not in need."

"No, my Lady, Landow knew you were not in need of the money," Nan said quietly, "but I think that you were the one person in his life whom he could trust to use his inheritance for good."

"If I am to do that, I shall want it to be used as a memorial to the Landow Family in his name. How can that be done? How shall I proceed? What are your ideas?"

Nan and Giles were both taken aback and remained silent at first. Then Giles said, "When each of us thinks of the person Brandon Landow was, what is our first thought?"

"He was greedy, deceptive, and abusive of his role in the church," Nan replied.

"In many ways, he was a terribly spoiled child whose parents refused him nothing," Apollonia added. "When a grown man, he continued to think of himself first with little thought of others except to exploit their fear and pain for his profit."

"But, my Lady, both you and Nan have told me that in every way, the pardoner became a different person. How would each of you describe him during your time with him in his last days?"

"I found him to be apologetic for his life, utterly grateful to me for every bit of care that I gave him," Nan said.

"Indeed, he was sorry for the life he had led," the Lady added. "He begged me for forgiveness."

"What if you were to return the money to Master Trumwin and ask for his assistance in using it to establish a school for orphaned boys in Cirencester? You could suggest that it be called something like, 'Landow's School of Grace', my Lady, and have a sign created for it with the image of two different hands reaching out to help each other."

Apollonia did not respond immediately, but her eyes brightened suddenly as if she had a vision of what Giles was suggesting. With a brilliant smile expressing her agreement, she said, "What a truly beautiful idea, Giles. Will you go as my representative to Cirencester with Master Trumwin? I shall engage his services for me. He is the perfect man to guide us and in a position in Cirencester to know how best to achieve such a goal. A school for orphaned boys will be the consummate solution to fulfill Brandon's last wish to achieve something good for the community in the name of his family."

"I shall take your idea with me to Cirencester and work with Master Trumwin about your suggestion, my Lady," Giles assured her. "Landow knew you would be the perfect person to complete his last wishes."

"Well, Giles," the Lady said as her smile expressed her gratitude to him, "this has really been your idea of how best to use the pardoner's ill-gotten gains and inheritance, but I shall gladly do my best to enable it."

Chapter Twenty-one

Growing Households

In late February of the new year 1407, it was a bitter, windy day when MaryLizbet burst into Aust Manor. As soon as she was taken into the presence of the Lady Apollonia, she simply could contain herself no longer.

"We have a date, my Lady. Waldef and I will be married on the first of June at Waldef's parish church door in Bristol. I shall become MaryLizbet Gilbert, wife of Merchant Waldef Gilbert, dealer in everything from hats to millstones. His dear father has been mightily impressed by Waldef's business acumen and says he will make him a partner."

"How wonderful. We are thrilled by your news, MaryLizbet," the Lady said as she begged the girl to sit between her and Nan. "Can you tell us more of Waldef's situation? How is his father's health, and how goes their business in Bristol?"

"My Lady, Waldef's father, Master Gilbert, is planning to come to Aust on the morrow to meet with my parents and discuss our marriage plans. It seems his recovery has been much improved, just to have Waldef home with him once again. He is instructing Waldef to join the Gild of Merchant Venturers in Bristol soon. Best of all, we shall be together, my Lady, because my family is preparing to travel to Bristol, having been invited by Waldef's father. As my Waldef is the only child of his parents, his father has found loneliness since the loss of his wife to have been the cause of debilitating weakness for him. Now that Waldef has been at home and sharing the successes in business as well as the news of our marriage with his father, his papa seems to have found his life enriched and strengthened in every way."

"MaryLizbet," Nan asked in response to her announcement, "do you have any idea where you shall live after your marriage?"

"It turns out that Waldef's father has a large house in Bristol, Mistress Nan, and Waldef has taken me there to show me how comfortable we shall find living with his father. Their home has a great hall with an extra chamber, kitchen, and larder on the main floor but also a solar with other upstairs bedchambers. I can hardly wait to show it to my parents when we travel to meet with Waldef's father."

"There can be no doubt that your husband-to-be is working hard to establish himself as quickly as possible," Apollonia told her, "and I am not the least bit surprised to learn of Waldef's dedication to his goals. Do you not think that Waldef finds this new occupation in keeping with his dedication to chivalry?"

"In every sense, my Lady," MaryLizbet said looking down shyly with a gentle smile. "He has shown me that chivalry directs his life, his faith, and his dedication to me. He told me that he discovered in serving a mercenary knight of the realm that knighthood can be as badly abused as any station in life. I shall always seek to join with Waldef as my own precious prince while we live our lives together in faithful regard for courage, honour, courtesy, justice, and a readiness to help the weak."

"It would seem that you and Waldef have thought this through carefully and together, sharing your goals in life in a very mature manner," Apollonia commented."

"And, if I may be allowed to add my congratulations, MaryLizbet," Nan said as she stood to hug the girl, "I do not believe you could have made a better choice."

"Do you think that you might ask Master Gilbert to come here to the manor to visit with me after he arrives to spend time with Joshua, Jeanne and your family, MaryLizbet?"

"Oh yes, my Lady, he has already asked if some arrangement might be possible for his chance to meet you whilst he is here. When during the day would best suit you that he come to the manor?"

"I pray you will tell him that I should be pleased to receive him whenever he has a few moments to spare," the Lady responded.

"Realising how busy your families will be in the days ahead, promise him that I shall not keep him too long."

"My Lady, Master Gilbert is well aware of the extraordinary opportunities you have given his son, most of all how you, especially, took him into your household when he was under the shadow of being an accused murderer. Both he and Waldef acknowledge you to be the preserver of Waldef's life as well as the enabler of his experience of true chivalry."

"Waldef has displayed extraordinary gifts in my service, MaryLizbet. Surely, Master Gilbert and I have much to share with each other."

* * *

It was not long after Master Gilbert arrived at Joshua and Jean's farm near Aust that the merchant sought permission to visit the Lady. Apollonia welcomed him warmly and begged him to retreat with her and Nan to the solar where they might speak together and become better acquainted. Waldef's father was a relatively short man who had to look up to the face of the Lady Apollonia, but she could see that he did so with a sense of value in his own success as well as respect for the variance in their class.

As soon as they were seated together by the fire, the merchant asked if he might offer his sincere thanks to the Lady for her gifts to his son, especially her willingness to take him into her household.

"My Lady, I was unaware of the situation into which Waldef found himself at the time of the death of Sir Hardulph and probably could have done little to save him. Because of his dedication to the concept of chivalry since boyhood, I had assumed that Sir Hardulph offered the lad an extraordinary opportunity in the service of a knight, but I confess, I knew nothing of the true character of Hardulph of Leicester. You, however, granted the grace to take my son, an accused murderer, under your protection."

Apollonia smiled and nodded but did not respond immediately. She was thinking back to those days when Waldef first came to her. "I can not say precisely what was guiding me, Master Gilbert, but having briefly met the disreputable Sir Hardulph and received a secret message from your son about the danger the knight intended against one who was living within my household at the time, I became aware of the risk Waldef had been willing to take on my behalf. Therefore, when I received word from my brother that this young man was claiming my protection after a very suspicious accusation of murder, I felt I owed him the possibility of a hearing. The circumstances of the murder were such that my brother and his friend the sheriff questioned what had truly happened.

"How could you take such a risk for a young person whom you truly did not know?"

"I have always believed that one should grant value to people until proven incorrect, Master Gilbert and I found I could grant no value to Sir Hardulph as a knight or a gentleman. Waldef made a valiant effort to protect someone unknown to him whom he had learned was being threatened."

"You could know nothing of my son, yet you took this extraordinary risk for him, my Lady."

"I did because I was grateful for what he had done for one in my household whom he did not know. Further, in the first days after Waldef came to Aust, I was able to have several men whom I admire speak with your son, work with your son, and share with me their first impressions of him. The more I began to know Waldef, the more I knew that we must prove the truth of his innocence. I have not been disappointed."

"Your grace and goodness are beyond belief, my Lady. As Waldef's father, I can only offer you my endless thanks."

"Throughout my long life I have learned that people should not be judged by their station in life, Master Gilbert, whether noble, religious, or common folk. Goodness may be extended by all, but evil can also be afflicted by those from whom we least expect it. First and foremost, the innocent must be protected," the Lady said emphatically. "Waldef not only proved his innocence to me, I have been able to learn the true identity of the man responsible for the murder of Sir Hardulph."

"Has that villain been brought to law for his crimes, my Lady?"

"Tragically no, Master Gilbert, though I continue to seek word of his pursuit and capture. But, enough of such criminal things. Pray tell me more of your home in Bristol and how it will accommodate your growing family?"

"My Lady, I can not tell you how pleased I am to have Waldef and his prospective bride plan to use our house in Bristol as their new home. MaryLizbet is charming and a very mature young woman who comes from a loving family. I dare say, she has already proven to me that she can take charge, and cleverly, I have seen that she has already made a friend of my housekeeper."

* * *

As the early weeks of February passed Saint Valentine's feast, Apollonia was surprised in a very special way. Her son, Hugh, arrived to visit with her briefly before returning to his home in Marshfield. He had been resident in King Henry's court and obviously had learned something that he wished to share with his mother.

Apollonia was pleased as always to see her son but even more excited when she could see that he brought her news from the court. She and Nan slipped away with him to her solar, and when they were settled by the fire, his mother simply turned to Hugh and said, "What can you tell me, my son? I dare say you have news and I am bursting with curiosity."

"First, I must tell you that I have become acquainted with Prince Henry, mamam. He is a truly chivalrous knight as well as being heir to the throne of England."

"Pray tell me more, Hugh. If you have spent time with the prince, what do you think of him as a man, as a leader of men, as a potential ruler?"

"Between us, mamam, I can tell you that our prince has a reputation for being a great leader on the battlefield as well as one who is known for his courteous behaviour in court. However, I thought I could also see him as being somewhat impatient with the presumptions of the Archbishop Arundel."

"What sort of presumptions, Hugh?" his mother asked. "The archbishop has done much to serve the king and has especially served him well through his reoccurring illnesses."

"Since Parliament, as a solution to the problem of the King's illness, insisted on the Thirty-one Articles to which the king finally agreed, King Henry has been significantly restricted in his powers. The council was to take over administration, and our king was subjected to the sort of supervision given to the child king, Richard, mamam. There can be little doubt in my mind that Prince Henry is not pleased to see the severe restrictions that his father's illness has placed upon the throne, and he has expressed some concern for how this might limit his royal power when he succeeds."

"Do you think that Prince Henry is attempting to build his personal support among the aristocracy, Hugh?"

"Well, mamam, I can only tell you that this month, when Archbishop Arundel confirmed the act legitimising the Beauforts, half-brothers of King Henry, the Archbishop added a clause which barred them from inheriting the throne. Since then, the Beaufort brothers have turned from working with the archbishop towards actively supporting Prince Henry. In return, the prince has increasingly promoted his Beaufort uncles."

"Do you think that we may have a growing struggle for power between our king and his son, Hugh?"

"No, one must not speak of such things, mamam. I merely share court gossip with you."

"Well, Hugh," the Lady said as she breathed a great sigh, "it seems there is no end to some sort of struggle for the throne of England. Earlier in my lifetime, I was witness to one king overthrown by a nobleman who declared himself monarch. Later in life, perhaps I may be witness to the son of that king struggling against limitations imposed upon his tragically ill father."

"I also have some other news for you of brutal but just actions against a man whom you have rightly feared, mamam. You remember the so-called Count Dravini?"

"Indeed, I do, Hugh, and I pray you will not tell me he has returned to the West Country."

"No, mamam, Dravini did flee to London, and I have learned under the name of Peter Declan, he attempted to become part of a well-known gang of the city. My good friend, the Sheriff of London told me that Declan tried to push himself onto the leadership of the gang by telling them that he could achieve entry for them into the great houses of London as a visiting nobleman from Sicily. The real leader of the gang said little about Declan's attempt to join them and instead asked him about his former henchman called Buldoc. Dravini lied, saying that he was unaware of anyone in his service by that name. At that, the London gang leader announced that he was family to Buldoc and blamed Declan for abandoning his brother to hang. I have been told that Buldoc's brother turned on Declan and the Sicilian's badly mutilated body was found stripped and abandoned on a dock by the Thames."

The Lady suddenly put her hand to her mouth as if to stifle a gasp. "What a horrible ending to his life, Hugh."

"Little can be said in his defence, mamam, but many would feel that a kind of justice was finally accomplished against a truly evil man."

* * *

Late in July, Apollonia received a letter from MaryLizbet to tell of the joys of her newly married life. First, however, she wrote of her wedding ceremony with Waldef.

My Lady of Aust,

How I wish you could have been with us, but your allowance of Mistress Nan to join my family celebration was a great gift of curtesy and affection to Waldef and me. No doubt she has told you much, but allow me to tell you that Waldef and Master Gilbert had seen to it that the notice had been placed on the front door of their parish church well in advance.

On our wedding day, I wore a beautiful blue gown my mother made for me. She told me blue was the perfect colour for our wedding as it symbolises purity. As Waldef and I stood together at the church door, the priest directed me to stand to the left of Waldef, because he said Eve was created out of Adam's left rib. We exchanged our vows, Waldef placed the ring on my finger, and the ceremony was soon over. My dear family was with me through the ceremony and had even brought with them my precious baby sister, Arild Marie.

What followed was a grand feast with our families and a number of Bristol merchants and their wives, friends to Waldef and his papa. We had never anticipated such a marvelous celebration, but Waldef's father has many acquaintances in the city who admire and respect him.

We have been busy making his father's house into our home, and I have been visited by local neighbours who remember Waldef's childhood before his mother died. The folk of Bristol have truly made me feel welcome here.

Grateful to be your devoted servants and friends,
MaryLizbet and Waldef

* * *

Apollonia was aware that though the condition of the King was not yet spoken of officially throughout England's church, she was told that the king's health was being constantly remembered in daily prayer. The Lady could see that Archbishop Arundel, now chancellor, seemed more and more in charge of ruling the country. King Henry spent much of his summer in the north of England, and when he moved about the country, it was rumoured that he no longer rode horseback but was instead transported on a sort of litter. For the king to attend the meeting of Parliament at Gloucester Abbey, it took more than a month for him to make the journey of less than two hundred miles from York to Gloucester.

The 1407 Parliament opened on the 24th of October in Gloucester Abbey, and from everything that the Lady could learn from its proceedings, it seemed they were being orchestrated by Archbishop Arundel. As chancellor, Arundel delivered the opening speech telling the members that Parliament's purpose was to honour the King because *he* had upheld the liberties of the cities and boroughs of the kingdom, *he* had maintained the law, and *he* had shown compassion and clemency towards those who had been willing to acknowledge their offences against him.

The King was not present to hear his chancellor's list of royal virtues, and the members of Parliament were somewhat taken aback to be told that their purpose was to honour the King. Yet, by the end of the Parliament, the Commons were being confronted with a stark reality. They could not blame the king for the problems of the realm. Because of his illness, Henry had been nearly a year ruling through the council at their direction, and their complaints had not changed. From the Lady's perspective, Chancellor Arundel had not only taken a year to halt the decline of the royal fortunes, he had seen to it that the battleground had been moved away from the throne. Arundel could do nothing to free his lord from the disabling illnesses that afflicted him, but as chancellor, he had been successful in the restoration of royal power to one whom many no longer dared to call "the Usurper".

* * *

Nan had returned from Waldef and MaryLizbet's June wedding feast full of enthusiasm. She seemed to have no end of stories to tell the Lady of the people whom she met in Bristol and the wonders of the big city, which she had never before visited.

Apollonia was pleased to hear everything her maid could share with her but could feel no regrets in remaining at home in Aust. The Lady knew that such a trip at her age would have been too great an effort, but she was pleased that Nan had been able to represent her. Apollonia felt a strong affection for Waldef and his new bride, so she listened carefully to every word as Nan rattled on, detailing each wonder of the wedding celebration and every new adventure she had encountered in Bristol.

What Nan could not be aware of during moments of silence, when the Lady's thoughts wandered from their conversation, Apollonia continued to offer grateful prayers for the growing households among her family, friends, and affinity. She had been cruelly wounded by the sudden death of her brother and indeed, she continued to grieve that throughout her life she had lost so many persons near to her-- husbands, a son, and friends--through age, sickness, and violence. Yet she reminded herself how grateful she must be having been allowed to witness her family, affinity, and friendships as they continued to live and grow.

She was grateful that King Henry seemed secure on his throne in spite of his body enduring endless illnesses, while his son and heir was reported to be a true leader, as well as a chivalrous person. Apollonia felt that she experienced real chivalry demonstrated to her as a Christian model for one's life, not only by her brother and her young friend Waldef but also by one of the king's notorious enemies who truly mocked it.

She smiled to herself as she said aloud, "I am an old woman but thank God, one who can continue to learn." Then she added quietly, "I miss you brother," as if speaking to Ferdinand, "but as long as my life goes on, I shall seek to grow and learn with it."

"Indeed, you must, Polly," she was certain she could hear Ferdinand say, "but know that we shall meet again."

About the Author

Ellen Foster and her husband, Lou, live in Valparaiso, Indiana, but both of Ellen's father's parents had come to the U.S. from England. In her adult life, she and her brother made efforts with their spouses to return to England to explore their family's villages of origin and meet surviving family still living in Britain. Then, over a ten-year period, 1988-98, Lou's connections with the University of Exeter enabled them to live for four different years in Exeter, England. These marvelous opportunities to spend extended visits in England were a key inspiration for her writing.

Ellen was a history major with keen interest in the Middle Ages. While living in Exeter, she served as steward and tour guide in the 14th century Cathedral Church of Saint Peter. The couple travelled extensively in Europe, visiting medieval pilgrimage sites and cathedral cities in the Netherlands, Belgium, France, Germany, Italy, and Spain. Foster was able to utilise her personal experience with surviving buildings and relics of the Middle Ages to create images, research ancient places, as well as create voices of English characters of the late fourteenth, early fifteenth century period in her writing.

Glossary

Abbey:	monastery supervised by an abbot.
Affinity:	medieval concept of loyal household, wearing the livery or heraldic badge of one's lord and granting full allegiance and acceptance of his rule in one's life.
Ague:	an illness involving fever and shivering.
Almoner:	a person whose function is the distribution of alms in behalf of a noble person.
Archbishop:	the chief bishop responsible for a large district.
Armigerous:	a person entitled to heraldic arms.
Bard:	a poet reciting epics, tales of distant lands, folk tales, or imaginary historical events.
Battle of Shrewsbury:	1403 rebellion of Henry Hotspur Percy against King Henry IV. Hotspur, favourite son of the Earl of Northumberland was killed.
Bishop:	member of the clergy who supervises a diocese, governing many parish churches and whose main seat or throne is found in his cathedral.
Butts for Practice:	a mound on which a target is set up for archery.
Canon law:	the body of ecclesiastical or church law.
Celibate/ Celebacy:	abstaining from marriage and sexual relations for religious reasons.
Celts:	Indo-European tribal peoples occupying England at the time of the Roman invasions and before the arrival of the Anglo-Saxons. Now Celts are represented chiefly by the Cornish, Irish, Gaels, Welsh and Bretons.

Chancellor of England:	head of the office which produced all the writs and charters which were sealed with the Great Seal. The Chancery and the Exchequer were the two main administrative offices of medieval government.
Chivalry:	rules and ideal qualifications of a medieval knight: courage, courtesy, generosity, valour, and dexterity in arms.
Churl:	in Old English: a peasant or rustic.
Diocese:	ecclesiastical district under the jurisdiction of a bishop.
Doctor of Physic:	medieval term for a physician or medical doctor.
Doublet:	a man's short close-fitting padded jacket.
Druids:	members of religious order of priests in pre-Christian Britain.
Earl:	an English nobleman ranking above a viscount and below a marquess.
Eiclips:	an ancient Irish spelling of eclipse.
Flux:	an abnormal discharge of blood or other matter from the human body including diarrhoea or dysentery.
Franciscans:	members of the mendicant order founded by St Francis of Assisi, also called the Grey Friars.
Gaol:	British variant spelling of jail.
Garderobe:	medieval privy often built into the walls of a castle or manor house.
Gentry:	well-born, well-bred people, an aristocracy; in England, the class under the nobility.
Gramercy:	an expression of thanks meaning "grand merci".
Grey Friar:	a brother of the Franciscan order.
Henchman:	a trusted attendant or follower, especially one who is willing to do risky things for a person of rank.

Holy Orders: the rank or status of ordained Christian ministry.

Indulgence: a document of the church containing a partial remission of punishment in purgatory, still due for sin after absolution.

Knight Errant: a medieval knight wandering in search of chivalrous adventures.

Lists: historical palisades; enclosing an area for a tournament.

Livery: a distinctive dress, badge, or device formerly provided by someone of rank or title for his retainers.

Man of law: 14th century barrister or lawyer.

Mendicant: a person who lives by begging; a mendicant friar is a member of a brotherhood who lives by begging.

Monastic: relating to monks, nuns, or other religious who live apart in a convent according to a rule and are unmarried practicing lives of celebacy.

Noble: distinguished by birth, rank, or title.

Noblewoman: a woman of noble birth or rank.

Normans: natives of Normandy.

Ocarina: small wind instrument with holes for fingers, typically having the shape of a bird.

Page: a youth in attendance on a person of rank.

Pardoner: an ecclesiastical official charged with the granting of indulgences.

Physic: in the 14th century, any medicine, or drug, especially one that purges.

Pitmaker: grave digger.

Poacher: a person who trespasses on private property.

Prebend: the portion of the revenue of a church given to a member of the clergy.

Prie-dieu: piece of furniture especially designed for kneeling upon during prayer.

Relic:	ecclesiastical term referring to the body, a part of the body, or a personal memorial of a saint or members of the Holy Family and worthy of veneration.
Sheriff:	executive officer of the crown in a county having administrative and judicial functions.
Shawm:	medieval wind instrument, forerunner of the oboe with a double reed in a wooden mouthpiece.
Solar:	a private or upper chamber in a medieval English house or castle.
Sovereignty:	the status of authority and independence.
Squire:	the first degree of knighthood, squire as servant to a knight; a country gentleman, especially the chief landed proprietor in a district.
Squirearchy:	landowners collectively.
Steward:	one who serves as manager of financial and business affairs, serving as manager or agent for another.
Table dormant:	a table permanently in place.
Table tomb:	a sepulchral structure with a flat, slab-like top.
Tapycer:	a tapestry-maker, weaver of tapestries, rugs, etc.
Tierceron vaulting:	one bay of a roof between supporting columns with ribs called tiercerons.
Tithe barn:	a barn built on monastic or parish property to hold the tenth part of agricultural harvest.
Transept:	the cross-like arms of a major church extending out from the intersection of nave and choir.
Treasury of Merit:	a treasury of the goodness, the merits of Christ and the saints, left to the keeping of the Church and which is the source of Indulgences. In the later Middle Ages, the sale of Indulgences became a significant means of raising funds.

Truckle bed: low bed usually pushed under another bed.

Tunic: an outer garment with or without sleeves and sometimes worn belted.

Usurper: one who takes a position of power illegally or by force.

Villain: a wicked person or a person guilty of a crime.

Vowess: a ceremony performed before witnesses during mass where a kneeling widow was asked by the bishop if she desired to be the spouse of Christ. The vow was restricted to the obligation of perpetual chastity and in no way curtailed the activities of the vowess. She was able to remain in the world and not be confined to a monastic life.

Wyclif, John (c1328-84):   a Yorkshireman by birth, Wyclif studied and taught theology and philosophy at Oxford. A major church reformer, he spread the doctrine that the Scriptures are the supreme authority and that the good offices of the Church are not requisite to grace. He was condemned as a heretic in 1380, again in 1382 and his followers were persecuted, but he was not disturbed in his retirement before he died.